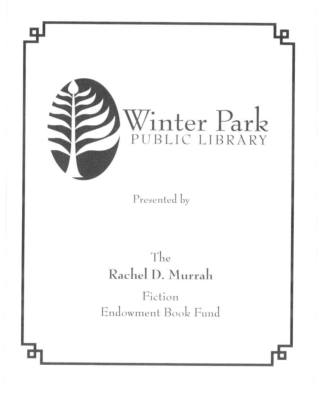

THE KING AT THE
EDGE OF THE WORLD

ARTHUR PHILLIPS

· · · · · · ·

THE KING AT THE EDGE OF THE WORLD

· · · · · · ·

A NOVEL

RANDOM HOUSE

NEW YORK

Published in the United States by Random House, an imprint and division of Penguin Random House LLC, New York.

RANDOM HOUSE and the HOUSE colophon are registered trademarks of Penguin Random House LLC.

LIBRARY OF CONGRESS CATALOGING-IN-PUBLICATION DATA
Names: Phillips, Arthur, author.
Title: The king at the edge of the world : novel / Arthur Phillips.
Description: New York : Random House, 2019.
Identifiers: LCCN 2019019018| ISBN 9780812995480 | ISBN 9780812995497 (ebook)
Subjects: LCSH: Turkey—History—Ottoman Empire, 1288–1918—Fiction. | Great Britain—History—Elizabeth, 1558–1603—Fiction. | James I, King of England, 1566–1625—Fiction. | GSAFD: Historical fiction.
Classification: LCC PS3616.H45 K56 2019 | DDC 813/.6—dc23
LC record available at https://lccn.loc.gov/2019019018

Printed in the United States of America on acid-free paper

randomhousebooks.com

9 8 7 6 5 4 3 2 1

FIRST EDITION

Book design by Simon M. Sullivan

for my parents, Ann and Felix, with love

We know our enemies are lying to us. But what intelligence coup could convince you that their claim is not a lie or a cover story? That there is no Soviet–American missile gap. That Hussein hides no WMD. If the absence of evidence is not the evidence of absence, then what the hell ever could be?

—T. MCCRADY HEWES, *A Life in Intelligence*

CONTENTS

PART ONE

MAHMOUD EZZEDINE, 1591

· · · · · · · ·

In her correspondence with the Sultan [asking for help against the Catholic Spanish], the Queen [Elizabeth I] emphasized the fact that as a Protestant Christian, she rejected the veneration of idolatrous images which the Pope and the Spanish king practiced. Her Christianity, she implied, was closer to Islam than was Catholicism. . . . Catholics were saying in [Constantinople] that "the English lack nothing to make them sound Mussulmans, and need only stretch out a finger to become one with the Turks in outward appearance, in religious observance, and in their whole character."

—NABIL MATAR, *Islam in Britain, 1558–1685*

IN THE PALACE of Felicity, in Constantinople, in the land of the Turks, early in the Christian year 1591, viziers to Murad the Great, third of that name, Sultan of the Ottomans, Custodian of the Two Holy Mosques, Caliph of Caliphs, dispatched an embassy to a far-off, sunless, primitive, sodden, heathen kingdom at the far cliffside edge of the civilized earth. The sultan chose as his ambassador a loyal and trusted man, but nobody of great importance, to negotiate with the people of that patch of damp turf.

Still, one must send someone to discuss trade and passports and the repatriation of unlucky Turkish sailors captured by the pirate crews who cowered in the harbors of that barbarian island. Those pirates thrived under the protection of the island's capricious sultana, cruel in her poverty, weakness, fearful isolation, and unnatural state of unmarried womanly rule. She also begged for the Ottoman sultan's support against her enemies, locked as she was in a bloody and endless sectarian combat with others of her kind about some incomprehensible quarrel over their false religion. The sultan felt it was time to send someone competent to the island of the English to wring concessions from her queen.

And so the ambassador and his entourage traveled to the end of the world. The ambassador, a eunuch who had been born a Christian in Portugal and recognized the truth of Mohammed when he was captured at the age of eleven, led a small retinue, only fourteen men: his chief adviser, a doctor of medicine, servants, scribes, guards. He carried for the island's sultana, among many other gifts, a pair of lions, a scimitar, a unicorn's horn, and ten English pirates captured by Turkish sailors.

This last gift assured that the ambassador and his men were welcomed to London by a torchlight parade through the gawping crowds near St. Lawrence Jewry church, winding to the large house where they would live for five months before returning to Constantinople.

MAHMOUD EZZEDINE, THE doctor responsible for the health of the ambassador first and then of every man of the embassy after, had tried to avoid this journey, but his presence was specifically requested.

He had enriched himself and gained a reputation, won favor and honor, wife and child, home and security, all from his carefully amassed medical knowledge. He had risen to become one of the physicians entrusted with the very bodies of the sultan and his family, and his life in Constantinople lacked for nothing. There was no pleasure in losing a year of his wife's company, of his son's growth, of attempting a second child. Despite a lack of success so far, he had enjoyed the process. And, nearly as important, there was no pleasure in being away from the royal family, whose health he protected and cherished even beyond his own.

He had dared to ask an influential courtier if there were any possibility of another physician being sent in his place. The man said he would inquire, but he must have done so clumsily, for a few days later, Ezzedine was visited at home by Cafer bin Ibrahim, who would be the ambassador's chief adviser for the expedition. "Dr. Ezzedine," said Cafer, over coffee and figs brought by the doctor's translucently veiled wife, Saruca, to the courtyard of the house and served under the shade and pink flowers of the Judas trees. "It was I who suggested to the sultan that he send you to England. And he was enthusiastic that you should protect us all. And you would now refuse?"

"Of course I would not dream of refusing."

"I'm glad to hear you say it. I misunderstood some idiot at court who misrepresented your words and heart to me. You should be careful whom you entrust with them. May I take another fig?"

The doctor's son, Ismail, cried for two nights after he learned of his father's approaching departure for Christian England. "I won't be gone so long as all that," he told Saruca as the boy sobbed himself to sleep. "I will bring him something English as a gift. It is gratifying to think I will be so missed." He reached for his wife's hand across the bed.

"He is afraid you will not return," she said. "He told me he was afraid you will be eaten by lions."

"I will reassure him. The English don't have lions."

The next morning, however, the boy was in no mood to be condescended to. "I didn't say lions," he said, stamping a foot. "I said Lionheart. You are going to where Richard Lionheart came from."

Ezzedine tried not to laugh. "But Lionheart died long ago. And all the Crusaders were defeated long ago. There are no more Crusaders."

"But his people may still be like him. And want to hurt you."

"I promise I will be safe," said Dr. Ezzedine, kissing the top of the boy's head. It smelled of something dusty but sweet, like a flower's pollen.

Saruca told him the night before his departure, "It is bad that you go. I don't want to watch you leave. So I practice imagining it and accepting it. I don't want to curse your absence." She kissed him in the morning as he stood outside, the boy clinging to his leg. "I accept this," she said, before she began to weep and pulled the crying boy away. The doctor walked down to the sea. He tried not to look back but didn't succeed.

Throughout their stay, the ambassador and his men had audiences with the English sultana at Greenwich and Nonsuch palaces and hosted her and her people in turn to feasts *à la Turkeska* at the ambassador's residence, where they slaughtered all their meat themselves in the correct manner. For months, official negotiations were conducted in the cold rooms of the queen's palaces or upon her green parklands. Conclusions were reached in matters of sea-lanes and free overland passages, the exchange of captured pirates/sailors, various immunities and protections for Englishmen voyaging in the empire of the Ottomans. Much of the diplomacy was a duel of imaginations, conceptions of events that had not yet occurred but were suddenly pressingly possible.

"And if an Englishman traveling in Qustantiniyya should wish to convert to the religion of Mohammed?" asked the ambassador's chief adviser, Cafer bin Ibrahim. This particular question amused those of the English negotiators who had never left England but deeply troubled those English who *had* traveled, especially in Mahometan lands. There was much to be said for any religion that promised wealth, opportunity, and wives in *this* world. (This was a truth as obvious as air to the Turks, one they lived with daily. Back in Constantinople, bin Ibrahim always hurriedly sold any of his Christian slaves who were considering converting to the true faith, or else he would have had to free them at a loss, enslavement of his co-religionists being illegal.)

Conversely, the question arose of Turk merchants traveling within England and of their free and safe passage throughout the kingdom, of what protections the queen might guarantee a hypothetical Mahometan buyer of, say, tin. Could such a one reside unmolested in London? Or travel to mines farther inland? And pray to Allah and his saints as his law demanded, five times daily? Even when it was pointed out that Jews (who were obviously worse and more dangerous) sometimes were free to move about, the English found the prospect of a freely roaming Turk so astonishing and obviously unsanitary to the body politic that the topic was temporarily set aside. But then one of the queen's privy councillors, Robert Beale, pointed out that if (as the Turkish negotiators insisted) any Englishman in the Ottoman Empire who of free conscience wished to swear allegiance to Mohammed could not be prevented from doing so, then any Ottoman wishing to profess his devotion to Jesus Christ was similarly at liberty to do so while in England. The Ottoman ambassador readily agreed to this reciprocity, unable to conceive of any Ottoman who would see an advantage—spiritual or economic—in apostasy or, for that matter, take up permanent residence on this island. England was simply too poor and Christianity too unpromising in this life. After all, they were scarcely able to convince some of the English pirates to return from Constantinople. Even those in prison.

Meanwhile, at the suggestion of Dr. Ezzedine, all the men of the embassy performed *zakat* by paying, as their wealth allowed them, for the release or well-being of Turkish prisoners held in England. Ezzedine went further and, under escort, searched in the darkest parts of London for a rumored community of Moors awaiting passports or funds to sail for happier places. Dr. Ezzedine would have given generously to these unfortunates, if he could have found them.

What would Saruca and Ismail think of this place? He sketched it for them, in pictures and words, the palaces and the creaking wooden buildings where mythological Moors could not be found. But it was impossible to properly capture with paper. Ismail often claimed he would explore the world, to see every corner of the sultan's empire, but he still was shy around other boys and hid behind his father's legs, and Ezzedine suspected that the sight of these houses painted with the sign of plague would ruin his sleep for days. "Sometimes, it's much nicer to stay at home," he had told his father almost every night for a few weeks when he was smaller.

Later, Ezzedine had brought Ismail to see the chamber of maps at the Sublime Porte, showed him the far-off corners of the empire, where Sarajevo and Buda and Athens and Jerusalem and Cairo sat, so many difficult months away from Constantinople and Ismail's beloved caged birds. As a mark of respect to his father, Ismail was permitted to see the globes and even to set one of them to turning. Ezzedine watched as the question of scale began to trouble the child. "Are we all residing on this one tiny dot? But how can that be?" It seized the boy's mind for a month to come, and at times Ezzedine despaired of getting Ismail to understand. "Even Mother? Even my birds? Even you? All of us live on a black dot? But it is not black on the ground outside. . . ."

Finally, Saruca succeeded where Ezzedine had failed. Ismail explained to his father, "Look how small the boats are on the water when we stand on the top of the hill. But they are not small when we are near them. They don't change, but they seem small. So if a bird flew very high, we would seem small enough to fit on a spot."

Saruca teased her husband that night: "If you would like me to take over the boy's education, I will make time in my day."

INTO THE INTOLERABLY wet and cold summer the ambassador and his men were entertained, feted by the queen, though they were often unable to eat much of what was served. They sat for plays and masques, dancers and musicians, even a Turkish acrobat long in service to Elizabeth. Ezzedine asked him how he had come to be in England, but the man was nervous to talk to his former countrymen and fled the doctor's gentle approach.

The embassy watched the queen's most beloved entertainment twice in the first month: A cat, dressed in the habit of the Catholic pope, was placed on the back of a horse and tethered to the saddle. The horse, draped in English banners, trotted in a ring until a bear, wearing the livery of Mr. Walsingham, the queen's recently deceased principal secretary, swept the cat from the horse's back, tearing it to pieces. "It's an allegory," a lady of the court explained to Ezzedine. The doctor looked away at the moment of the animal's death.

The most senior Turks went out riding with the master of the horse, the queen's favorite (and, to Turkish eyes, quite obviously the English sultana's sexual consort), the Earl of Essex. The earl was pleased to hunt with the pair of falcons brought by the ambassador as gifts to the queen. He deemed the ambassador a good and companionable gentleman and found his chief adviser, Cafer bin Ibrahim, to be "an uncommon skilled hand at the noble falcons." It was bin Ibrahim who taught Essex the spoken commands in Arabic that the predators understood best. Bin Ibrahim was then honored to be a guest at Essex's table and to hunt with him alone. He conversed often with this chief of the English military, asking naïve questions that led the earl to talk and talk and talk, taking obvious and predictable pleasure in educating the childish foreigner.

Members of the embassy who spoke English, or some tongue in common with the Englishmen, were encouraged by bin Ibrahim to pass hours in conversation with the strange inhabitants of this strange place. Later, at the embassy's residence, they would be called in, one at a time, to make private report to him of all they had discussed, every English word and intonation. Each then received further instruction as to whom they should speak with the following day and on what topics.

Cafer bin Ibrahim condensed all these reports into an oral summary for the ambassador, delivered in his master's chamber every evening, removing and adding certain details so the ambassador would best comprehend. He would then return to his table to prepare a written statement for a particular vizier back in Constantinople. This report bin Ibrahim would dispatch whenever a vessel departed while the embassy remained in London. Though the vizier had told bin Ibrahim that no English person—not a single soul on the entire island—could read Arabic, still he enciphered the reports. Long after the soft and plump ambassador was snoring contentedly, bin Ibrahim would be twirling an engraved spiral of mahogany upon which rode delicate tiles, each with two letters inked on it, one upside down. After completing his work, he would invert this ciphering wand and reorder the tiles for the next day, according to a system prearranged with the vizier prior to the embassy's departure. Still, bin Ibrahim woke at least once a night in fear that he had made some fatal error in code, rendering it illegible.

CAFER BIN IBRAHIM dreamed of knowing all things at all times, and in his dreams his body enjoyed the sensation—in his cheeks and groin and kidneys—of what such a stuffed pregnancy of facts and secrets might feel like, how close total knowledge might feel to paradise. He dreamed of paradise not as it is written but as he might hope it to be: every answer to every question, a perfect knowledge, while his eternal and youthful form was caressed by so many perfect duplicates of women he admired in earthly life—the sultana, the ladies most recently retired from the sultan's seraglio, the wives of other men at court, and most decidedly and deliciously the wife of Mahmoud Ezzedine, the daughter of a rich man, a prize absurdly wasted on the doctor from the provinces, a woman whose face had been nearly visible through her light veil and whose eyes unquestionably revealed her lascivious nature.

In waking hours, bin Ibrahim settled for less than total knowledge, though he watched with particular interest as Dr. Ezzedine—by nature shy—was befriended by John Dee, the queen's wizard. It seemed unlikely that Ezzedine knew how valuable a source of intelligence this man could be, but that ignorance might serve bin Ibrahim as well as anything; at least the transparent doctor would not be asked to lie or perform. He would simply give reports of table talk.

Mahmoud Ezzedine, born in Beirut, was as fair in skin as men of that sun-bleached corner of the Turks' empire could sometimes be. "You might be an Italian," said one of the English courtiers. This man was styled "knight," though he wore no armor, and the weapon at his side was as thin as a twig, not feasible for combat. The stories of Crusaders that Ezzedine had heard all his life, tales of Christian marauders told to frighten and control wicked children—this knight was not possibly such a devil as those men had been. Ezzedine was excited to tell his son that the Christians had become weak since those days, it seemed. He wished he could be home that very night, to wake the boy and tell him, "Ismail, I saw the Christians. They are not Crusaders at all. Rather, they are like stick men you make with your friends."

"Yes, no question, you might be an Italian." His tone implied that this condition might be only slightly more palatable than if Ezzedine were a Moor. The English knight was, as many of the Englishmen were, so languid and thin in arm and leg, so peculiar and effeminate in affect, that Ezzedine wondered how many of them were eunuchs. Later assured by a laughing page boy that this was not the practice among the Christians, the doctor then diagnosed that most of them suffered from blood too thin to carry much warmth or vigor. The island's damp simply could not in most cases produce men of physical beauty or virility. The nation was doomed by its weather (all praise be to Allah) to weakness, in the individual and the aggregate. Perhaps as Englishmen sailed south, they grew stronger, so that when they had arrived in Africa or Jerusalem they had grown powerful.

The willowy knight spoke to the doctor in French. "I have been to the south of the Italian lands. The people are like you, dark from the sun but not like Africans, you know, or even your other Turks there. Have you seen portraits of the savages of America? Two were brought here to court. They did astonish some of us, it must be said. There are, perhaps, some *millions* of them, do you know? They know nothing of God. Nothing of the world. And nothing of your empire, either, Doctor. It is . . . ." The knight poured himself more wine, then looked at the carved and painted ceiling of the chamber in Greenwich. "You people really won't take wine? Well. It is a troubling thing to contemplate. How could there be quite so many of the red devils? How many centuries have they existed? And we knew nothing of them? Might there, do you suppose, be other such lands full of other such nations of whom we have no knowledge? The counting of . . . how many millions might reside to east or west—I have never thought of it at all, for why would one? But if the total number of Christendom—I'm not a scholar—but if it were not the bulk of human—I don't quite have it straight in my mind, what it is I am trying to say."

It was difficult for Ezzedine to know how much of this strange and anxious talk he should report back to bin Ibrahim.

6.

D R. EZZEDINE FELT his own form softening and fading, as if it would soon resemble the English bodies. His vigor and heat drained out of him in the diseased air and gruesome streets. He shivered, even in daytime, even when dry. He coughed with no material result. He slept poorly at night and fell asleep eagerly at noon. He was far from his family and the family of his beloved sultan. He told himself he was still trusted, that home did not alter in his absence, but some days the distance felt unpassable and permanent, infinitely far from the palace and the body he was most responsible for. He sometimes childishly feared the future, and he suffered from three dreams of himself as a vastly old, gray, and withered man, entirely alone amid the offal and human waste that ran through the useless roads of primitive London. He awoke angry with his own cowardice.

Ezzedine's duties during the embassy's months in London were, after all, usually light. He was here to protect the health of the ambassador, but somehow that eunuch was, without effort, in good health, unaffected by the English air. Perhaps this was because he had been born a Christian, which might have protected him, as some who are born to plague victims cannot themselves fall prey to plague. The ambassador was ceremonially protected from the English food, too, and mechanically untempted by the grotesque

Englishwomen and their humid, steaming pox, smelling now of roses, now of onions.

Ezzedine prayed, expressed gratitude to Allah. He was there, he reminded himself, to be a figure of strength and confidence in the face of endless strangeness, of threats to health and mental stamina. He must fortify the bodies of the embassy's men (himself included) and fortify their minds against all that was wrong here: the half-naked women, the food, the fog, the filth, the intoxicating drink, the intellectual softness, the islanders' several varieties of devoted and violent false faith. On days when he was able to work and breathe properly, to feel gratitude and anticipation rather than bitterness and fear, he fell asleep recalling anew that the prize of return would be well earned. Saruca's touch would be the reward for walking bravely among these strange creatures; Ismail's laughter for listening to their conversation; Saruca's cooking for the sour fruit offered in flimsy palaces; Ismail's company, his small hand in his father's, for the Christians' whispered mockery.

And he woke ready to face his duties again. Beyond conversing with the English and reporting their words to the insatiably curious Cafer bin Ibrahim, Ezzedine prepared astrological charts for the ambassador and attended to the physical complaints of the other men as well, distributing powders and ointments for stomach ailments and skin bumps, preparing a useful balm for those who had foolishly entertained an Englishwoman. In the time remaining to him, he studied the island's herbs and plants and became cordial with the queen's alchemist-astronomer and philosopher of nature, Dr. Dee. This Christian was kind and sought out Ezzedine's conversation. He revealed himself, astonishingly, to have considerable knowledge of mathematics and medicine and had even read translations of Averroes, Avicenna, and al-Khwarizmi. The two men were seated together at a feast at the embassy because bin Ibrahim arranged it, saying, "You both like to inspect grass and dirt, I'm told. Perhaps he knows secrets he will share with you."

Dee invited Ezzedine to his home after that feast, and bin Ibrahim approved of the visit, asserting a power—increasingly over the length of the embassy—to control the movements of the men in the retinue. "Tell me what you learn there. And if he should know of medicine new to you, the sultan will be pleased at your enterprise. If he should be willing to speak of the queen's use of magic for her foreign wars or our negotiations, even better. And any horoscopes he has cast for members of the court, these you should memorize and report to me at once."

But there was no conversation of intrigue or palace secrets. Instead, the learned Dee shyly displayed for his new friend his philosophical instruments for reading the stars, his library, his own glass house of medicinal herbs. It was far better than Ezzedine had expected to see outside Turkish or Moorish lands, and he complimented his host, expressed the hope that he might someday return the favor by showing him the expansive facilities at his disposal in the New Palace. Dee eagerly accepted the invitation, sincere in his desire to make that voyage, and Ezzedine was pleased to have inspired some envy for Ottoman knowledge in the Englishman. Dee even confessed ruefully that what the sultan had subsidized would likely dwarf what could be built here in England, where "men were too often nervous to learn of things that contradicted their dearest falsehoods."

Dr. Ezzedine liked Dr. Dee, would have liked him in any circumstances, admired the wisdom of a Christian who could take steps toward light, could perceive glimpses of truth in darkness. When Dee led him one day outside London to a forest, explaining to him in Latin the English soil's bounty, Ezzedine was deeply moved by the other man's enthusiasm and knowledge and by the plentiful wonders of these foreign trees. It was a vanishingly rare moment in which Ezzedine did not wish to be launched immediately from the sickening island.

"I have a boy. Ismail is his name."

"Ismail," Dee repeated slowly, trying out the sounds in his mouth. "Is he a child to make you proud?"

"Very much. A wise boy. He is eight years old. He has an affinity, I believe you would say, an understanding of the animal kingdom, with animals individually. I do not recall the same attitude in myself at his age. I came upon him recently lying on the stones in the courtyard of my home. At first I was frightened. I saw only his small fat legs stretched out on the ground, but as I came around the corner, I saw a little dog sitting on Ismail's chest. I did not know the dog or where it came from. I watched. They had not noticed me yet. The boy was scratching the dog's ears. The dog seemed obviously, I think, to feel affection for the child. I watched them until the dog wandered off to smell something in the corner."

"I have seen such things. But he sounds a kind and gentle lad."

"But wait: The dog left, but the child remained supine there. He did not rise or move. I think he knew I was watching, but I am not certain. And then, to my amazement, two birds flew down and landed upon him, one on his chest where the dog had been, one on his arm, near his hand. I tell you the truth. And he seemed in no way surprised by this. He thought it entirely proper that birds should trust him like this. They stayed upon him, walking a bit and making birdsong, for several minutes! I began to sketch them there.

"That evening at supper, my wife had prepared us a chicken. She prepared it in the way she always does, with pomegranates in a sauce of yogurt. It is a favorite of both mine and Ismail's. But that night—"

"He refused it?" said Dr. Dee.

"He did. I asked him if he felt ill. He is a plump fellow. It is unlike him to turn away from any food. 'I am not ill, Father,' he said. His mother said, 'If you want to be strong and wise like your father, you must eat.' And do you know what he did?"

Dr. Dee considered, then guessed: "Did he mourn?"

"Exactly. He wept. At the table. And could not be consoled."

"Of course," said Ezzedine's English friend. "Of course."

7

EVERY NIGHT, AFTER the *Maghrib* prayers the men performed together, Ezzedine wrote to his son, a long journal he would carry to Constantinople himself at the completion of the embassy rather than risk individual letters to messengers on merchant ships, which might well be taken by Algerian (or English) pirates before they saw Constantinople and his boy.

The doctor wrote his unguarded impressions of the foreigners and their practices, their rare flashes of common intelligence (Dee's praised as a separate matter worthy of its own category), their prevalent uncleanliness. He wrote of their queen, whom he had seen at table and in her court, and who, on a few occasions, had spoken to Ezzedine directly. She had looked with interest at the Turkish men, even looking long into their eyes.

The English court is not so richly built as ours and would not suit even a pasha. Their finest buildings are handsome, with walls and ceilings carved in wood and painted with scenes of their stories, but it is a small kingdom, unimportant in the world, and poor. One might easily speculate that their refusal to recognize God has made them weak. Once, they asked our sultan for assistance against their enemy the Spanish. I was present when the sultan read this queen's pleading letter to the court, and his laughter, and the laughter of all the court, was loud.

The sultana of England is not beautiful, as our sultana is reputed to be, nor as wise as our sultan, though she speaks Latin well. She is an old woman, and her face is painted with strange colors. Her hair is the color of a persimmon because her people come from the land of Wales, where everyone is so strangely colored, though I have not traveled there to confirm this with my eyes. But the Wales men are fiercer warriors than the other tribes of the island and so have seized almost all of it. The men of Wales conquered the island under this queen's grandfather, though I do not know if he was as strong as a Turkish soldier, since the king he defeated was a hunchback. The queen's principal vizier is also a hunchback. It seems common to these unfortunate people. Their bodies break easily, or they are born incomplete. It is a strange place.

The most northern piece of the island is still held by the weaker (yet weaker!) Scots people and their king, who is cousin to the queen. He is sometimes the queen's friend and other times her enemy, if I understand correctly. The mother of this little king attempted to take Elizabeth's throne, through sorcery and wiles, but the English queen discovered her plots and took her head. It is no wonder that Yakub, the King of Scotland, should hate Elizabeth and the English, and no wonder, too, that when he claims not to hate them, and claims to love her as his cousin and woman-lord, that many men should think he lies. I do not know if he lies or how one might ever know such a thing, for he wants, I am told by our ambassador's adviser, to be king of all this cold island when Elizabeth dies. And so men struggle in blindness, like rats in darkness, a crust of bread all the world to them because they know not what light shines just outside their cellar door.

This queen of theirs—I return to her, despite myself. She never wed and everyone too loudly says she is still a virgin, though she is old. She is old, yet still she behaves as if she were a young woman with flashing eyes. It is embarrassing when she looks upon you, but the ambassador seems able to compliment her beauty without blushing. His is a difficult job. Perhaps he is best equipped for it of all of us. The sultan may be very wise indeed for having selected him for this task. The women here walk quite nearly nude within the court and in the city. They all show their faces. All of them. Do not tell your mother!

One is not amazed to discover that one Christian nation dislikes another and would make war upon a neighboring kingdom of Christians. Such things occur among men of the true religion as well. But one is shocked to learn that the Christians would kill one another not for land or power or money, but more often than not rush to slaughter one another from a shared inability to comprehend the nature of God. What is obvious to all of us— even if we should fight for power or land or wealth—so confounds the half-sighted Christians that they slash and burn their neighbor, their own countrymen, their holy men.

They have their book, certainly. And yet they cannot agree even among themselves what it says! They cannot agree to understand it. Like children (like children much stupider than you, my child), they are frustrated at a problem whose solution eludes them, and so they vomit up wrath. They do not look at the true source of their frustration: their own blindness. Instead, they rage against those who stand beside them in quite identical frustration. And such rage! In Paris, I am told, in the kingdom of the Franks, the Cross-worshippers tore to pieces men, women, even children, who understood Christian stories differently.

Before this queen, England had another queen, this Elizabeth's sister, but she was a Cross-worshipper, so she burned her religious enemies by the hundreds. Not for a moment did it occur to them (or to Elizabeth's Luther-men, who in turn have been hunting Cross-worshippers in England, chopping them to bits when they find them cowering in a cellar) that they are both wrong!

But there are men of wisdom among them. My new friend, John Dee, invited me to his home again this evening. A dinner in my honor at his house in London. A meal mostly of vegetables and fruit tart, intended to avoid any contradiction with our laws. He even obtained a pomegranate, which is rare on this island. The generosity was noble of him. Some of the conversation was conducted in English far too rapid for me to follow, though I have improved in their language.

8.

MONTHS BEFORE, SARUCA had sat in front of the house, pulling feathers from a chicken. She spread her legs wide and laid a cloth across her lap. The child picked feathers up and dropped them one at a time over the wall above the hillside. The breeze would occasionally capture a feather and set it in a long flight the full length of the hill, all the way to the sea. The woman wiped the back of her hand across her exposed forehead, and a little of the chicken's blood marked her skin there.

His appetite for her was almost like the appetite for food. He stepped closer to her and made his presence known. She looked up, startled. "My husband is not at home, sir."

Cafer bin Ibrahim feigned a mild disappointment. "A pity. I have some news for him about our departure for England. But may I sit and rest a moment before I return to my day?"

A man of middle size, middle intelligence, and middle talent, Cafer bin Ibrahim did have the supremely well-developed survival instincts of an old jackal. He had been dispatched to England as chief adviser to the ambassador for good reason. Not only could he speak English, but he had, far more than the gentle ambassador, a clear eye for weakness and strength, for softness and indecision, and for (an English trait, the sultan knew) incompetence and ignorance disguised as haughty indifference.

In the Palace of Felicity, bin Ibrahim was one of many the sultan trusted to sniff out plot and conspiracy without becoming attracted to its scent. The sultan recognized a man to whom the logic of life as it really was came as naturally as breath. The sultan knew that Cafer's self-interest would identically match the interests of the sultan in his negotiations with the queen of the English. Cafer was the sort of man the sultan allowed to rise to a certain height of glory and then carefully and regularly examined for signs of toxic ambition, much as Dr. Ezzedine insisted on examining the sultan twice yearly for any small incursions of some subtle disease upon his skin, within his sputum, or in the bubbled currents of his passed water.

"Dr. Dee showed you herbs," bin Ibrahim repeated Ezzedine's last words back to him, then called for more drink for them both.

"And demonstrated their properties, in some cases." Ezzedine was aware of using language that might dazzle bin Ibrahim a bit. "Their natural properties and inherent philosophical value."

"Explain."

Ezzedine attempted to explain, though bin Ibrahim's eyes were closed, and, if Ezzedine were candid about the question, the man wasn't intelligent enough to understand a fraction of what was involved in physic. "Nothing troubling. Merely the medical or magical properties of certain herbs and grasses that appear in this island and not in our country. Their ability to harm or heal. I rather thought"—and here Ezzedine congratulated himself for being clever, expecting to win Cafer's praise—"that I was doing the task you set us. I am bringing secrets of this country back home for the good of the sultan and our people."

"Excellent, Doctor. Now tell me of all those present, in order, around the table." Ezzedine strained to recall, not having the skill some men had to create a picture in the mind of faces, and many of the English resembled one another so closely that he had, more than once, called one by another's name. There had been a great deal of drink, which he had been assured was not liquor but which, he must admit, may have clouded his mind nevertheless. "Tell me of the talk, please, Doctor. Do they support their queen? Or conspire? Do they want a king upon the throne, as would be natural? One of themselves? Will they abide by their agreements with us? Which of them seems the poorest? Did you speak of the true religion? Would any of them consider, do you think, making private reports to you in exchange for gold?"

This was a task for which Ezzedine was ill-suited. To recall what every man at a long meal said? Some had likely spoken of France and Spain, this or that about King James of Scotland and Elizabeth. But most of the talk was of horses—whose was fastest, handsomest, boldest. They threatened to fight on these last questions, and peace was made with difficulty but always before actual combat.

Ezzedine had left the table at Dr. Dee's invitation to examine his library. Dee had a book in Arabic and wanted Ezzedine to read a passage to him. It was Averroes. There was some conversation, as they returned to the table, of Ezzedine, in the time remaining of the embassy's stay in England, teaching Dee how to read and write a bit of Arabic.

"You agreed to instruct him?" asked bin Ibrahim.

Ezzedine answered cautiously, fearing something in the man's voice, fearing that he had stepped over a bound. "I said I would consider it." This lie sounded implausible even as he spoke.

"I think it an excellent notion," said Cafer, who seemed nearly asleep. "To be in regular close conference with the queen's trusted wizard. Cleverly done. And when you returned to the company at the table?"

Ezzedine was doubly relieved: The Arabic lessons, which he had already begun out of enthusiastic delight, were permissible; and he had another clear recollection of table talk he could now deliver to bin Ibrahim. He felt almost gratified to be able to give the man what he wanted. "A young man—a poet, I believe—was boasting, trying to impress all the older men with his talk. Like a naughty child."

"On what subject?"

It now returned clearly to Ezzedine. "He said the Christian holy book was false. That the Jewish books, too, are false. That they are mere stories with no truth, tales of tricksters and filthy men. He said these words: 'filthy men.'"

Bin Ibrahim opened an eye with interest. "Was there agreement with him among the company?"

Some. Some heads shook in disapproval. Some of the conversation became too rapid for Ezzedine to follow. There were some—knights and lords—who laughed and urged the poet on in his flights of words. "'Moses was a juggler,' he said, and another man, a large man I have seen at court, laughed loudly at this."

"And your host? The master Dee?"

"A man interested in all things, prepared to listen to all things, whether he agrees or not. He acknowledges our own physicians as his masters, as in mathematics and astronomy." Ezzedine paused to recall what had pleased him in the evening, and he described it with unthinking candor. "They are men who, I suspect, *wonder* at the blindness of their fellow Christians. They are, perhaps, men who would see the superiority of our ways. But in the meantime, they dance, it seems to me, near other ideas. They are accused by some of atheism, though I do not think they truly—"

"You spent the night, then, my trusted doctor, drinking with men who reject the truth of *any* God?" Bin Ibrahim opened his eyes at last and smiled slightly with this question. Ezzedine only now heard a threat, like the first throbs of fever or infection. Had it been those, he would surely have seen the troubling symptoms much earlier. But he was, in streaks and moments, a child, and he was angry with himself for this. He stuttered: "If Allah . . . If Allah . . . If . . ." as if the idea he meant to eject from his body, bloated with anger, could not push past his tongue.

"Yes? If Allah what?" Cafer heard that anger and opened a space in front of Ezzedine where he could place it.

But calm returned: "Perhaps these men must stumble blindly first and then, when they fall often enough, learn to see after."

9

DR. DEE STOOD beside Dr. Ezzedine, a fair distance from the birds and hunters, and watched the falcons take their meat. "To listen to the earl," the English doctor said, nodding toward the queen's beloved Essex, "the birds are noble. They know respect, courage, loyalty."

"But you believe they have learned simply to follow the food," said the Turkish doctor.

"I believe they know habit as we do. Perhaps even preference for familiarity. That wrist. This hood. I do not think they *love* one gloved wrist above another. Although that story of your boy and the birds gives me pause. And the loyalty of some dogs and warhorses does make me wonder if they feel or comprehend something more."

Across the park, beside the Earl of Essex, Cafer bin Ibrahim loosened the straps of his bird's hood, releasing the blinking raptor's head to the light. The animal peered at the sky, and bin Ibrahim threw it into the blue as the beaters and dogs flushed the songbirds and sparrows from the trees and bushes. Essex called for wine. As it was served, bin Ibrahim declined, then turned to nod and slightly bow to the two doctors from across the green expanse.

"Let us walk," said Dee, and took his Turkish friend's hand.

Ezzedine followed his favorite Englishman farther into the wood.

Dee pointed with excitement. His pleasure at sharing was evident: "Poison . . . pain relief . . . reduces boils . . . urinary difficulty . . . other insufficiencies of the male organ . . ." Unlike English faces, these buds and leaves and sticks differentiated themselves graciously for Ezzedine, explained themselves plainly. Some he knew from Turkish soil; others he recognized as kin to those plants; most interesting, of course, were those unique to English earth. Dee broke a twig in two and held it to Ezzedine's nose. "To slow a wound's bleeding."

Ezzedine took several cuttings for his bag. "It would be illustrative, I think, to cut, slightly, the flesh in two locations and to apply to one a paste made from this English root and to the other a paste made from the herbs I carried from Qustantiniyya. And then to see which stops the bleeding more rapidly."

Dee laughed like a child. "We must! Let us you and I do it this very night. It is most clever of you, my friend. If only every question could be settled so brilliantly."

"You are kind."

"Your party returns to Constantinople soon. Are you ready to leave our island?"

Ezzedine told his one friend, "I will be sorry to come to the end of our walks and conversations, but I will see my wife and son, and I can feign no unhappiness about that, even to be diplomatic. They require me, and, if I am honest, I feel the loss of them while I am here."

Dee laughed. "My friend, that has been quite evident, even for one as diplomatic as you."

As they pushed farther into the wood, Dr. Dee spoke of the strife he had seen in his life caused by an inability to answer questions with solutions as elegant as Ezzedine's proposed experiment. "The unquestionable greatness of our queen lies in her wisdom on one particular topic. I do not know how matters stand among the Mahometans, but, sadly, Christian kingdoms hate one another and are divided on how best to show their love for Jesus Christ. How mad, you think, to hate over how best to love. But there it is. One makes allowances for children and souls that quake like children's souls. For many, it is the way things have always been.

"Every man as old as I knows of three different alterations of all they knew, and all our ways were upside down, and in despair at knowing the right way to believe, men did sometimes choose to believe nothing at all, yet that spared them not from the flame and the ax, wielded first by the Catholics, then by the Protestants, and then back again and then again. Until our queen, in her wisdom, has understood, with a divine spark of love, that we must not look inside other men's souls. We must—and I believe she knows this, though sometimes she forgets when Catholics threaten the throne itself—learn to be indifferent to other men's errors, even unto their damnation. For what we, in our frailty, take with certainty to be their errors . . . let us accept that just possibly they are not errors but we are in error? I believe she sees this. Let us all act the same on Sunday, as good English, and then discuss it no further. Perhaps men could accustom themselves to living with a small amount of doubt. I think doubt a necessary ingredient to live."

Amazed by Dee's words, Ezzedine remained silent and listened, until the philosopher came to an end and the silence became perhaps offensive. He finally allowed himself to speak but was nervous of what he would need to report to bin Ibrahim, and feared even what someone might say (although none was present) about Ezzedine himself, and so he was cautious, even to the point of dishonesty with his words: "Is there a limit to the permissible error of other men's thoughts? Would you love your English neighbor were he a Mahometan?"

"I love my dear friend from the land of the Turks and feel no need to correct him."

Ezzedine could not help himself: He admired this humility, this open heart. "And if your neighbor, like your poet-guest at your house the other evening, held his belief in no god at all, by any name, neither mine nor yours?"

At this, Dee laughed, and Ezzedine flinched that any might hear. "We mustn't take a wicked child's pulled faces too seriously. Do you know, in France, there are English Catholics who study violence and mean to infiltrate themselves into England to do mischief, and they know full well that they will be caught and tortured and killed, and they *long* for this! And they call themselves *martyrs*! It sickens the heart. And for this, in front of a Mahometan, I am ashamed of ourselves, Catholic and Protestant alike."

All of this Ezzedine attempted to remember word for word. He wrote it down after he and Dee embraced in parting (and made plans to cut each other's arms and apply pastes together), though first he wrote sketches and descriptions of the leaves and roots his friend had taught him.

He wrote Dee's words to be sure that he forgot nothing. This was his duty.

He wrote Dee's words to someday show his son how wisdom grew. This was his pleasure and his duty.

He wrote Dee's words because Dee's mind brought Ezzedine pleasure. He would enjoy, when home in Constantinople, recalling his friend's words at his leisure. Perhaps they would continue a scholarly and warm correspondence. Perhaps he might send medicaments back to England for him.

But first, his duty to report to bin Ibrahim: He would do so, of course. Or he could report only that the conversation pertained to natural philosophy, medicine, botany. He did not wish to imply that Dr. Dee's clarity about Christian weakness made him a potential secret servant of bin Ibrahim.

Dee and Ezzedine passed three ladies as they exited the wood into the open park, where in the distance Essex and bin Ibrahim still hunted. Ezzedine followed Dee's example, bowing while turning, walking backward as the ladies turned their heads and prettily smiled with only their lips. "That one is a lady of the chamber. She dresses the queen, attends her in her bath, cleans her in all manner of things. Do your sultan and sultana have such a one as this?"

Ezzedine felt it would be unkind to state the truth: that for any one English page, serving girl, or beauty such as this woman, for every man-at-arms, musician, or cook, the sultan had a dozen in the

Sublime Porte, some paid, some slaves, some loyal for love. The sultan lived amid a clamor of those who wished to touch the royal hair or paint the face or clean a tooth or wipe away filth. The English court was richer in nothing except green grass, which Ezzedine did enjoy kneeling down to caress.

"Because," Dee continued, "I happen to know that this one has asked about you. You have caught the eye of a great beauty, my friend, with your exotic ways and Mahometan wisdom. And the red beard, I suspect."

Ezzedine did not at first understand the implication. "I am honored," he said simply, though he was not a complete innocent. In Constantinople a court woman might well desire a man who was not her husband. The result might be heads cut off, or merely poison drizzled into goblets, and so illicit desires were kept at bay without much difficulty. Of course, the nearer a man sat to the sultan's favor, the more freedom he was able to exert, and, as one of the sultan's physicians, Ezzedine could, he supposed, have been nearly as free with himself in the Sublime Porte as any man might wish. He knew some men who acted according to their desires and the license of their rank. And yet he felt no desire whatever beyond what he felt for his wife. It never occurred to him that this was unusual. Nor did he notice the appetites she whetted in other men.

The two physicians strolled around a curve of wood and into an enclosure of green lawn, a bay nestled on three sides by forest, shadowed paintings of tree branches cast onto the grass. Three acrobats—a skinny man of surprising height, a boy, and some person whose sex Ezzedine could not have guessed—were awaiting passing audiences and now hurried into their performance at the arrival of the two chatting doctors. "Hop, hop . . . Hey!" The mysterious third climbed upon the man's shoulders and set to juggling three balls. The boy ran in circles, pretended to fall, then leapt and scrambled up, not stopping until he was on the shoulders of the second figure, and from this perch, high above the doctors, he pulled four balls from a pocket and set to juggling, a ring of orbs set above the smaller ring below. "I can throw these balls to heaven!" shouted the boy, hurling the balls higher and higher in their crossing arcs and orbits, these harmonic circles. The two doctors leaned backward, like reeds blown by wind, to watch the balls fly and form a little universe of their own above the tower of people.

A voice behind them replied, "That is what I meant to say at your house the other evening." Ezzedine had not heard anyone approach on the thick grass, and the voice was nearly in his ear.

It was the young man from Dee's home, the friend of one of the lords, the poet who took such giggling, vicious pleasure in playing with hot ideas and trying out sour words upon his tongue. "*That,* my doctors: The juggler, like a priest, tells us he can see right up God's nostrils and we, just a few yards below, beg him to report to us how long those celestial hairs grow."

Ezzedine could not remember the man's name. Dee just shook his head, calmly disapproving but ready to forgive, as at an infant smeared in filth. "Kit's a difficult boy," Dee said to Ezzedine, smiling but apologetic. "Exactly the sort of talk I was saying we need less of." But today there was something about the young man that Ezzedine liked instantly, before any voice of censure arose in him. The poet blasphemed as if he expected to be praised rather than punished, praised for wisdom and for naughty daring. In normal circumstances (blasphemy against Mohammed), Ezzedine would have been glad to see him punished, but there was something in this arrangement (blasphemy against Christians, among Christians) that freed Ezzedine to weigh the boy's worth on some other scale than doctrine. And then he liked him. He liked the boy's desire to be loved, to make Dr. Dee laugh, and Dee did laugh, shaking his head in unconvincing disapproval, the boy going on and on with his jests and provocations and claims to historical evidence. He had said over dinner (words Ezzedine had forgotten to report to bin Ibrahim), "Do you know, there are people in the New World whose nations have been upon the earth well beyond six thousand years. Beyond the span of all human history laid out in our misshapen book."

The boy juggler atop the tower shouted down, "Can you catch what heaven throws you, lords?" The child let fall from the top of its arc one of his balls, kept the other three converging into a blur, a halo. The released orb fell from the sky, shooting past three bodies and six other balls. Ezzedine tried to catch it, but he had no skill at such things. It fell between them, and the poet leapt at it. Kit chided him, "Can you not catch, sir Turk? Why, even the papists I've known can now and again catch and tickle the odd hairy ball."

Ezzedine attempted to play with Kit's words and wit: "Does God think the earth but a child's ball?"

Quoth the poet: "He thinketh it but a turd." Ezzedine caught his breath, but no one from his embassy was in range to hear such talk. "And I do return his low opinion."

"Do you not risk chastisement for this . . . speech?" asked the doctor.

"Of course he does," clucked Dee. "He thinks his friends make him immortal."

"Oh, the men without wit are not so foolish as to think me menacing. But if they should grow tired of me, I would flee with you to Constantinople and take up residence in the seraglio."

"I doubt the sultan would welcome your intrusion. Or that he would enjoy your wit."

"Good Turk, I have higher hopes in your people than that. I will give you a gold coin of your own realm if you invite me to the Sublime Porte so that I might inform the sultan that, just like the god of the Hebrews, the god of Rome, and the god of the English, so, too, the god of Mussulmen is born of the same muck: the conceit of man. I shall convince every man there in the sultan's court, and all the harem, too, that I speak the truth. When I leave, they will not one of them spend another day on anything but tobacco, wine, and lust."

"I should need the gold coin paid first, because I do not think you will be able to pay it after your lecture."

10

A WEEK BEFORE THEIR departure to Constantinople, after prayers, Dr. Ezzedine came as was his custom to the ambassador's private apartments, nodded to the guardsmen outside, knocked twice, announced himself even as he was opening the door without waiting for assent, so comfortable was he in their routines.

But tonight, unlike all other nights when he was dressed for bed, awaiting only Dr. Ezzedine's sleep-inducing preparations and a discussion of the day's health concerns, the ambassador was seated behind a writing table, a single candle illuminating a flickering portion of his round, beardless face, his thin brown hair. "Sit," he sighed.

The doctor sat across from the ambassador, who now waited some time before speaking, rubbing his eyes, looking at the ceiling, rubbing his eyes again. "Are you feeling discomfort?" asked Ezzedine.

The ambassador was silent a few unhappy moments longer, then sighed again, undamming a rush of words: "You have done something so foolish. I have no choice now but to involve myself in this nonsense. It is aggravating to me. I would have thought you more careful of yourself and more considerate of my needs."

"I do not know how I have failed in my duty to you."

"A boy said to you that God thought the world a turd."

"How did you hear this?"

"And you accepted his offer to pay you to arrange his visit to court, where he would then mouth apostasy to the sultan and take his pleasure in the sultan's seraglio, after he rendered everyone in court drunken and lustful."

"Oh, no no, it was all in jest. In the English style."

"A jest? Did you laugh? Did he?"

"That is not their style of jest. They speak the opposite of what they believe."

"Was he doing that?"

"I certainly was."

"So you did say all of that? The report is true? And you did not report any of this to Cafer."

"I didn't recall it when I made my report," said Ezzedine feebly, but he could recall the moment he chose to tell Cafer of nothing other than discussions of herbs and the Earl of Essex's sexual reputation.

The ambassador stared at Ezzedine's chin for a long while and finally breathed deeply, almost smiled. "You do know that you possess in Qustantiniyya certain things he desires."

"Things? Who desires?"

"How could you have exposed yourself to all this." It wasn't a question. It was stated almost pityingly, and then, self-pityingly, "He will make a matter of it at court when we return home. I cannot see how you will escape unpunished. Accusations will be made and answered; some vizier who protects and promotes Cafer will be called upon to judge; one of you will be punished. And I must tell you, my doctor, as a man who respects you, who is grateful to you: Cafer is better than you at all of this. I do not think you will prevail in shaping your words or catching the ear of the men who will have the sultan's ear."

Ezzedine was dazed by the rush of information. "But I have served the sultan well and with loyalty."

The ambassador looked at the ceiling and said, "Yes, perhaps you are right." His meaning was clear.

"Who desires what things? I don't understand."

"Do you really not?"

Cafer had come to his home, had accepted coffee and figs from Saruca. He had admired her grace, and the house, the garden. He had told Ezzedine that it had been Cafer himself who had convinced the sultan to send Ezzedine to England.

Ezzedine's career as a healer prepared him not at all for the diseased moments of his travels, for those fleeting diagnostic opportunities where a different decision might have led to a different outcome. In the comfortable life in Constantinople, as physician to the family of the sultan of the Turks, he could identify a symptom, and from a symptom a cause, and from a cause a cure, whether herbal or dietary or astrological. Even in moments of growling medical crisis—a fever, a pustule, a fracture, a rupture—there was always a procedure to initiate, an ointment to apply. But away from all of that, when life-and-death decisions were political or personal, not medical, he had only uneducated guesses with which to protect himself. His recognition of danger blurred or dulled, or simply abandoned him. He did not know a disease was infecting him until it was nearly fatal.

He attempted the voice of a courageous man. "Even if he has me killed, she is a free woman. She can refuse him. She is not a slave to be granted to my conqueror."

"Of course. But let us not waste our hours or spoil our night further. My feet ache."

But the reality of power—a field of study Ezzedine had ignored, even as he benefited from it—could not be denied infinitely. He would be subject to its immutable laws whether he studied them or pretended they didn't exist.

Many years later, the doctor would recall this scene, and finally he would fight, would demand, would calculate and strategize. But at the moment, Dr. Ezzedine was childishly frightened for his life, as if it still had value, and he thought it best to say nothing, until, slowly understanding the meaning of words he had heard and glances he had noticed, going back so many months, illuminated now by the reference to *things he desires,* he asked, "If I do not prevail in the sultan's judgment, what protection can you give my wife and child from Cafer? They must not be his. To ensure their safety, I can perhaps offer you something of value now. Anything you might name."

The ambassador appreciated that Ezzedine had hurried to catch up to the implications, at least: "I will think upon it. But now, please, Doctor, my feet ache."

11

WITH LESS THAN a week remaining until their wind-dependent return to Constantinople, the embassy was invited to the queen's presence in honor of the third anniversary of the failed Spanish conquest of England. The chamber was hot and close, and the shadows and light from the fires and the torches played upon the ceiling in a show of tongues and demons. Ezzedine tried to stand near the window, where there was some cool air and a little gray daylight, but was pressed by crowd and shyness and his own preoccupations to the back of the Presence Chamber while the Master of Ceremonies glided through the room, signaling when a song should stop and a speech begin and another song rise from another corner.

Ezzedine, having spent months now in London, had almost accustomed himself to the cold, dark, childish little court, the parody of the wealth and pageantry awaiting him at home. He had, though, come to like the music, a little. His mind wandered as he listened, and he decided he would ask for written pages of it to take back with him to Constantinople, if it was written in the same codes as Turkish musicians used. If he was to be imprisoned in Constantinople for his behavior, for his polite (and diplomatic, he would argue) tolerance of other men's apostasy, if he was to be made to look like a sympathizer of blasphemy, merely because bin Ibrahim lusted after Ezzedine's wife, he would at least come home with something of value. No, no, no: He would not be imprisoned, because bin Ibrahim would not be believed. The service Ezzedine had done the royal family was too valuable, too clearly the service of a devoted and pious man. Or Ezzedine would not be imprisoned because bin Ibrahim would not be satisfied with only a temporary opportunity to steal Ezzedine's property; he would insist on Ezzedine's death. But the ambassador would protect Ezzedine. He would explain to the sultan. This was a question of loyalty first, and in that Ezzedine was above reproach.

The ambassador smiled upon the proceedings. The queen asked that the story of her address to her troops be retold. The Earl of Essex bowed and began to declaim, "No woman soft, but *monarch* stern, before the bristled men of Tilbury did raise martial voice and call down heaven's—" before a lesser noble pushed to the front of the leg-sore lords and ladies. He seemed to demand attention, shoving aside several, including the queen's favorite in the midst of his oration. "Ruffian, are you touched?" someone cried. A page laughed. A countess slapped at the stumbling noble's hands as he reached for her, and then he fell to the floor and trembled in every limb and foamed at his lips and spoke in unknown tongues. A giant man in the back began to step toward the commotion, then was stopped by the lightest touch of a lady's hand on his arm.

Essex thought to ignore the intrusion and continued his speech, his timing in political gesture never being perfect. But the cries soon outperformed him. "A demon is locked within him!" murmured one of the queen's ladies, and another shouted the exact same words an instant later, though with a poor player's lack of conviction or even of alarm.

Ezzedine watched: the lord palsying upon the floor, his eye rolling, his chin wet, the queen observing but unmoving, though she leaned slightly forward on her throne to have a clear view of the event. Ezzedine might have asked his ambassador's permission, but he did not think of it. Had he done so, perhaps he would have been reunited with his soft wife and fat son, in his house upon the hill over the bluest water in creation. But perhaps, too, he would have been murdered on the French ship back to Constantinople (Cafer's open hand), or executed for apostasy upon his return (Cafer's closed hand), or . . . Those possibilities don't signify, those other lives and deaths he didn't live or die. Because he did not ask his ambassador's leave to attend to the stricken Englishman.

Dr. Ezzedine was dressed in the clothing of a Mahometan, of course, and so when he bent over the thrashing body of an English lord, there was scarcely a man in the chamber who did not clench his whole body, fist and tail, at a collective national memory: a Saracen kneeling over his Crusader victim. And when the Mahometan doctor removed from within his robes a curved implement of polished wood, a hand's span in length, the image of one of Suleiman's turbaned assassins with his carved killing dagger was complete. And yet no Englishman stepped forward to rescue his fallen comrade, if that is what he was, and the queen herself only tilted her head to one side in fascination at the theatrical unfolding before and beneath her.

Ezzedine knelt beside the trembling man and wedged the shining crescent of wood fast between the man's jaws. A man-at-arms felt enough was now finally well past enough and began to step forward, lowering his halberd, but none less than the queen told him to be still. Ezzedine seized the lord's flailing arms and pressed them to his flanks, again pushing the slipping bar back between his teeth. The doctor only then recalled at last some shred of protocol: "Forgive me, please, great Majesty," he said. He then pushed Henry Fairleigh, Third Baron Moresby, onto his side, facing away from the queen (turning both his and the lord's back to the monarch, but what can one do), because, seeming to know exactly what would happen next, he collected Baron Moresby's voluminous outflow of vomit in rags withdrawn from his own robes. The queen moved one bejeweled foot slightly forward and out from under her skirts, as if considering standing for a better view, but she remained seated at the farthest edge of the Presence Chamber's throne.

At last, held tight by the Turk for another long minute or two, the baron ceased to flail. His shoulders drawn to his ears, his eyes closed, his head turned away, his fists brought close to his cheek, the baron became at once a sleeping child. His vileness was wiped away and hidden by the graceful doctor who, in the same motion, stored away the curved piece of wood by which he had prevented the Englishman from swallowing his own tongue.

The observant queen, with the speed and strategic brilliance for which she was renowned, noticed at once that Moresby was not possessed of a demon and that the Mussulman did no harm but rather healed the Christian, and that Moresby was now visibly incapable of living at court and so would have to return certain valuable royal patents to royal hands. She was not entirely unprepared for this, having previously instructed two of her ladies to squeal something about demons if they ever saw Baron Moresby shake, as many-tongued rumor sneered that he sometimes did in private or in the company of a single trusted groom.

12

CAFER BIN IBRAHIM would have preferred to keep the arrogant and conniving physician locked in his room, then locked away on the ship home, not brought out until he faced accusations before a vizier. But this was a ceremonial moment, and the ambassador had insisted on the full company of men attending. Still, Cafer took the doctor aside before the queen entered the chamber, and he smiled alarmingly through a few words in Arabic: "I hope that you are able to explain your position to the sultan more convincingly than you could to me or the ambassador. I truly hope it. It would be a loss to us all otherwise." Perhaps that might be enough to make the doctor flee before they reached Qustantiniyya. The man's house was placed so delightfully on a hill. There was a well-water fountain in its courtyard, clean and drinkable water, cool year-round. The child would have to be dealt with in time, but the sultan would certainly not stand in the way of a marriage. The widow would be considered greatly fortunate to make a new match. Told of her husband's crimes and disappearance, she would leap at the offer.

Not forty minutes later, while Ezzedine attended to the thrashing, vomiting English lord, and the ladies cried "Demon!" and the lazy lords stood idly by as a Mahometan tossed and turned the body of their peer, while the queen poked a single jeweled toe from under the farthest skirts of her gowns, Cafer bin Ibrahim reduced himself to nothing but freely floating eyes and ears, and in that potent state, he sped and flew through the chamber, collecting priceless knowledge. Such physical pleasure to leave the body like this, to drift at any speed, at any distance, to glide invisibly above the room and below the feet, into the mouths and thence to the minds, all possible with effort.

Cafer floated beside the ladies shouting "Demon!" and saw their glances to each other, and then heard the words kept within their hearts: They did not think there were any demons here but only mouthed this claim upon instruction. Bin Ibrahim's body, far across the chamber, shivered with pleasure at this purloined knowledge. He felt less aroused when it was his actual body at work, when, as an example, he had placed himself alone in the library of the city home of the Earl of Essex, while he was that peer's guest, and read, rapidly, such letters as could be seen upon a writing table. There, alone, his actual body in the perilous act of intrusion, he felt pleasure—even a deep pleasure—but nothing comparable to the rush of blood and the quivers of waist that rewarded this disembodiment. The spirit of Allah's angels inflated him as his own soul freely flew up the skirts of these ladies and into the mind of the Earl of Essex and the Baron Moresby and even his own countryman, Dr. Ezzedine. What did bin Ibrahim learn? What was not revealed to him as his body felt such heavenly caresses, as if his eternal pleasure in paradise had begun ahead of all logical time?

Upon a royal barge that night, artificial fires blooming against the sky and weeping red into the Thames, in which river mechanical porpoises with men inside them leapt and gamboled, the queen told the Ottoman ambassador that his physician was a man of great skill and that she was grateful to him for having preserved her loyal peer. She wished to present the embassy's doctor with a gift to symbolize her royal esteem. She raised her hand at an attendant, who passed to the ambassador a ring set with a blue stone. The ambassador recited all appropriate words, such diplomatic matters having scripts and, after numerous performances, a certain reflexive dullness. Would the ring ever find the finger of the physician for whom it was intended? Such things could not be easily known, and neither party cared.

For at that exact instant, Allah whispered into the ambassador's ear a solution to all the troubles and unpleasantness awaiting his return to Constantinople, when he wanted to arrive to laurels and the sultan's love. Allah spoke to the ambassador the precise words to repeat to the English sultana, and all trouble was cleared away with a breath of celestial wisdom.

13

UNAWARE OF THIS conversation between the queen and the ambassador, Ezzedine spent two days preparing his belongings, letting his mind wander, then walking in the gardens of the embassy residence to restore his confidence. He would, somehow, address the sultan directly. He would plead. No, he would not plead. He would speak openly of his love for the royal family and explain that Cafer desired his wife. The sultan would take pity on him the more honestly and manfully he explained himself.

Or, if he was sentenced to die, he would at least make a plan for Saruca to flee first. Who would help him?

Despite his eagerness to return home, his fear of what would come next slowed him down, sometimes nearly to immobility, for minutes at a time. Shaking himself free of fear's shackles, renewed with hope, he spent extra time wrapping and storing his vast array of new and fragile items: liquids and seeds and cuttings his friend, Dr. Dee, had presented him, in shared love of knowledge "and our Creator, by whatever name we choose to praise Him and by whatever means we worship Him." His English friend's typically provocative way of speaking. "Someday you will show me your gardens."

Two nights before the delegation was to leave London and travel to Deptford to their waiting ship to Constantinople and the New

Palace, the ambassador entered Ezzedine's chambers. It was the first time he had come to his physician's rooms in all their months in England.

"My doctor. My friend." This was a peculiar choice of words, even if Ezzedine were not already susceptible to alarm. The little ambassador sat on his doctor's bed, his legs sticking out straight, almost giddy with some excitement. "The sultan has communicated his desires to me. He is pleased with our expedition to the English and with the terms we have made with them. He mentions you, in particular, as one worthy of high honor."

"He mentioned me? I am undeserving of this gift beyond measure." There! The threat of bin Ibrahim was already dealt with. Ezzedine had been acting like a child, and he was ashamed of ever doubting the protective love of the sultan.

The ambassador leaned forward, his soft hands on his fat thighs. "It is exactly a gift of that value, and to earn still more, why, one would do anything. At least, I would."

"Naturally."

"And he is especially pleased to make use of you for the greater glory of the empire and for the foundation of confidence in further negotiations between himself and the English infidels, great in his wisdom, all praise to him."

Ezzedine did not reply.

"You do not doubt his great wisdom, his strategy in his decisions?"

"Not at all. How could I begin to be such a fool as that? I do not claim to number the stars in the sky."

"Then rejoice, my dear friend. For he has chosen you to do something great. Something only you can do. To be the cement, the very bridge he is constructing between London and Qustantiniyya."

"You sound like you are reciting from a peace treaty."

"Do I?" The ambassador giggled. "Mahmoud! Like a treaty indeed! You are to become a treaty in your person! You are receiving a gift of incalculable value! He has given you this gift! I am envious!"

"When did he communicate this to you?"

"A strange and irrelevant question. Better to ask how you can continue to deserve his extraordinary trust and generosity. Now, prepare yourself, dear friend. Prepare yourself to flood with gratitude. For when it happens, I must mark exactly what you do and say, so that I may present myself to the sultan and say, to the word, what effect his gift had on you. Are you ready? Your every gesture, your every word, I am prepared to record to the slightest detail."

"And I will not be present to offer him my gratitude myself?"

"It is unlikely. But your wife and child will be present when I describe your reaction. And he will look upon them accordingly."

Ezzedine stood unmoving, silent, wishing his heartbeat would obey, heard his slow thoughts roam in useless circles, lost, lost.

"Are you prepared to express what you will feel? Quite absolutely prepared?"

There was a kindness in this, interlaced with the cruelty, knotted inseparably with it. In later years, when Ezzedine replayed this scene, retold the story in silence or solitude, he could appreciate the ambassador's care at this moment. The ambassador allowed Ezzedine time to exercise the skill that any man at court must master: to hide one's thoughts. He had warned Ezzedine that the effort would in this case be extreme but that failure would be worse, threatening his wife and child.

The ambassador reclined and busied himself with the pleasant task of sipping ale, a taste he would have to shed with great difficulty before their return and that no man would dare report, as all of them had sampled it except bin Ibrahim. (The water was not clean enough to drink on this filthy island; one of Ezzedine's judgments after some weeks, with the ambassador's blessing, had been to instruct all the men of the embassy that English beer and wine could be consumed without sin, as they were not alcohol but, respectively, English rainwater and bull's blood.)

Ezzedine did not prepare for the worst thing he could imagine. Instead, he thought at once of his home, of Saruca and Ismail and the animals and herbs in his garden, of the hours spent in the sultan's court and the pleasure all of this had brought him in his life, of his wife's eyes and the smell of his son's breath when he was a baby. He even savored the anticipation he had felt, while in England, of returning to all this. This was deeply wise: Since he would have to protect all of it in his reply, he held it all in the forefront of his mind, its value and importance placed above the pain he might feel at its loss. This was the best way to care for it and to love it. He swallowed again and again and again; each time, a blade caught in his throat and acid boiled in his stomach.

He breathed deeply, and when he was ready—the ambassador did not hurry him—Ezzedine murmured through tears, "I am eager to learn of how best I might please our sultan."

At the end, when with curlicues of language the ambassador had made clear Ezzedine's gift, Ezzedine asked if the ambassador would carry a letter back to his wife, to keep it private for her and read it aloud to her, of necessity. "I will gladly," said the puffy man, lovingly grateful in turn to Ezzedine for having played his role so gently, without any strife. He was now so kind to his physician that Ezzedine in turn regretted having caused the ambassador all this trouble to begin with, and he hoped that the sultan would praise the ambassador for the solution he had discovered and the lies he had told, since of course it was not at all possible that this had been arranged in Constantinople at all. The letter to his wife was a large request, and in later years Ezzedine was sometimes even forgiving of the ambassador for having ignored it.

14

A T THE CONCLUSION of the play—the comical story of a woman who was cruel and disobedient to her husband until he starved her into proper behavior—the ambassador stood before the queen, in the space the players had left. He summoned Dr. Ezzedine from out of the crowd to join him. Some of the players circled in the back of the chamber, jostling to find a space, the better to study how their betters spoke and stood, the better to play back to them, convincingly, the image of themselves and their ancestors.

"Tomorrow, great queen," began the ambassador, "we sail from your shores, successful in the task our lord and sultan set for us, for we have found upon this island peace between peoples and love for your great kingdom. A people as contented and fatted as can be conceived. Councillors as wise as any we have ever known. And atop this commonweal, a queen who rules without a king but with all the strength and wisdom that any king, or even sultan, might be loudly jealous to possess."

Elizabeth smiled upon the speech, and her councillors and attendant lords and ladies bowed and applauded lightly. "Think you could play a Turk eunuch?" a player whispered to one of his slim young colleagues, still in a gown from his performance as the shrewish wife. "If we put a cushion under your shirt? And tied your eggs back between your legs?"

"Murad the Great, third of that name, Sultan of the Ottomans, Custodian of the Two Holy Mosques, Caliph of Caliphs, knowing that Mahmoud Ezzedine has been of service to Her Majesty, Elizabeth, Queen of England, France, and Ireland, Defender of the Faith, and greatly proud that Master Ezzedine's knowledge of physic being among the most esteemed of all who reside in his lands, so most certainly does our sultan wish to present you with a gift that in every day of health will bring to your mind a thought of kindness between our kingdoms, the friendship bridging our empire and your own. For you to command and to take such benefit as might please you, that you may reign in health for so long as monarchs reign, Mahmoud Ezzedine, physician to the sultan of the Turks, will remain and wait upon Your Majesty's desires for so long as he does bring you satisfaction."

"Such friendship and comity between our nations will forever be one of the great prides of my reign," said Elizabeth, "and it pleases me that you will tell your sultan that his friend in England does thank him for his kindness." She noted carefully what she could see of Dr. Ezzedine's expressions, such that were visible above his beard and mustache. "Doctor. Is this destiny what you yourself may desire? To live among us English?"

"Great queen, it is my desire to serve my sultan, and if he so desires that I might serve you, then I desire it, too, and with all warmth. To serve Your Majesty is to serve him. It is my duty and joy."

"Prettily pronounced," she said as the doctor bowed to her.

Essex laughed loudly. "But he will not live here among us forever? As a Mahometan?"

She eyed the insolence into silence, then turned her softer gaze to the kneeling, bowed Turk.

AND SO, IN late August of 1591, Mahmoud Ezzedine was for the first time made into a gift.

The boat left without him. They left him. Before he could even give them the letters to his son and wife.

He was stranded by chuckling fate or reeking devils on a tiny, wet, and blustery island, impossibly far from civilization, from home, from love, castaway and outcast in one. He stood, alone, on this island populated, as in a children's story, only by savages and heretics and imbeciles and, most of all, by professional liars, speaking only and always in misdirection. The speed of events was bewildering, perhaps even to God, if He ever chose to cast His eyes over the circumstances: In just a few months—in just a few days—a respected and fortunate man was reduced to a slave; a man who knew his honored place became a token of others' generosity or scorn. He was in almost no time at all sliced from his devoted family, from his country, severed even from his loving God, and dropped to wander alone in a wilderness far from all he loved.

And they congratulated him, behind false smiles, for his abandonment.

When men win prizes from life by their cleverness, they begin to believe that their cleverness is infinitely protective, that they have earned an unshakable and privileged place in Allah's creation, that they are essentially and eternally unlike the world's poor victims. But—having begun his long stumble into diplomacy and espionage, court politics, foreign intrigues, religious war—as a man ensnared by events beyond his understanding, Mahmoud Ezzedine was stupefied: He was made stupid or forced to accept that he had always been stupid. He was never aware of a symptom, and when made aware, he responded with useless instincts. And so it was that in a time when a man might be lucky to see fifty years, ten years were lifted from Mahmoud Ezzedine as easily as a purse is snipped free in a crowded theater.

Of arrogance and stupidity, he realized, ten years later, standing alone on a heath in Scotland, vomiting, he had never been cured.

Dr. Mahmoud Ezzedine was to be presented as a gift—was handed over as the personification of someone else's generosity—four more times.

My son,

 God the all-knowing and merciful will place such obstacles in one's path that He deems necessary, and it is not for us to demand an explanation or to bewail our fate but to love our travails as we love Him. Allah knows all, and Allah listens not to the whine of a man or a dog.

 I will not return to you when I had expected, and when the embassy returns to the Sublime Porte, I will not be among them.

 Whosoever brings this letter to you is my friend and yours. He may judge it wise that you and your mother should travel with him away from our home, possibly even away from Qustantiniyya, until such time as I am able to rejoin you and protect you.

 Here is a difficult task for you, but one I ask you to perform as a young man: Please tell your mother that I will return when God arranges for it and that my return will never be delayed by any desire of my own. Her husband is alive and hurt only by our separation. Please read her these words as often as she desires. I am delayed, only delayed.

PART TWO

GEOFFREY BELLOC, 1601

· · · · · · · · ·

There is less danger in fearing too much than too little.

—SIR FRANCIS WALSINGHAM

1

"STILL NOTHING?" ROBERT Cecil asked, wiping his eyes as if he were the one exhausted, self-starving, entertaining Death at his bedside.

"She took a sip of wine."

"No food?"

The lady shook her head, so Cecil walked past her and lowered himself, with some pain in his crooked back, onto a low stool beside the royal bed. "Majesty."

"My pygmy," croaked the queen on her fifth night of refusing food.

"I have sampled the broth. As fine as any you have ever tasted, if I may be bold to imagine." The queen closed her eyes. Now she was so thin that her bones could be seen beneath the fragile skin of her arms; nothing remained of her that was stately to Cecil's eye, nothing regal, nothing beautiful, nothing that should make her queen, and yet sitting beside her still ignited in Cecil some small spark of the excitement he had felt as a boy, watching from corners as his father tended to her blossoming reign. He watched her doze, rubbed his own sore shoulder, and waited for her to return.

She opened her eyes, and Cecil renewed his insistence that she eat, but she whispered, "I have received such marvelous intelligence. From abroad." She waited, wanted him to ask what it was, even now tried to flirt with his interest.

"Madame?"

She smiled weakly. "I am with child," she pronounced. Cecil bowed his head and tried again to guide the bowl to his monarch's lips. "England," she proclaimed, then turned her head away. Perhaps the child was to be named England; perhaps she was carrying the entire nation in her ancient and virgin womb. Perhaps, Cecil thought, she was speaking poetically or even cryptically: She was prepared, in her hunger and disease, to discuss, finally and at painfully long last, the matter of her successor. It was a bit late for that.

At the door, Cecil asked the attendant lady if the queen spoke often of this fantastical notion. "She has once or twice said something similar." And so the principal secretary asked the lady, as kindly as he was able, that she not repeat that to anyone, but still his voice sounded in his own ears like a threat. He wished it were otherwise, that his voice could glide and charm, that his face could evoke affections and confidences. It would make his life easier if he didn't seem always to be conniving or demanding, complaining or menacing. But it was yet another skill his body refused to acquire.

2

And even as a threat it failed to close mouths or ears or doors, for the day after next, Cecil found Geoffrey Belloc in all his giant bulk sitting in wait in Cecil's annex, asking a moment of the principal secretary's time, and not terribly politely. "Before a royal child is born, sir," Belloc said quietly, when Cecil tried to put him off, and so Cecil, feeling bullied, opened the door for the intruder, said he had a very few, very brief minutes.

Inside the inner cabinet, Cecil gestured with his nose for Belloc to sit on a low folding stool with a leather sling, the lowest point he could offer. Even then, with Cecil settling into his tall chair up on its platform, still Belloc looked down at the secretary. "What are you up to nowadays, Geoff? The Gentlemen Pensioners?"

"Queen's Messengers, sir," said Belloc. "More than ten years now. The generosity of Mr. Walsingham when he died."

"You are from the very old days indeed. The old Earthworms."

"Earthworms, my lord?"

Cecil laughed without making a sound. "What my father and Mr. Walsingham used to call you fellows, out in the mud of it all."

"Your father and those other gentlemen were kind to recognize my small service."

"Stories since I was a boy of fellows like you. Derring-do. Hiding under the Catholics' beds, in the teeth of it. The sharp end. Saving us all from papal conspiracy, from the bad old days. You were catching Catholics starting when?"

"Since I was nineteen, sir, maybe a bit younger. Mr. Walsingham had me in France around then."

"And today? Do you come asking for a favor?"

"No, my lord. I come as a messenger of sorts. On the very same question."

"Catching Catholics?"

"Yes, sir. And I come on behalf of better men than I."

"Ah." Cecil leaned back and tilted his head.

"We understand that she isn't eating, my lord."

"You hear that in the Messengers' office? Rumor."

"As I said, sir, I'm sent today in a private way."

"Very dramatical, Geoff. You're still a bit of a player, aren't you? Drama in all things."

Belloc had volunteered for this task, had agreed over dinner to represent Mr. Beale's and all the other gentlemen's views to the principal secretary and to demand action; he would push on until Cecil listened. Crooked in heart as much as back, Geoff thought; if you met Cecil in an inn, you wouldn't trust him with your luggage. "You're still new to your position, sir, and perhaps certain matters haven't yet risen to your attention. And in your father's day, this might have seemed distant enough in the future to leave unanswered, but now, sir, the gentlemen have sent me to raise the matter's urgency to you. Their question is now pressing, as she's not eating. She wanders in her mind, as you know."

"Who told you this? How dare you speak of—"

"Events threaten to gallop past any preparations, Sir Robert. If matters are to proceed peacefully, we require certainty. It's no disgrace for us to discuss it here, behind doors." Geoff pushed to the end: "King James may believe England is his for the taking, but not as matters stand."

Cecil winced and rubbed his humped shoulder, to Geoff's eye an amateur performance of having been stabbed in the back.

"As they stand? With whom? You dare a great deal—"

"There is worry."

"There just *is*? Like rain?"

Belloc said nothing more. Size always helped in these matters when there was nothing to be gained by speaking. He learned that years ago, making money by helping to collect rich men's debts, real or implied.

"So." Robert Cecil spread his hands on his table, his legs in his chair, his back against the light from the window. "A clique of whispering men will be anonymous. And will send their giant messenger to question Her Majesty's principal secretary and demand that we all ponder the illegal question of what the future holds. I don't have a *vote* in the matter, you know. Inheritance just *is*."

"They ask, my lord—as men who have seen the darkest and worst of Catholic crimes and have loyally protected Her Majesty from invasions and intrigues—whether the claimant to the throne can bring peace and be relied upon not to burn his subjects alive in the streets. It seems a small matter to be certain of this. They demand an answer, definitive: Is he Protestant or not?"

"Ah." Cecil waved distractedly as if at a fly, and his body began already to lose the illusion of size he had strained to create. "Who has ever thought he wasn't? He says he is. He goes to Protestant church every week. If that's all that worries them—"

"If he is a Catholic, they won't let him in. If they *believe* he's a Catholic, my lord, it will be war or civil war, sooner or later. It will be slaughter again. The Catholics will rise up to greet him, and they will murder. I was in Paris with Mr. Walsingham during the St. Bartholomew's Day massacre."

"I saw the play."

"It was worse than the play."

"That's saying something." But the topic seemed to exhaust Cecil. His pride and bluster were thin. He rubbed his shoulder again and poured himself some wine, offered none to his tormentor.

Belloc pressed on: "James has a Spanish boy who gives him counsel in bed."

"Oh, James has always had favorites. They never last long."

"They are always Catholic."

"Do you still have webs of intelligencers in Scotland, Geoff?"

Instead of answering, Belloc opened the leather case he had held at his side throughout. "We have prepared something for you. An abstract."

"This *we* again?" Cecil couldn't long maintain an air of calm. "How many dare?"

Belloc unfolded the sheets and placed them on Cecil's table. They were headed, in fine secretary hand, "Chronology of Certainties. Of His Acts."

If Cecil was impressed or surprised by the dossier, Geoffrey Belloc couldn't perceive it. Instead, when he saw Geoff wasn't going to answer who had sent him, the smaller man grunted and condescended to lower his eyes to read. He asked questions without looking up. When had Belloc received this entry? And how much later until he had written it down? And whom else had he told of this or that? Did he keep similar abstracts for other questions of intelligence? Who was the pseudonymous Ursinus? And why, if Belloc— "sorry, if your *anonymous gentlemen*"—had all of this information, why were they still not able to settle this largest of all questions but rather came to pester Cecil about it: *Was King James VI of Scotland, likely heir to the English throne, secretly Catholic or not?*

The information was all ambiguous, almost intentionally teasing, as if the answer were always held in balance with its opposite. By way of example: A chandler in Edinburgh won a contract to supply Holyroodhouse Palace itself with a certain number of candles each week. This was a significant opportunity to place eyes and ears inside King James VI's royal residence at last. But, after the chandler had increased his prices to what he thought the royal household would pay, he no longer cared about the small money he had been earning by selling information to London. The closer he crept to James's world, the less interested he was in answering coded letters. What little he did write, though, tantalized: In his final report of 1590, he wrote that of those candles being ordered for the palace, a certain number were fit, by the chandler himself, into silver sticks *with crucifixes on them,* kept in a small chapel separate from the main chapel of the palace. "And when I was to fit them, sir, to these sticks, I was allowed to enter only the front-most alcove of this chapel, the rest of which was covered away from my eye by a long black curtain, through which I could not see a peep, nor dared to, as this was sure enforced by the guard. He did follow me throughout the palace as I made my delivery and set my wares, allowing me to enter this room but not that, this far but no farther, to turn away and face a wall whensoever someone was coming or when a horn or bell or voice was heard."

London had pressed the chandler to recruit servants within the palace, but he replied with silence. Asked if the chandler had tried to converse with his guard about minor matters first and major matters later, the chandler returned again silence. By the time Belloc had planned to travel to Scotland to enforce his will upon the reluctant intelligencer, Belloc's master, Walsingham, had died, and plotting had been reorganized. From that moment on, intelligence reports were to be handled by Mr. Cecil or the Earl of Essex only, and Belloc began his retirement from secret matters, entering his years on the stage, years as a Queen's Messenger, years of worry, boredom.

Chronology of Certainties. Of His Acts.

1566—Born and baptized Catholic. HIS mother having been queen of enemy France.

Cecil looked up. "Shocking, Geoff. Whoever knew such fine secrets as this? Come now. James was raised up properly by the Calvinists. No one thought him Catholic as a boy."

Belloc answered with the same words that he and the gentlemen who had sent him today had so many times used: "The pope excommunicates Elizabeth and tells her subjects to rise up and murder her, but he does no such thing to James, who equally claims to be a Protestant."

Cecil shrugged and went back to reading.

1579—HE begins to welcome into HIS bed HIS French and Catholic cousin, Esmé d'Aubigny. Saith the spy Prideaux, they do count the rosary together in private.

"Yes, yes, and when he married, he married a Protestant princess."

Came back Belloc: "Who, in '93 . . ."

1593—Queen Anna turns Catholic and is allowed to keep Romish priests in the palace for her use.

"And, my lord, some believe that marrying a Protestant might be done with the pope's blessing to make us believe he is not an idolater."

"Ah. So behaving like a Protestant is proof of his Catholicism?"

"In some cases, as you well know, my lord, yes."

1587—The year HIS mother's head rolls off the scaffold for her treachery against Elizabeth. In Glasgow, HE—

"Where were you in all that?" Cecil interrupted himself. "When Mary was held in Chartley?"

"I was there," said Geoff.

"I thought I remembered that." Cecil considered him.

"She spoke to me of him. Of James."

"You were as close to Mary as that?"

"I was. She spoke of her son as a Catholic."

"She spoke to you? Of him? You were there at the very end, too?"

"I was."

"That must have been . . . Why, Geoff. I think you might be frightened. You hate the whole family. No wonder you want this clear. Do you hate him? It's fine to say so now." Cecil mused, "Though I wonder how you could ever believe him to be honest if you are inclined to think him a liar."

1587—The year HIS mother's head rolls off the scaffold for her treachery against Elizabeth. In Glasgow, HE is approached by a hermit. HE gives the man a coin and says thus: "Let this be our saving good work to you." Good works for salvation, as Rome demands. This action is witnessed by Spottiswoode and recorded in that one's daybook with the comment CONCERN. This is secretly read by Spottiswoode's servant who is in our pay and placed in his letter sent via Glasgow group to Walsingham.

Cecil was envious of the secret work there—eyes set close enough to read the king's Protestant minister's daybook—but he didn't pay Belloc the compliment of looking impressed.

1588—Escorial Palace, Madrid. Sorcerers in the employ of the Duke of Parma are instructed by him to prepare weather and storms, including hurricanoes, to destroy our fleet in harbor prior to the Spanish invasion. The sorcerers toil at dark hours in two tall scarlet towers within the gardens of the Escorial to cast spells upon the skies of England. They are able to determine and command the very source and direction of the winds and have received from the bellicose Spanish dukes the dates upon which the wind must perforce blow invariably toward the coasts of England. Yet the duke commands the sorcerers to leave Scotland untouched by storm but to lay a blanket of fog along the marches, "thick as a wall between England and Scotland." Reported from our man Ursinus in the duke's coterie.

"They didn't do so well, the sorcerers," said Cecil.
"Not, I think, the point, sir."

1580s—Multiple incidents of Spanish agents discovered entering Scotland.

1594—Rome. Cardinal Mastricci dines with an English priest from the Catholic English seminary in Douai, France. The cardinal reveals to the priest that in the highest councils of Rome, the pope himself has declared that HE is not to be assassinated, excommunicated, or troubled in any way but rather to be cherished as "our wayward but well-loved son."

*There will be practice to protect HIM and to make stumble any who
would stop his progress to England. Later talk of the English Catholics in
Douai was of hopes placed in HIM to be the Catholic savior of the realm,
as HIS mother would have been. Reported through the baker Zephyr to
me by letter.*

*1590—The bishop of Durham says he thinks HE is a Catholic, subtle
and careful but unmistakably an "animal of Rome." These words
reported by member of household, delivered through the fishmonger's.*

*1588—HE is informed of the Spanish Armada's destruction and
Elizabeth's safety. HE does make upon HIMSELF the sign of the
cross—this reported by a man in Berden's employ. Berden told me
directly.*

Cecil breathed deeply, noisily, nodded wearily, the weight of all
the evidence finally breaking his ability to find innocent explanation. "It's annoying," he admitted. "At the very least he certainly
doesn't go to any effort to make himself clear." He twice began to
speak again, then stopped himself, until, "It won't do, obviously. I
do know that," he finally muttered. "But look here." He tried one
last time to advocate for the devil: "If James favors the Catholics,
would not our friend Mr. Nicolson, in situ, have witnessed it? He
tells us of weekly worship in proper manner, mentions no secret
popish nonsense."

"Sir, eleven years George Nicolson has been Her Majesty's representative in James's court. If, as we fear, James's practice and faith are
but for the world to see, then the world at the moment is no larger
than George Nicolson, trusted to observe the comedy and report it
to London. Mr. Cecil, allow me to say what it's like when you're in
the teeth of a thing and far from home. Mr. Nicolson lives every
day alongside the man everyone has come to assume will be . . .
next. He knows that some men in Whitehall have accepted or are
no longer asking questions like ours. If things proceed without al-
teration, there will never be another English embassy to the court in
Edinburgh. And when it ends, Nicolson returns to London, alongside the new monarch. Maybe an ambassador starts serving only

himself. Mr. Nicolson thinks, 'I am here with the next one, not down there with the . . . older one.' And that Scotsman thinks, 'Why, here is Mr. Nicolson, my first and most loyal English subject, who will do as I say, who will report to his *temporary* masters in London as I tell him to, tell them I'm Protestant, even, so that when the day should come that—' "

Belloc watched the truth arrive irresistibly with Cecil and then pressed his advantage home: "Surely a man can perform on a stage as often as every Sunday if his audience profits by believing in his performance. How small a cost to him to play a Sunday Protestant, when all he needs do is go to damnable Roman *confession* when the play is finished, and all London is ready to give him the one favor he desires above all else." Cecil looked as if he were having stomach trouble. "Mr. Secretary, it is late. Dangerously late. And we feel England must have a definitive answer."

"Tell me at least—as I do see and agree, Geoff, I do—who is this *we*?" Cecil was openly irritable, taking it out on the messenger.

"Councillors to Her Majesty, members of Parliament, lords, commanders of men."

"Are they? Perhaps you are only one man, understandably frightened of the Stuart family, since you practically walked the lady to her execution. How do I know men of import speak to *you*?"

"I know the question troubles you, too."

Robert Cecil did not stand once in this conference, unwilling to show his height against Geoff Belloc's, or his weakness in body. "You were Mr. Beale's creature, I know, so I will take it he is one of the courageous nameless. He has a whole circle of similarly minded men, has he? More than I can keep track of?"

But Geoff held his tongue until Cecil nodded. In pain from trying to keep his body large and upright, he slid a small ways down his chair. And Geoff pushed to the conclusion: "If James is his mother's son, and Rome's, if he is Catholic in his heart and his intentions, the country cannot survive swallowing him. They will stop him before he crosses the Tweed. It will be bloody. Citizens will slaughter citizens. As in Paris. And if he is lying to us and fools us all the way until he is here? It will be much worse. For all of us. The streets will run with blood. And those of us who helped catch his mother? Yes, I should think we—I am not alone—would be happier in Amsterdam."

"As my father's son, you mean."

"Your father would not allow—"

"Well, I'm not him. None sorrier about that than I, Geoff." Cecil was finally surrendering; Geoff saw it; the repeated comparison to his great father did it, and Geoff was satisfied, with the intelligencer's relief at having found the spring to a lock, while Cecil melted further: "Let us therefore speak it crudely. Perhaps James is performing a role, to hide a Roman tiger's heart. I have heard them whisper that Mr. Walsingham's ghost would groan for our lack of serviceable intelligence on the question. My fault as well, I suppose. You and Mr. Beale and your circle think I have been credulous in accepting James's performance."

"My lord, neither I nor any I know would ever doubt your care for the realm, but if left unconvinced, they may support other claimants. With strength."

"There it is at last." Cecil's hair was black, but his beard was red, giving one the (false) impression that one or the other was tinted. "You know as well as I do that of the—what are they now?—twelve with passable claims, none is much more appealing than James. I don't suppose you or your nameless friends want the Spanish princess or Antonio of Portugal any more than I do." He poured himself more wine, still offering Belloc none. "And if your friends are wrong? If James is as Protestant as he says, but he can't convince you of it, or you can't convince them of it, and your friends fight him and kill him, what do you think will happen? Invasions again. Spanish, Portuguese. Another war. And this time the sorcerers might get the winds right."

"We cannot put our faith in ignorance."

"Fine, Mr. Belloc. If your group had the impression that matters were *settled,* why, that's not how matters actually are. One has to be a little cautious at times, that's all. So what do you suggest? If I've done such a poor job of protecting the kingdom from imminent disaster?" He was wheedling now, with momentary bursts of battered pride: "My father, it must be said, wouldn't have put up with this sort of whispering and menace. . . ."

"We must have a plat of inquiry, my lord. Crafted with your support. The results of which you will rely upon, as will we. One last conclusive effort to know James's heart before it's too late."

"Yes, yes, very well, I understand. You save the realm, a secret hero from Walsingham's boys. But do you think, if he is lying, that such a secret could be discovered without doubt?"

"With money and effort and careful plotting, yes, my lord, I do. That is my faith, I suppose."

"And the answer, either way, is better than ignorance and hoping for the best. I accept."

"Thank you, my lord."

"Now, you tell me," said Cecil, trying to tamp down his persistent irritation. "What would be sufficient proof of the invisible state of James Stuart's soul to satisfy your friends? I'm not unsympathetic to their concerns, so go ahead and prove it to your liking. But how will you do it? He can lie to you as well as he can lie to anyone else. Your years of gathering reports have only left the matter cloudier."

"Let me think on it a day or two more, now that we have your blessing. Something will occur to me."

"I cannot see how you could produce any answer certain enough to satisfy you. But fine. Go. Get your damned answer, but please keep your mouths shut. All of you. You choose the man. You'll trust his answer if I don't interfere, but I would like to approve of your plat, please."

"Certainly."

Cecil closed his eyes, rubbed them, moved his jaw from side to side, which made it click. His voice changed, less aggravated. "I do feel that responsibility. We are in a difficult moment. I would have arrived at the same question as you, I suppose. I just . . . hadn't yet." The man suddenly seemed embarrassed, and Geoff let him stew in it. "I blame myself for not having been suspicious enough. Do you still have friends in the north? On the border? Or perhaps farther? Anyone in James's court I am unaware of?"

"No, my lord. I'm sorry to say no. But might you send me to his court openly, to organize watchers from near at hand? Give me letters as your servant."

Cecil smiled just enough at the ceiling to clarify unbridgeable social distances. "You're not, I don't think, exactly the diplomatist type, Geoff. Rather more a dagger in the tavern, no?" Cecil poured himself more wine and considered the man in Messengers' livery, the sheer size of him in the small room. "And you are known in Catholic circles after all your success. It's not played like you used to, not anymore. The prison cells. Not like how the old Earthworms did their work. You must think of other ways. To let us see clear beyond any question. That's what we want. Complete Clarity, a transparency of James's heart."

"And if we learn the worst, my lord? If James is Catholic?"

Flinching a little at the bluntness of the question, Cecil concentrated on running his wine-wet finger round the gilded rim of his glass, and it began to sing. He raised his eyebrows at Geoff at the sound. "The Spanish tried to assassinate my father, Geoff. I'm not a fool. If James is a papist, we should have to think hard about how to protect ourselves. And how to prepare, quickly, for other futures."

GEOFFREY BELLOC PASSED through the corridors of Whitehall to take his leave for some weeks or months from the Queen's Messengers office, bearing a letter from Cecil excusing him on sensitive matters of state and forgiving him, ahead of time, for whatever he might do while attending to Her Majesty's secret business.

The queen, God save her, old and childless, had outlived all the murderers dispatched by popes, by kings of France and Spain, by the Queen of Scots, by England's own Catholic furious and militant. The war against the Catholics—sometimes a shadow war of honey-tongued spies and sneaking priests, sometimes a proxy war stuck and muddled in the Dutch marshes, sometimes a half-blind hunt for whispered plots dreamed by Scottish queens, sometimes the cannon blast of a real invasion from Spanish armadas—was not over, might never be over, even if it was not, in 1601, so dangerous or so plainly seen as it once had been. It was unsurprising that even Cecil had been lazy or wishful. Some spoke of it as in the past or somehow irrelevant now, the sort of talk Geoff Belloc had too often to endure—from players in their cups, from gentlemen at court, from the widow who rented him his rooms.

For all the pleasure and rebirth Geoff felt at being set back into action, today, of all days, the court seemed especially stuporous. Everyone from the hot days was dead or nearly so, or so it felt. Everyone was deaf or nearly so, even if young men in court still fought for attention, begged and negotiated and boasted for permission to walk into a room attached to a room leading to a room. He stopped outside the cabinet of the captain of Messengers. He waited. Next to him in the hall, a golden bowl of brown apples sat atop a table cut in one piece from a single felled tree, and upon the apples slid three small centipedes. Belloc watched a young page pull back his sleeve and press his thumb slowly down onto one of the worms—not hard enough to injure it, only enough to stop its progress over the pole of the brown planet it was circumnavigating. The beast stopped its ascent, its many legs rowing futilely against no waves. The page looked up from his microscopic cruelty and saw Geoffrey Belloc staring at him. He showed Belloc his teeth and pressed harder, spreading the green bowels of the worm across the fading apple.

Geoff was not much older than this brainless boy when Robert Beale had found him.

GEOFFREY BELLOC WAS four years old when he watched a person being burned alive and, for the first time, was aware of what he was seeing. It wasn't the first time he'd been near a burning, but this was the first that he would remember all his life. Elizabeth's Catholic sister was Queen of England, and Protestants burned by the hundreds. This day, alone in a crowd, he understood the unique smell, knew at once he had smelled it before, sometimes for several days and nights in a row. It was a recurrent element of London's air, but he hadn't until now known it for what it was. The sounds the man made were sounds Geoffrey had heard before, too. He had heard men make noises like this when burned by metal in a shop or cut by blades or when eaten by plague, so it was not the sound or the smell that was new, even to a boy of four.

From beginning to end a man disappeared while Geoffrey watched.

Death wasn't new to him. Sometimes people died, or dead bodies were taken away, removed from view after some days. Sometimes a living person (the woman across the road who gave him half a sweet apple once) was there one day and the next day was gone, and someone explained that she was dead and wasn't going to come back (or share more apples).

But this man had been standing atop the wood and packed straw, and over the next hours he disappeared to nothing. Geoffrey watched all of it happen, watched them add more fuel, watched them remove any fuel that smoked too much (so the man wouldn't suffocate too quickly). The man looked Geoffrey in the eye, even asked the boy for help, though Geoffrey didn't know what help he could or should provide. But he watched the entirety of the event. It wasn't a trick; they couldn't have somehow taken him away when Geoffrey wasn't looking, because he never stopped looking, and at the end the man was gone: his hair, his skin, his insides. He had disappeared entirely.

Geoffrey's father found him sitting on the ground, staring at the gray and charred remnants of the event, trying to understand the magic and the feelings of what he'd witnessed. "Not a good place for you. Shouldn't have to see this." The boy didn't look well, or somehow didn't look like his usual self, and, though the child was almost too large for it, his father lifted him up and over his shoulders. He walked them away from the sight, and Geoffrey twisted backward to see if any trick was now being revealed, but it was still all the same. "Have to do what the Roman priests say, you hear me?" his father advised. "They have God's ear now and that's that. Can't let them do that to you or me, eh?"

Both of Geoffrey's parents died when he was twelve, plague having taken nearly everyone in two houses. Geoff himself was spared because the year before he had been apprenticed to a spurrier, a fair distance from the old house, and only learned of his parents' deaths some weeks after.

The spurrier's had been a fortunate placement for the boy but not difficult to arrange: He was already of a size that suited the task. He was strong enough by thirteen to squeeze the iron pincers as well as his master and to twist the thin blazing sheets of metal into the tightly sealed cones or flattened spikes of a spur's rowel.

Until he grew larger than his master, Geoff took his beatings at the spurrier's hand with no complaint, even though his own father had never struck him. Geoff knew the spurrier was a Catholic (increasingly quiet about it in Elizabeth's London), and Geoff suffered the blows knowing that cruelty was somehow the nature of those people.

If spurs were the spurrier's only line of trade, the boy's food and bedding would have been a worthwhile investment, but soon Geoff was tall and broad enough to help his employer in his more profitable business, which was the collection of debts. By fifteen the young man started out gathering money that forgetful but trusted customers still owed. Soon after, he stood quietly behind the spurrier to collect payment on bills for other items, for loans intricately engineered to avoid violating laws on charging interest. Before long, Geoff's skill had become a matter of public knowledge among those who loaned money, and other creditors would pay the spurrier a fee to lease Geoff's bulk for their own affairs. Rarely was actual force required; Geoff's presence and easy glower usually sufficed. When violence was essential to produce coin, Geoff showed an even more valuable skill: He could calibrate the quantity of force necessary to achieve results and then went no further. He had no trouble stopping himself in mid-beating, and he seemed to take no pleasure in administering punishment.

Geoff was likely seventeen in 1570 when Robert Beale, with two sullen attendants, came to order two sets of spurs. A gentleman's presence was always of interest, and Geoff, alone when Beale arrived, made conversation with the wealthy customer, who needed the spurs ready before his expected return to Paris in ten days' time.

Seven days later, Geoff was sent outside to give his ambitious master time alone with the returned customer. Geoff, across the road and facing the shop, spoke to Beale's two escorts, begging for information on how they came to join their master's service and what life was like in Paris. Beale stepped into the road, his merchandise in hand. As his two attendants had their backs to the shop, Belloc saw a cutpurse snip away Beale's wallet in a passing stroke, and he was running after the fleeing thief before Beale or his men knew anything had happened.

The thief made two turns, knocking over handcarts behind him, leapt a fence, and would have been gone but for Belloc, who was over the fence in a bound and ran the criminal to ground three roads away. It was less than five minutes before Belloc returned with bleeding fists and Robert Beale's purse. Beale's own men had seen nothing and given up the chase by the first blind turn.

"It wouldn't do, sir, to have you robbed at all, but surely not in front of our shop."

Beale was equally grateful to the boy and mocking of his own men. "Are you badly hurt?" he asked as Geoff wiped the blood from his skinless knuckles with a rag. "You'll take this coin with my thanks, and you'll allow me to take you for your supper tonight."

Supper was the two of them alone in a back room while Beale's two useless men waited outside. "It was well done," Beale said.

"Sir?"

Beale took one of Belloc's giant hands in his and unwound the wrap over his knuckles. "Wall or ground?" he asked.

"Sir?"

"Surely the other fellow doesn't let you beat him if you make it out of view."

Belloc's face was blank with confusion while, behind it, his mind ran through his options of lying, fleeing, fighting the men outside the door. He bought more time: "I don't understand, sir."

Beale watched Geoff's calculations proceed and finally said, "Oh, I think you'll do just fine."

And so Geoffrey Belloc found himself released from the final years of his apprenticeship, no money needing to change hands once Belloc described to his new master, Beale, the spurrier's Catholic practices and rages. Belloc was removed from London and from England, taken to the English embassy in Paris to serve as a messenger, a bodyguard, a pair of useful hands and eyes for Robert Beale, deputy to the ambassador, Sir Francis Walsingham.

Seventeen months after Belloc's arrival, Paris exploded with slaughter in the streets, and again he saw what unleashed Catholicism meant. He helped keep the door of the embassy shut against the murderers as the blood streamed in the roads like rainwater. They impaled infants on pikes. Protestant men, women, and children were hacked to bits as they clawed the doors of the English embassy, while Walsingham and Beale and Geoff Belloc struggled and sweated to hide a lucky few in the basement. The Catholics were as if drunk or sexually engorged. Geoff saw from the window a Catholic soldier rape and kill a Protestant woman at the same time, as if the acts were inseparable; his two desires were so strong, neither would wait for the other to complete. (In later years, the pope had a painting of the St. Bartholomew's Day massacre on his ceiling; Geoff knew a man who'd been in the Vatican and seen it. And on the anniversary of the butchery every year, the pope murdered a Protestant prisoner with his own hands or reclined and watched one killed for his pleasure. At least that's what the intelligencer reported.)

Back in London, the nature of the enemy clear beyond all question, Geoff was trained for new responsibilities. Mr. Beale brought him to a boardinghouse in Finsbury, teaching the boy the methods and devices, the plots and plats, that would keep Geoff alive and in money for the next part of his life. Beale quoted Walsingham, who, newly inventing himself as the master of all the kingdom's secret affairs, taught that men were "but boxes with spring-hook lids, and within each box more boxes, with more hidden hooks to find and unfasten. Work the next one open, and at once begin looking for a still-smaller latch. Until, at last, one arrives at the heart of the matter, wherein what we seek is cloaked and padded snug in shadows. Unless it be yet another box. We never know with certainty if we have arrived at the end."

Extracting salable information from men was a better life than being someone else's paid fists, and so Beale trained Geoff in what the vague and distant gentlemen in Whitehall wanted and how to get it. England's most pressing need was to find out where the Catholics hid and what they planned. "The boxes inside a man will open if you are beloved, but that is very rare. More commonly they feign to love you, the better to blind you from seeing truth. The boxes will of course open for you if they are forced, but then one risks damage to the contents. Boxes open for *fear* of being forced, and that is an improvement, but then you may not know if you have reached a true or feigned secret. And finally, men will reveal themselves for pleasure, but each time you return, the demand for pleasure will be greater: more drink, more women or boys, more money.

"And so, we must confess, no solution works forever. We must repeatedly find new paths to truth, never taking our location in the forest with certainty. Pleasure, force, love, fear: now one, now the other. What we may never afford ourselves ever is the comfort of trust. Ignorance will kill us. Blind trust will kill us. Faith in men will kill us. We must never believe we have arrived at the end. There is too much danger to wallow in such ignorant luxury. Better to assume we are being lied to, always, by enemies far more clever than ourselves." Geoff loved them both: Beale the teacher, and Walsingham the wise father, so distant and rarely spotted that he was almost a dream or a deity, but both necessary to fight the Catholic enemy and to lift Geoff, another orphan in London, from abandonment to belonging. He ached to make both of them proud, to become a master of opening locked boxes, finding ever smaller, ever more darkly shadowed cells in the hearts of men.

The first work was simple: Go where Mr. Beale sends you, then sit and drink without growing drunk, and listen to the talk around you. And then tell Mr. Beale, or the man who knows Mr. Beale's password, what you heard. And some of that was worth money. Simple.

Belloc enjoyed the money, and Beale paid (only for results, not for effort). But far better was being told by Walsingham that you were clever, being told you'd done something good and necessary:

"Geoff's our boy, cunning as they come." Walsingham could read your desires before you knew them yourself, could read your heart to you when you were blind to it. The hint that there would be a life in court for Geoff at the end. The promise that he had landed at last upon a safe shore, and Geoff would never again suffer the tedium and ache of poverty or vagrancy or being set loose in the world without a father. And, of course, even better than that: The assurance that the Catholic danger would be kept far from England (or rooted out in England) thanks to Belloc's work. This was a precise blend, concocted by Walsingham for Geoff Belloc's appetites: money, safety, success, love, pride, praise, future, victory, justice, God. No fear was necessary to control Belloc. Later, Belloc saw men who did fear Walsingham, and well they should have, but Walsingham had judged Belloc malleable and loyal enough, had fitted him with custom gloves. Walsingham could choose his keys and open men up to read with scarcely the creak of a hinge. "We must awaken *desire* in our man to do whatever task must be achieved, if the man will not do it by *nature*. Only failing that must we remind him of *fear*."

LEAVING WHITEHALL WITH his letter of permission and his leave from the Queen's Messengers, Geoff trotted an hour west to Chiswick and paid a ferryman to carry him across to Barnes.

"Geoffrey Belloc. My boy. My *bulldog*." Robert Beale was, like everyone else, impossibly older than he had been; all the heroes and villains of Geoff's youth were now penciled and painted to play ancients, as if Geoff had fallen asleep in the annex to the Messengers' chambers and woken thirty years later. Beale had retired to his home out in Barnes, to his study, to books and papers and long afternoon naps, trying to make his influence felt and his wisdom useful seven miles away in Whitehall. When he was Walsingham's deputy, the innermost node of the secret kingdom itself, he took reports directly from agents, kept them away from Whitehall or rewarded them by walking them into Walsingham's presence, all those groveling men and women who came at midnight to claim their expenses, rehearsing and performing their bravery and hardship and coups of reporting for a professionally dubious paymaster. They were happy when Beale paid a fraction of what they demanded.

After Walsingham's death, Beale tried to write a manual for how to properly run a secret service, how to duplicate Walsingham's success and learn from his errors. He tried to write it all down: not just who and where the agents were, not just where the secret pay was flowing, but how to *do it*, how to operate this invention of Walsingham's, explained for the incoming generation. How to run agents and networks, how to identify targets and draw up plans, how to compare reports from multiple sources and triangulate upon something like the Truth. Beale assumed that whoever came next would have the same worries and fears of Catholic incursion; it was perhaps an eternal struggle. Beale completed *A Treatise of the Office of a Councellor and Principall Secretarie to her Ma[jes]tie*, but there's no evidence that Robert Cecil, the new principal secretary, ever read it.

And now old Robert Beale, pushed out of his office by Robert Cecil, spoke to Geoff as if he'd always loved Giant Geoff above all the other Cunning Boys, and maybe he had. The idea certainly appealed. "Geoffrey, you good and dear man, it makes my spirit sing to see you." He raised himself up with some difficulty and, to Geoff's surprise, embraced him. Geoff returned the leather case and abstract to him, and he in turn offered Geoff an orange.

"Tell me the news. Your snout is bloody, I think. You hung on to his face, gasping for breath, until he succumbed, didn't you?"

Beer and wine were called for, and plates of meat and bread began arriving in the study, and there was indeed the orange with an inside like jewels. But Beale also wanted Geoff to see his energy, offering a walk in the gardens. The singing spirit, the dancing words, all of the old mannerisms—the fast politeness, the desire to help, the fussy energy (standing as soon as he sat, walking as soon as he stood, sitting as soon as he stopped), the display of frustrated inability to find just the letter he was looking for on a worktable of towering paper cliffs—all that was still there, but the effort to perform these old bits of business showed, at least to Geoff's theatrical eye. Perhaps they had always been performances, years ago, in the annex to Walsingham's cabinet. "We walk, let us walk." He gave Geoff his arm.

But the old fellow was soon out of wind, and they sat on a bench beneath a willow by a man-made stream. "Now tell me. You are here and not arrested, so that is promising."

"Yes. Cecil is willing, maybe even convinced. But he is so small in the job."

"He is not the ideal of English strength and guile."

"He guessed your involvement immediately, sir."

"Of course. That was to be expected. It makes him feel he has his finger on matters. That doesn't worry me."

"He is stung to know how much resistance to James remains. And that he can't guess the others. At the end, he agrees. A Catholic James will not come to London."

"That's true, I hope, whether Mr. Cecil agrees or not. Men are moving now in case of it. James will find that his road to London is impassable, if you tell us to make it so, Geoff. But you have done well: Cecil knows. He knows we know. He accepts the unavoidable. And he will abide by whatever answer we find. So then the question: It is a pretty puzzle—how will you do it?"

"I have been thinking about using players. Poets at James's table, talking of elevated matters. Players in his presence, performing to his fears and dreams every evening. A play about witches might move him to confidences. I can introduce a company of a dozen spies in a single day. Handsome young men of open minds might be able to gain certain access, either to him or to the pope's ambassador, or the Spanish one." Beale smiled, and Geoff felt himself embarrassingly pleased at the old man's easy laughter. He ate Robert Beale's chicken and grapes, drank his wine, and they spoke of how to tickle the most secret truth from canny James the Scot.

"Which reminds me, you might warn your player friends of something." He led Geoff back to his study, where Beale moved rapidly through papers in his cleverly joined cabinets with their hidden panels. He found a page in the caverns of one of those paper mountains. He cleared some matter from his throat and grandly orated, in honor of Geoff's third career, after spurrier and spy: " 'It is regretted that the Comedians of London should scorn the king and the people of this land in their play; and it is wished that the matter be speedily amended, lest the king and the country be stirred to anger.' " He looked for his audience's reaction. "That was written to the council. It's from Nicolson."

Matters were as far along as *that*. The people of London were not to laugh at Scotsmen on the stage anymore. And the Englishman at James's side would make it clear he spoke for James. And it was enforced: London was already trying to *please* James.

"Did you ever see, what was it, *Edward III*?" asked Beale.

"I was in it, sir."

"Ha! What about the *King Arthur* the Chamberlain's Men had at the Globe? The Scots connive for the throne of England because the English king has no heirs."

Belloc had seen the play. It had not been subtle, to be sure. Belloc had laughed along with all of London when Francis Cobb waddled across the stage as the ancient king of Pictland, with his coat of arms of a squirrel rampant, and delivered his speech in as Scotch an accent as he could produce, promising "whirling bangstry," carrying a banner with a French cross and the keys of Rome quartered with Scottish thistle, a Spanish friar in his company as he leered out at the crowd and taunted:

When Britain all, this island whole entire—
All England, Wales, this Pictland, and the Scots—
By one crown all is ringed, and that crown mine.

Thus Nicolson's letter, complaining of how the Scots were portrayed upon the London stage. King James VI cared what the English thought of Scots. King James VI wanted an end to Scots kings who strutted, ambitious and crude, scheming for the English throne.

For so long, no discussion of tomorrow had been permitted. As the pressure of the approaching future grew almost unbearable, the act of ignoring it required the mind to turn feverishly in exhausting circles. For some years now, everyone had adjusted their speech, if not their mind, to the idea that the future would always look precisely the same as the present, politeness puffed and inflated to its furthest limits. One began a secret life in one's own heart, increasingly at odds with what one spoke in company. Yet tomorrows invariably come, and now gentlemen in Whitehall, smoothing James's mind, shut down offending entertainments. James was to be coddled rather than mocked and corrected, even as it was still against the law to imagine England ever having a ruler besides Elizabeth.

Somehow, after all these years of blood and fire, the Catholics might simply place one of their own on the English throne, without even a battle. No armada, no murder, just a Catholic Scotsman walking into Whitehall. And then the blood would pour.

Beale chewed a grape, winced, spent some time maneuvering it around a bad tooth, pushed half of it back onto a cloth with the tip of his tongue. He tried another grape, forgot to chew it on the easier side of his mouth, if there was one, and it met a similar fate. "James will kill us all. I suppose he won't kill Cecil, but those of us who were there? If he's Catholic, we may as well fill our pockets with stones and walk into the river."

4

IN GEOFF'S DREAMS, the King of Scots is a large man, like a Scot he once met in a tavern, barbarian in style, quick to make fists. (Though this was not at all what Walsingham reported to Queen Elizabeth and Beale and what Beale in turn had told Belloc: James VI was small, weak in body and limb, swayed by the last person he spoke to, terrified of witches and goblins, today's dinner in his beard and yesterday's staining his tunic, comfortable only on horseback, walking awkwardly from the fright he took when he was still in Mary's womb and some thane or other threatened her with a blade.)

But in Geoff's dreams, James VI is regal, subtle beyond almost any spy's ability to perceive. James checks his doors, covers the keyholes, throws a coin across the room to fool whoever listens, to make them step and give their location. He covers the windows, looks under the bed, slashes and thrusts behind the arras. And at last King James, the public Protestant, endorsed by Calvinist ministers to impress all of England and its residents' half-closed eyes, withdraws his popish toys and relics from a locked box. An Italian massmonger babbling Latin lowers himself from a perch near the ceiling, and together they cross themselves and bow down to an engraved silver wafer canister, confess to each other, lay the bloody biscuits on each other's tongue. The ritual becomes more involved now, the bodies entwined, blood of Christ, blood of the two men, nails of the True Cross, six perpetually growing hairs of Saint Agnes.

Geoff wakes in the dark. He tells the girl in bed with him to leave. Kicks her until she obeys.

Who accompanies the king in his most privy moments? Who sleeps at the foot of his bed? Some lover made an earl, and often enough Catholic. Do the Scots have gentlemen of the cloth? Do they have a cloth at all? All the Scots Geoff has ever known stank as if they would never know a cloth or let it wipe their asses.

Someone lower in court, then, one whom I could replace, or bend to my will, to open his lips by coin or menace, but high enough to move freely within the court, to view the king in private meditation and prayer.

And Geoff wakes again. The girl is still there, asleep. The dream has carried on past when he thought he was awake, and that tells clear enough a message: James will make me think I see the truth when I am still dreaming. He pulls the girl close and smells her head in the dark, glad he hadn't really told her to go. She makes a noise and twists away, snoring.

Enough of dreams. What could my spy see or hear, and what could prove to Cecil what Beale and I know, saving England before it is too late? My spy sees the book kept beneath the king's pillow. It is not enough: Cecil will sneer, "Perhaps it is someone else's book." My spy sees James take communion the Catholic way. It is not enough: Cecil will shrug and sigh, "He does it to pacify his Catholic wife."

What might my man see, the sincerity of which cannot be ignored or explained? The king upon his stool, struggling to pass along the remnants of some difficult meal, crosses himself and lifts his eyes to heaven. Will that suffice? The king keeps within a hidden niche in his apartments a box containing some false relic. The king in private conversation with the Spanish ambassador or the pope's legate promises that when he is King of England he will reveal the truth, invite the Inquisition and the Jesuits to come and make merry with England, burn Protestants in the fashion of Bloody Mary, imprison the men who caught and killed his mother (that other damned Mary), men like Beale and Belloc and every rank in between. King James VI, who would on our backs be remade King James I, be washed and somehow reborn English, reborn the first of his name and not the sixth, crosses himself in his bedchamber when he thinks himself alone, but somehow my man is there to watch him do it, somehow can tell me what he saw, and somehow I convince Cecil, and he allows some other man to sit upon the throne when Elizabeth leaves it, and England is saved, my people are saved, I am saved, there is no slaughter in the streets, no babies on pikes, no men turned to ash, screaming as they melt. Somehow. What proof would be enough? How to make a dishonest man be clear? What makes the finest actor crack and, for a moment, forget his lines, his role, his audience? What makes him stop and show the truth upon his face?

The king, before he sleeps, kneels to pray. He thinks himself alone. He lifts his hand to his forehead. Does he pause there, scratch, and be done with it, or does his hand continue down his invisible cross? Does his Catholic queen kneel beside him? Or does he pretend even to her that he is Protestant (as he pretends to her that he enjoys her company in bed), allows her to believe it in cold Edinburgh, and only when he sits atop the throne in London will he finally present her his greatest gift: his Catholic soul.

Geoff dreams again. A crucifix made of blood and fire bears a living Christ: "Listen to me. Listen to me."

5

GEOFFREY BELLOC WAS twenty-two or twenty-three in 1575 when he sat in a public room, in front of too much drink and too many ears, and told all who would listen that he would not pay the fine he had been assessed for refusing to attend his parish services of the Protestant English Church and for denying Queen Elizabeth's supremacy in religious matters. He wouldn't pay any such fine, damn her, and he swore again, loudly, that the Catholic faith, the old faith, which had been good enough for his English family back to the creation of the world and the beginning of time, was the only true religion, and he would not let his soul burn in a fiery lake forever simply because the heretic daughter of the illegitimate mistress of the lecher King Henry said otherwise. It shocked no one (least of all the aspiring professional informants who drank with him, encouraged him in his reckless talk, then wrote reports about him as soon as he fell asleep) that Geoff Belloc was soon arrested and thrown into the Clink, another Catholic recusant imagining himself a martyr for the Roman Church, stubborn, or idealistic and dreaming of saints, or nostalgic and longing for the nice pictures that used to hang on English church walls before the Protestants had painted them over, melted all the silver, torn down the statues, splintered the colored glass, made the priests talk in plain English and not the magical sound of Latin.

Imprisonment in wretched circumstances didn't soften him to Protestant society or theology. He passed four weeks of quiet prayer alone, gathering pebbles from the walls of his cell and hair from his head to craft a fragile rosary, scratching a cross in the stones that held him until his fingers bled, that same blood staining his shirt at three points as he crossed himself. Four weeks of this mad solitude passed before he was invited to join the Clink's other Catholics, the mission-men and captured Jesuits, for their prayers and transubstantive communion mass, and Geoff, weeping, took his absolution from the sanctified among them.

When he was released three months later, he and his fellow Romish papists were allowed to leave England immediately and forever, thanks to the queen's gentle mercies. Geoffrey Belloc accepted the other Catholics' invitation to sail with them to Douai in France, where he was welcomed in the Catholic English seminary as a fellow refugee from England. The English Catholics could not bear the tyranny of the excommunicated heretic queen and her satanic, puritan principal secretary, Francis Walsingham, the whore's spymaster. They would sooner live away from England and plan for an eventual return, theirs and God's, whether that return was peaceful or necessarily bloody.

Geoffrey lived in this colony of English exiles for nearly a year. His reports about what he saw and heard began to arrive on Walsingham's desk in London twenty weeks after his drunken (and pre-licensed, in writing) performance in the tavern, four weeks after his wailing, gesticulating exile from England's shores. Throughout it he played his role, all while he described in invisible ink (wrung from his own bladder) the infighting and the schemes, the treachery and the plots to seize England back to the Catholic fold through armed assault and murder of the Protestant faithful. If he had not already feared and hated Catholics, what he saw in Douai would have settled it. They spoke of God and then of vengeance, of salvation by good works and then of the English blood they would spill. Belloc learned of plans to raise armies from Catholic noble families along the Scottish border, to pay them with Spanish gold, to arm them and preach to them in the Roman style until they felt blessed to rebel and murder Queen Elizabeth and place her cousin, Scotland's Catholic Mary, on the English throne, and Mary's son, James, after that. He wrote of priests who preached that Elizabeth, as an excommunicant, could be murdered without fear. "They teach this; I do not conceive it in my mind," he wrote in his report, a carefully balanced sentence with two perfect meanings: a declaration of his honest reporting but also his simultaneous defense, for it was literally treason even to imagine her death. Somehow, he asserted, he was transcribing the idea without ever having allowed himself to think it.

Geoff hid in the woods outside Douai and reported gossip as well as conspiracies. He described personalities and weaknesses for later spies to use as leverage: "The Catholic John Hurley is fond of fine victuals and will *possibly,* in exchange for tasty bits, hold less tightly his loyalty to Douai, where the meals are *bitter,* says he, and the beds more creeping maggot than soft feather." Huddled in shadows, he wrote, urgently, the names and descriptions of the English Catholic priests who would enter England posing as Dutch traders and how they planned to hide in the cellars and chimneys and horses' hay of great northern families as agents both of religious lies (holding secret mass) and of subterfuge and civil strife (arranging weapons routes and Spanish gold for Scottish pretenders).

Belloc's reports were corroborated by others, although he did not know who else was working for Walsingham until after he returned to England. Even so, his accuracy was proven by the results: The insurgent priests arrived where Geoff said they would, followed paths Geoff said they would, slept in Catholic cellars in the Catholic homes Geoff said they would, and were seized by pursuivants far from their landing points under Dutch names, for carefully contrived reasons far from the sour truth, which was that Geoff Belloc had betrayed them. When they were taken, to spend their few remaining days in the Tower or Marshalsea, before their lives ended on the scaffold, cut open from navel to neck, their innards and genitals displayed for the crowd, not one of them knew Geoff Belloc had led them here, only that they had made some mistake upon arrival, had crossed themselves without thinking who was watching. They died cursing themselves for having blundered in their celestial mission to save England from damnation.

Returned at last to beloved and blessed England, Belloc met other gentlemen from Mr. Walsingham and Mr. Beale's cabinet: Mr. Faunt, Mr. Milles, Mr. Gregory, Mr. Waad, Mr. Phelippes, all those senior gentlemen working in perfumed Whitehall while men like Geoff—the Cunning Boys, they called themselves—served them in cells and camps and behind enemy lines. The gentlemen met him in Belloc's rooms, then in gardens of private homes; finally, invited by a Queen's Messenger, Belloc came to Whitehall. He ducked his head to fold his giant frame under the doorway, then stood tall, filling the room, while Mr. Beale told Francis Walsingham himself, "Of all the Cunning Boys, none is near as cunning as our Geoff. He crept, Sir Francis, into the papists' hearts in less time than it takes to grow a moon or for a pear to spoil." The sickly gray man behind the table loaded with papers and seals looked up at Geoff with sad and sympathetic eyes. He wore simple black and gray clothes, a Puritan, when those all around him at court strove to out-color the next. He stood up, stooped and thin, though a handsome younger man was still visible within him. He may have aged himself a bit for Geoff's benefit, recognizing one who needed a father. "I remember you from Paris. You must have been most painfully troubled by the hardships you bore for us. We thank you, and so indeed does the queen." So indeed does the *queen*.

A man of Belloc's size would surprise anyone who saw him overtaken by strong feeling. He pretended to feel pain and sorrow in prison (or at least he pretended new causes for the suffering he truly felt), but now, in the office of the queen's principal secretary, he wept from his heart, sobbed like a boy, grateful for the attention, proud of what he had done for a woman he had never seen, aching for some kind words spoken by an old man who called him "my son." And then he laughed—at his own strange tears, at himself for shedding them, and out of some joy he felt in equal measure. His laughter seemed to affect the other men, as plump Robert Beale and the tired old secretary both began to laugh with him. When a chit for money was written out for Geoff to take to another office to collect, Walsingham was far more generous than Geoff had ever hoped, even in French woods, fearing discovery, quieting his heart with fantasies of future gain.

He spent a few of his new pennies to watch plays: Lord Howard's Men and other troupes, *The Solitary Knight, The History of Error*. The better companies made him believe they knew what they were talking about when they shouted curses and fought, when they poured poison into the ears of kings, when they spoke of vengeance and hatred, when shepherds wooed maids, when the philosopher sold his soul to the devil, when the Scottish king made mischief while the dangerously distracted English fought the dangerously distracting French. He watched with envy and wonder. He felt a strange satisfaction at every play's ending, when, with the epilogue, all questions were answered. The fate of every character was revealed. There was a deep pleasure in simply knowing what happened to everyone at the end.

Geoff, too, had been a kind of player, after all, but without knowing all the endings. He had performed his part well enough to live undetected among the enemy. He, too, was a kind of play writer, and had written the truth well enough that dangerous men had been stopped before they could do their evil. He had been one of the Cunning Boys, Mr. Walsingham's Men, the Secretary's Men.

He met others of his costumed guild. Mr. Beale introduced him to a new man who would carry all further instruction, for Geoff couldn't be seen meeting Beale for the next task, and this new man in turn introduced him to four others with whom he would do his next job. Geoff recognized some faces among them, had seen them in other places. They drank, they joked, they took one another's measure, they spoke of the game, of what they had done, surprised at having been on the same side all along. "The Clinksmen," Geoff proposed they should call themselves, a company of actors after all. Some of them got the joke. It didn't catch on, though.

6.

Y OU'RE A MOUNTAIN *of a man, aren't you, brother?*
Geoff had been there, at the pinch, at the sharp end, in the
cold, damp late summer of 1586, in woods beyond the park of
Chartley Manor, playing his role in events that would define him
forever after.

A new star had appeared in the sky the week before, prophesying
great events, and Geoff now stood in twilit woods, almost alone.
He was tying an unconscious man to a tree and wondering whether
he should cut the man's throat, or if that would overstep his authority, or if it might be useful to the larger task. He imagined the man's
family, not without a nip of envy, but that was outweighed by the
pity. No matter the bleeding man's beliefs and disloyalties, Geoff
didn't hate him enough to murder him cold, unconscious, tied up.
Besides which, that was something *they, not he,* would do. The
work, the physical struggle, and now that clear decision: Geoff was
very happy, and he knew he was very happy. He had accomplished
extraordinary things. He had been present at the most important
events of his or any time, the very definition of the world, the protection of all that mattered. He had witnessed events that people
would remember forever, would write of in books, would put on
the stage. More practically: He had made some money (by no means

easy for a man who'd been most of his life an orphan); he was trusted and well used by the gentlemen who employed him, gentlemen whose influence at court was considerable, and whose promises to pay Belloc still more handsomely were deliciously plausible; he was not without future expectations, and, even better, he was not without current protections, and, better still, he stood in these woods the master of his immediate surroundings, a task clear in mind, with no man to tell him how to proceed or to scold him. He was participating in the defense of England, of God, and of his queen, whom he had now seen once, from a distance, and who was something other than beautiful, something better and rarer, for which he did not have the word. He wore the invisible livery of Francis Walsingham, which he preferred to any velvet in the land. He fought on the righteous side of an infernal struggle, against forces human and demonic both. The bound man made a soft noise, a pathetic face, and spat at him: *Geoff of all people? Sweet Geoff?* He made an insulting counteroffer for Geoff's services, so Geoffrey Belloc struck him back into silence before stuffing his mouth and tying it shut.

The larger purpose of Geoff's work became clearer to him with time, though that day in the woods it had been necessarily unclear how any given task fit the larger story conceived in Walsingham's mind. It was, when Geoff thought about it, a battle between two imagined stories. Only one could come true: The stronger imagination would be rewarded with reality. Scotland's Mary conceived of overthrowing Elizabeth. Walsingham conceived of allowing her story to unfold to a point of near fruition but then stopping it, stillborn. The child of his conception would live; the child of hers would emerge, only to wither while she stared in horror.

Mary, Queen Mother of Scotland, Catholic pretender to England's throne, would-be murderess of her cousin Elizabeth, was taken, all the proof of her intrigues made clear in her letters, decoded by pocked and bespectacled Tom Phelippes, read by Sir Francis Walsingham. And when the arrests began, Geoff single-handedly prevented several of her men from interfering. A few months later, Mary the Scot was parted from her head, and Geoff was there, too, in the hall at Fotheringhay when it happened, saw her little dog lap at the blood and scream like a human child when they lifted away its treacherous mistress's body.

So many conspirators were rounded up, so many Catholic northern families broken up by Mary's evil, that rewards were in order. Rob Beale visited Geoff the night after Mary's execution, and he said the strangest thing: "I think we may be safe at last, Geoff." Geoff looked at him in some amazement. It was unlike Walsingham's perpetually worried second-in-command. As was his giddy, jovial embrace of the larger man. It was a sort of drunkenness without drink, Geoff noticed (and of course it turned out to be as false as any sot's optimism).

But at that table in 1587, with Mary dead and Elizabeth safe, Geoff allowed himself to be convinced. He took Beale's money, his messages of love from Secretary Walsingham, and he left secret work, accepted its gentle farewell.

In March of 1587, Geoffrey Belloc changed careers, an unusual transformation for a man of his class and time. He was thirty-four or thirty-five, and England was safe at last. That's what everyone kept telling him. So he became a player, taken into another community composed largely of orphans and penniless third sons.

7

IN EARLY 1588, a house in Cheapside revealed that week's thirtieth, thirty-first, thirty-second, and thirty-third plague deaths, and so the theaters were closed. Geoff Belloc fled pestilent London with the rest of the Earl's Men company to make a tour of courtyards and town halls and private manors all the way up to Cumberland. Their licenses to travel the country without being arrested as errant vagrants were issued in a few days, reminding them all, not for the first time, how profoundly their existence and livelihoods depended upon their patron. Without him, without the theater, they were masterless and doomed. Their earl wished for them to be able to travel; they could travel; they traveled. And were spared death by plague.

Walsingham's invisible livery was surely the strangest, but to be a player was to be dressed in livery of many colors, dressed as lords, as kings, as queens. And when Geoff played the role of an ancient and foolish king of Scotland, he wore a bit of robe that had been given to him as a farewell gift by Beale, who said it came from none other than Walsingham himself. The retired spy wore the spymaster's clothes to dress as the ancient enemy.

They traveled in the mornings and played courtyards in the afternoons. Their evenings were their own, though they were not rich men, of course, so evenings tended to resemble one another and to resemble the evenings of touring actors across centuries: boisterous drink, regrettable sex, poor accommodations, all while bemoaning dim and violent audiences, the envious politics and intrigue behind the enviable allocations of roles.

But then one afternoon in '88, after a performance of *Edward III,* where Geoff again played his bullying and much-booed king of Scotland, little Jack Carson appeared, up all the way from White- hall, waiting to take Geoff for a drink and tell him Beale needed him to head up to Scotland, and not in play. That year the Spanish fleet came to try to seize the whole country, murder the queen, enslave the English, and Geoff left his beloved theater behind, returning to Walsingham's service to play his part in grander dramas. The Span- ish were all over Scotland, looking for help from James VI, who was panting ready, to be sure, to avenge his mother's death. James took a leering interest in the attack, but resisted the urge to aid the Span- ish on to London, glad for them to kill or weaken but not to succeed so far as to make his goal of becoming England's king more difficult. Geoff was not far away, helping other secret men track those Span- iards as they skulked in and out of Scotland, dressed as tinkers, sail- ors, barbers, shepherds. Geoff would never again believe anyone who offered up the sweet and tempting enchantment that the Cath- olic threat had passed, that it wasn't nursed by vipers in the north.

In '89, with Spain sunk or wind-scattered (a lucky few of them becoming Irish husbands), Geoff was back onstage, changed, a little less patient with apprentices who forgot their lines or groundlings who threw apples at the players. After a few months, during which he seemed to be growing calmer and his stage friends claimed they had tamed the bear, he was visited after a performance of Kit Mar- lowe's *Tamburlaine* by Robert Beale himself. Beale took Giant Geoff for a drink and a meal—goodbye, theater, again—and the rest of '89 and much of '90 were spent in Lancashire, with Belloc reporting to Beale through sub-agents about the Catholic hopes that even then lingered, embers of the great fires of '86 and '88, inextinguish- able hopes to peel Elizabeth from her throne with a blade and crown this or that Catholic nobleman, or James of Scotland, in her place.

The final danger in this sort of work, after all the other dangers, was in doing it too well. Geoff played so brilliantly the role of Catholic attendant in the service of a Catholic lord that in 1590 he was arrested, along with nearly every other member of the household. His sputtering Catholic rage at the English soldiers who beat and chained him was so convincing that he was tossed in the Tower, sharing a low and narrow cell with the lord's master of the horse, an old fellow whom Belloc rather liked. Belloc could appreciate the sad old man's love for old rituals and childhood habits from a life lived far north of London. To be dropped in a cell with a man as large as Geoff was an extra punishment, and Geoff pitied him.

Geoff slumped against the wall and could hear from down the corridor as his sort-of friend had his conscience scraped on the rack. Geoff tried a few words of comfort when the tough old man was tossed back in, weeping and unable to stand. Geoff was still of necessity playing his part when he tried to nurse the broken man, but his pity was real. Whether Geoff was a good man or a great actor was impossible for Geoff to decide, and there was not much time to sort it out, because he was taken out of the cell the next day and was on his way to that same rack room.

Richard Topcliffe, the queen's "investigator," awaited him. Geoff had never met him but had heard for years of his skills, whispered to him by Catholics who limped and hunched and hobbled and cowered and cried in their sleep for the rest of their lives. Geoff, brave since he knew his true situation would soon be clarified, felt a bit superior to the weedy bald man with the thin arms who waited for him in the rack room. Geoff could snap him in two, under normal conditions.

"I'm here as Walsingham's man," Geoff told him in a low voice, and the indifference on Topcliffe's face caused Geoff the most fear he had ever felt in his life. "You have to tell him I'm here. I had license." Topcliffe kept adjusting something on a table in the corner and touching himself, readjusting his cock in his slops. Geoff fumbled a bit: "You have to let Robert Beale know that I am here. Geoffrey Belloc. He'll tell you. I was licensed, from the start."

It was possible, Geoff later thought, that Topcliffe believed him. "I have license, too," he said. His voice was soft. The torturer didn't take Geoff as another man wailing his innocence. He simply wanted to have his fun before his new toy was taken away. That Geoff was a man of such strength and size probably made the day ahead even more appealing to the scrawny interrogator. He stripped off his shirt and hung it from a hook, put his hands in his pants again.

Such things did happen now and again. Back in '81 (all the Cunning Boys knew), Cuth Poulter was all the way to the gallows, tortured and about to hang, crying all along that he was a Cunning Boy and someone should go fetch Beale or Walsingham quick. And maybe Cuth was, and it was a bad mistake. But maybe he wasn't, and it was a lie. And maybe even Cuth didn't know for sure, couldn't remember from day to day which he was: Catholic or Catholic-hunter pretending to be Catholic, Catholic like his dad really was or Catholic-hunter like his paymaster, Catholic like his friends in Rheims or Catholic-hunter like his friends in London, mocker of Catholics like he was in a tavern or devoutly Catholic like he was in mass. Or just a boy of twenty-two who couldn't keep all that tidy, who found both spying and friendships easier when he told the truth always, even if it was the opposite truth of the day before. Either way, they hanged Cuth and slit him and chopped him to bits.

Now Belloc was shouting at Topcliffe to wait, begging, threatening, "Just a few hours until someone can go check with Sir Francis, damn your eyes if you touch me, he'll have you flayed, please, man, now listen to me."

But Francis Walsingham was at that moment dying in his home outside London, and lucky it was, since, in a spasm of sentiment, he asked to see a few of his old Cunning Boys and asked Beale—who kept a vigil at his master's side—where Giant Geoff was these days. Beale sent someone to inquire after Belloc and whether he'd reported in yet on his time in the north. Belloc was spitting at Topcliffe when the chamber's door opened and the warden led in a Queen's Messenger saying Geoffrey Belloc was released, at Mr. Beale's word. Geoff never forgot the face Topcliffe made as he released Geoff's straps and shackles, disappointment and curdling anger badly hidden behind a wet and yellow laugh: "We'll meet again in happier circumstance."

By 1591, after all these exploits, Geoff was one of those with a face and a name too well-known to ever go again into the enemy's presence and try to pass. Beale was kindlier than ever, and he sometimes stood a meal for Belloc, and they would talk of days past. Beale was bored, too. Since Walsingham's death, this pleasant work had been taken up by other men and other favorites, and Beale wasn't much involved. But still they talked, and worried, and shook off their worries. They were men who knew the secrets, who knew the enemy's relentless ways, who knew what it was to be surprised by the bloodlust of Catholics, to be almost too late to stop the threat, who knew that wishful thinking would get good honest people killed. Neither of them would ever say again, "I think we may be safe at last." But most people looked around and thought the country *was* finally safe at last.

With Walsingham dead, Beale was good enough to see that some trusted men were given pensions and work, where he could. Nicky Berden was made Purveyor of the Queen's Poultry. Beale was noble and generous enough to have Geoff made a Queen's Messenger, granted £36 per annum, for easy and safe work: Keep his ears open, deliver dispatches with discretion. And as an officer of pursuivants, Geoff was also entitled to make some extra money serving arrest warrants and tracking those Catholics who still attempted to enter England with death and destruction in their papist hearts. Geoff's pursuivants themselves were hard to plumb—men who made their wages by hunting papists but would often take a wealthy papist's money to let him escape. They traveled easily among Catholics because they used to be Catholics themselves, and who was to say they were not still able in their hearts to justify arresting Catholics while all the while knowing they would confess to a priest someday and slither off to heaven?

He spent days in court, sending Messengers to and fro on open and secret business for Lord Burghley and then Robert Cecil, whom he hadn't even met. Sometimes he carried important dispatches himself, within London, within England, even to Paris or the Low Countries. At times he would savor the fleeting sensation he had felt in the woods back in '86, with the world tied at his feet, that feeling he was doing something of the greatest importance. But not very often anymore. He missed the stage and considered going back yet again, but the money would never match what the Messengers paid.

With Robert Cecil in Walsingham's old office, Geoff's work rarely demanded he rely on his wits. There were no more parts to play, no more intelligencers to recruit or question, no more coded letters to write, no more invitations into the offices within offices to discuss what new plots against the Catholics could be conceived or which Catholic plots to foil. And, outside all those offices, delivering sealed messages and then sitting and waiting for other sealed messages to carry back, it was difficult to sort out facts from stories. He saw Mr. Beale now and again, and Mr. Beale was always friendly. He watched old stage friends play by candlelight before the queen. One day, after such a performance, he was standing not ten yards from the queen herself when a nobleman collapsed in killing tremors to the ground, his fists drawn up to his cheek in stiffened palsy, only to be restored to health by a Turkish sorcerer.

8

THE MORNING AFTER Belloc received Cecil's approval to con-
struct a plat to ascertain the color of James VI's soul, Geoff
woke with a feeling he used to have sometimes when he was doing
the work in prison or in Douai among the papists, pretending even
when sleeping: the shock of fear in the belly that he had missed a
message sign, deciphered a letter incorrectly, stepped past a warning
left for him in a hole. Mystifying dreams had carried on all night
and offered no more clarity: the laughing phoenix, the smoldering
Catholic stepping down off the pyre and smiling at Geoffrey in tri-
umph, the mountain falling down on Belloc and all his faceless
friends, Scottish Mary's severed head seducing him as her laughing
dog licked at the pooling blood: *You're a mountain of a man, aren't you,
brother?* No rest, no clarity.

That afternoon, Geoff sat upon the highest galleries of the Rose,
the performance of *Sir John Oldcastle* complete. The yard had nearly
emptied, just a few women far to the back finishing their slowest,
drink-delayed customers. The youngest apprentices of the company performed their own tasks for the coming night, working
around the women, gathering up the leavings on the ground, collecting the penny cushions to be locked away, the costumes and
properties to count and brush clean and lay in trunks before the sun

fell much farther and the work would require the expense of candles and torch, annoying the partners.

Geoffrey Belloc had sent down word, and soon his friend joined him upon the highest, easternmost bench, the last few rays of sun racing up their faces, up the theater's horsehair wall, until the dome above them still sang blue but a blue aspiring to black. They drank the liquor Geoff had brought by way of inspiration and reward. "Plot with me," said Belloc, an old invitation.

"Tell us the conceit," said his friend the playmaker.

And so Belloc framed the story like this: A young king wishes to possess a neighboring kingdom, larger and richer than his own. He would rule both of these kingdoms. But first he must convince the larger kingdom of his true faith. "The king knows he has no hope to conquer his larger neighbor. His ancestors tried and failed and were lucky to keep their own lands after."

"Like Scotland, then?" asked the playmaker loudly.

"No. Not that. Not Scotland."

"No?"

"Decidedly not."

Ben Taylor pressed his lips together, amused himself by pulling faces at Geoff, then nodded and drank deeply. "Not at all like Scotland."

"Illyria. And now as punishment," Geoff continued, "the King of Illyria is kept to strict military limits by the larger kingdom, Bohemia. No warhorses, a set number of men-at-arms, of cannon, whatnot. This king knows all this—"

"But will the audience know it, man? It can be quite tedious to explain such history. Even in my own plays, I can't bear to listen to the first fifteen minutes one more time, all that explanation of who has cause for vengeance against whom and—"

"Then let's rush to the first surprise. Soliloquy: The king believes that if he is patient, the larger kingdom will simply be presented to him as a gift. Perhaps he is the legitimate heir, perhaps not, but many believe so, and he believes so. But he dare not ask outright."

"Ah. Good, there's the story: The king of large Bohemia sees the danger, weds some girl quick, and begins littering out heirs. That enrages our little Illyrian man, and we're into Act Two."

Belloc began again, with a tone somewhat less fanciful: "Let us say instead that Bohemia is ruled by a queen, an aging queen, too old to litter out any heirs. And she will not wed. The King of Illyria knows this."

"Oh." Ben Taylor's face changed, though he felt the physical excitement of marching right up to the edge of a cliff before turning away, giddy. "Oh," he said again. "Oh. So nothing like Scotland."

They drank some more, and the blue dome darkened. Belloc waited, but as his friend did not speak, at last Belloc said, "It's just a story. Ancient. Nothing to do with today."

"Won't pass the revels office. You'll never get a license to play it."

"Doesn't have to. Private performance only."

"Oh" again. "Below," said Taylor, and they descended to the next gallery and then into the empty yard and from the yard up onto the stage. Ben Taylor sat on the stage's edge, held between his legs the bottle Belloc had given him, and Belloc waited, standing below. "What plot do you perceive here, man? I see no story but the story of a patient king, waiting for his old neighbor queen's death."

"That's the main action, but the other plot is the crucial one. I need the story of discovering, beyond any possible question, the king's most closely guarded secret." To write a play, one must imagine what a character will do next; to make use of a spy's report, one must imagine what the target of espionage will do next. "How is a canny man tricked into revealing treasure? I want to know what is inside the man's heart. In its nooks. When even his soliloquies all lie."

The playmaker slapped the stage next to him, demanded Belloc leap up and sit close beside him, their legs dangling off the end of the boards, the floor of the yard almost invisible below them in the fast-gathering night. "You ever met him? King of Illyria?"

"No, but I was there a fair bit. Caught his confederates. One was a barber-surgeon, of all things, traveling along the border offering his services—except that his traveling case, filled with all his tools of tooth-pulling, also had a secret panel that, turned upside down, revealed ciphered letters from the King of Spain."

"Extraordinary," said Taylor, "that such things exist, and men like you are there to stop them." The playmaker drank down the last of the bottle meant to reward results.

"Your help now. Call upon your genius. What does he truly believe and how do we determine it before it is too late? Please. Plot with me, Ben. Make yourself *useful,* wouldn't that be nice? Instead of just a player."

And Ben Taylor began to imagine an act of theft, the victim no lighter for the loss, never knowing the thing was snatched.

It was dark when they left the theater, Taylor just sober enough to check all the chains and locks himself. He reached up to take Belloc's arm, turned him past the Rose brothel and the Clink prison, pushed through the street's stench and night business to the river. The mounted torches behind them still left plenty of shadow, and there they sat, backs against a wall, to see anyone approaching from either side.

They could, it occurred to Geoff, be overheard from above, and he was relieved to see Taylor look up at the wall behind him before he spoke a word; they saw no balcony or casement. "I think it might be done like that. One hears of Jews, upon their dying beds, who ask to drink Christian blood in hopes it will protect them if, to their surprise, the Christian faith is true." Ben was well and truly drunk now, but Belloc was shaking, sober, shaking at the thought of what was to come, thanks to a good storyteller.

9

GEOFF HAD SPUN a respectable web in Scotland back in '88 at the time of the Spanish attack—hostelers and brothel keepers, his own Cunning Boys, actors, lovers, grocers, customs men to seize imported rosaries and crosses, dockworkers, prostitutes and stablers, servants in noble northern houses with Catholic tendencies indulged almost openly—but no one within James's palaces, no one inside Holyroodhouse or Edinburgh Castle. Now he needed a rope long enough to plumb the depth of Scotland's deepest lake.

The prison population had in the past proven useful in certain specific tasks. Thieves' skills were often worth the price of their unreliable honor. In this case, though, it was futile, Geoff confessed after he had wasted days in Marshalsea and the Gatehouse interviewing the least capable of such men ("empirically" the least capable, as the natural philosophers would say, seeing as any thief in prison had been caught in the act of failing). When these whining cutpurses and lock-melters and queer tenants weren't protesting their innocence and marveling at their illusory good fortune (having won, in their lightless puddled cells, the attention of an eminent man), they revealed themselves to be—every one of them—merely dexterous of hand. Limited of imagination, not one of them could pass as anything other than what they were. Thieves resembled nothing so much as thieves; no face paint, Roman priest's costume, lady's wig, or perfume could make them otherwise. They had devoutly applied their minds to their fingers since they were children and carelessly allowed time and circumstance to shape the rest. Geoff wished to lift a secret from a man's heart, not a coin from his purse.

(Irritated by the lost time, Belloc left them wondering what the gentleman had wanted in the first place, regretful almost to insanity that they had been unable to find the words that would have won them liberty from the ax when fate had granted them such a chance. They shouted after Belloc's fading steps: admissions of guilt, threats, offers to pleasure him or kill his enemies. Some claimed intelligence of Catholic plotters against the queen. "I will lead you to them. I know the holes where they hide." This formula alone charmed, if only for a bit: The clever ones were kept alive a day or two longer while Belloc sent word up and other persuasive men returned with questions about the pope's myriad agents.)

If the task was too subtle for the thieves, asking too much wit and improvisation, it was also too daunting for most of the players Belloc could trust to keep a secret. Too many other skills to teach those improvisers, too much effort to calm them over the risk to their lives and souls, too many who refused this kind of work anymore, since Kit Marlowe's murder. A dry well, he suspected, worried that further delay would cost him against whatever was happening in Elizabeth's bedroom. Still, one night among his old friends might bring to mind someone new, someone charming, someone dangerous, someone devoted.

All massacres complete, all villains punished, all lovers wed, all endings final before the sun was going down, the company was released into their true vocation as men of the stage: drinking. Geoff found them leaving the players' gate and sat among them at the Pard's Head.

On one side, a plea from little Tom Prescott that Geoff use his influence at court (vastly larger in the players' imagination than in life) to get the queen to attend a performance of his new play. "Oh, but she has to. She'll watch this one. Promise me. Geoff, I'm begging you, talk to someone. Please. Whoever will listen to you. Get someone to come to the Rose, and they'll want it in court for her. She's who I dreamed of watching it, when I was writing. For her Christmas revels or—"

"Stop. I don't run the place. I'm just—"

"It's as great a thing as anything you ever read or played in. Anything you've seen by Kit or Middsy. I did it all on my own. Every line." Tom Prescott had one of Geoff Belloc's giant hands and was squeezing as hard as he could, pleading. Geoff laughed, stood, and lifted him with one arm like when Tom was a boy, because he was making the same face as when he was a boy, when he would beg Geoff to steal him sweets from a noble house for Christmas. "Give me my hand back. That'll do. All right: *I'll* come and watch. That's something, right? If it's as good as you say—"

"Geoff, it's a *miracle*. I did it, and it's . . . Terence or Seneca. It's the best thing I've made. Philip will have to start paying me better than six pounds a play. You know what the Chamberlain's makers get at the Globe? Munday told me. The playmaker gets a portion of the box, same as the sharers. Their writer gets *first* dip! But it's more than the money, this one." Tom looked into his drink, at the backs of his hands, at the ceiling and the heavens lurking somewhere just beyond, and he began to leak half a smile only for himself.

Tom Prescott was born in Silver Street, near where Geoff had been living. Tom told him so the day they met, when the boy appeared begging for an apprenticeship: "Silver Street, sir. Saw you all the time." Good enough, and so in Geoff's days with the players he had murdered Tom a hundred times as the Husband killing the Wife in the Yorkshire play. Belloc's tenderness for his slaughtered Wife lasted all the way to this day: "Of course you're as good a writer as they are. I'd rather have played your worst shit than the second part of *Tamburlaine*."

"I'm writing a play about Mary, Queen of Scots," said Gil Ames, on Geoff's other side.

"I wouldn't risk it. The revels office is a bit touchy about anything set in Scotland."

"I'll make her out to be consorting with the devil."

"Not far off the truth, but I still wouldn't risk it." Geoff finished his drink and called for more. "Did I ever tell you? You both would have been boys when I was in the woods catching her, laying snares. I knew her. She couldn't wait to betray, call for slaughter." But then he saw the young men's faces: Yes, he'd told them this one before. He couldn't remember doing so, but they were laughing at him.

Tom said, "I will give her this: Seems wrong, her end. Trying to find a way to write about that, not make the audience sorry for her even a little. Couldn't get *that* cleared by revels."

"Won't argue with you there. I saw it, her end. I was there. Don't like to think about it. Had to help dress up the stage and scaffold ahead of time. Make sure the sight lines were clear. Just like theater work. But the end . . . Her little dog ran up, licked up the blood, cried. Little dog absolutely cried."

Tom Prescott pinched his giant friend's red and bristling cheek. "You always bring in the dog."

He batted the boy's hand away. "Stung a little to see it, that's all I mean. Even if she deserved it."

Ames whistled at the image, closed his eyes to be there. "A crowned queen."

"True. But so is ours, and the Scotch would have done her worse. Don't ever forget it. She did her own husband, you know."

"I know."

"They're like that."

"Who? Queens? Scots? Catholics?"

"Take your pick. Well, not queens, obviously. But otherwise."

"Glad that's all done now," said Tom Prescott.

Geoff said, "I'd be as glad as any man to see it done, but it's not done. The pope won't let it be done. The Spanish. The Scots. We're not ever walking out of those black woods. Wolves."

And did young Prescott and Ames laugh at him for his unquenchable fury and readiness to fight an ancient war? For the speech he could be provoked into giving when drunk, so reliably that Ames now owed Prescott a penny? They did.

But then Geoff heard from the other end of the table the unmistakable sound of intelligence: ". . . until you hear what I know has come out of France . . ." At once, Geoff's ability to seem rapt in one direction while straining to catch every meaning from another direction engaged: His face betrayed no change while he awaited word of what might be reported from France. Could be useful, maybe salable, or turned back against its first whisperer: a foolish thought that came like breathing. Foolish because, of course, those practiced abilities were madness: He was not among men of state or at a table of conspirators or Catholic regicides; he was with actors and their women and their boys. Drink had slowed his thinking and brightened his camouflage, so he finally realized he could simply turn to the would-be intelligencer and ask, as he did, "What reports from France? Fleets?"

Richard Breidel, player of epic knights, giants, monsters, murderers, and, today, Mephistopheles, was toiling hard, without any luck yet, to get drunk. Geoff's question seemed enough to tip him over, at last, into laughing inebriation. "You think we're receiving news of fleets, you shit? Much more urgent than that. Tell him," he instructed his woman, laying a giant palm across the back of her golden neck, his loving fingers nearly meeting at her throat.

"It seems," she continued, with a tone Belloc recognized at once: the satisfied reporter, bursting with secret story, made powerful proportionate to the hungry attention of her customers. "It seems they have discovered in France—but I should take you back a step with me, so you can better understand." Again the inhalation, the inward hoarding of news, the pleasure in kindling all anticipation while others must wait and wait.

"I have," she began again, "a friend. She and I served in the same house for a long spell. I saw her last week, after some three years apart, and still a girl to talk. She looked just the same, a true beauty this one, gentlemen, and one who seemed no older at all, while the rest of us gather time in little pouches on our cheeks and arses. She now serves a woman whose husband came and went to France for the trade of this and that, and he liked her well, so when he came back to London, he brought her gifts of French silk and flower-waters. Unlike certain people."

Breidel squeezed her neck until she lifted her shoulders and squealed. "Tell us your story, can't you?" he growled. "Geoff's masters at court are eager to pay him for this."

"The husband tells my friend—take your hands off me, you filthy bear—he tells her this great secret from France, the news from Paris. Do you want to hear? Do you?"

Belloc, a little drunk now, allowed himself to wonder if this gossip at fifth hand could possibly have value. He had seen stranger things in life, true pieces of intelligence that fell from one mouth to another in bed or at table. He missed the game more than he had realized. There never was a thrill in life or love or onstage to match these strange and glittering moments.

"It seems that in Paris, in the very court, they have discovered"—could this woman really have somehow heard information that might explain some secret corner of the constantly shifting map of war and religion and monarchs, Catholic schemes and venom?—"a way for a man and woman to enjoy each other that answers all five of the fundamental questions."

Belloc exhaled and poured himself more drink.

"No laughter, good Messenger. This is gospel: There is a position—he shared it with my friend, and she tried to draw me a sketch—in which she cannot be made to have a child. This is one."

"I think we in England have discovered *in ano* as well."

"No, no. Not that. In this position, neither can give the other the pox or anything like it. This is two."

"*La bouche?* The French discovered that in my father's time, I think."

"No, not that, either. He will in this position enjoy the most complete and transporting joy. This is three. But so, too, shall she. This is four."

"This seems difficult to credit. Who will try it with me?"

"And finally this. Five: She will present as a virgin even after this, if she did before. She can be enjoyed without ever being spent. A treasury never depleted. And so this is five, all answered."

"Has anyone ink and paper? Can you draw it, girl?"

She made a show of shivering with delight. She drew her shoulders to her ears, closed her eyes, turned her head to one side, brought her closed fists to her cheek, and shook from head to toe.

And two days later, God having granted him that inspiration, Geoff Belloc was heading north at speed, with Beale and Cecil's approval of his plat.

PART THREE

MATTHEW THATCHER and DAVID LEVERET, 1601

. . . .

[James] the King of Scotland . . . was reared in the heretical doctrine of Calvin, which he now holds, nevertheless he is mistrusted by the Scotch heretics and the Queen of England; and the Catholics, recollecting his pious mother, and trusting in his naturally good disposition, hope that he will one day open the gate to the light of truth.

—SIR WALTER LINDSAY, 1594, in an intelligence report to Catholic Spain

1

MATTHEW THATCHER WALKED in the park most days in most weather, almost always alone, stumbling on a stone or branch if his attention strayed. He would sit alone, sometimes for hours, considering the firth, that tongue of ocean and infinite boundary. In stronger health, at the beginning, he drew sketches of each variety of bird in the lord's realm, tried to capture in words the quiddity of their twittering, until, when every bird he saw was familiar from his own pictures and captions, it was another year.

He attempted to catalog for his lord's library all the plants and herbs, the buds of each in spring, the leaves of summer, the mushrooms that came the following autumn on the wet and naked roots and under the soft and crumbling fallen logs. He sorted the grasses, ate from each green and berry and mushroom, tried in his rooms to determine their effects and value, in tinctures and distillate and paste, wrote what guidance he could be certain of as he followed each bite of foliage into his sleep and digestion, into his legs' aches and the spots and threads drifting through his vision, and through the shadows where memories had once glowed, where he raced to extinguish them before they burned him.

Dreams were rarer and less specific with years, less true to the past, and so they could now be tolerated. Early pains, which had once pierced so sharply, had left behind in their place a rotating crew of smaller, childish griefs, as if the process of forced forgetting had turned him into a boy. These petty complaints could trouble Matthew Thatcher beyond reason, and he would at times find himself alone—in his chamber or in the grounds—weeping at the unkindness of beast or child or servant, even while loathing his own weakness.

For example, he feared one of the kennel's dogs more than the rest. The kennel keeper knew this and so let it run at Thatcher in the park, or so Thatcher suspected. The lord's youngest child, whom Matthew tutored in natural history, mathematics, geography, and Latin, found amusement in stealing his tutor's ink, until one day the boy fell and struck his head and recovered only to fall again, this time to a swelling that never healed, and the boy died. Another loss, and surprisingly painful to Thatcher.

Matthew Thatcher sat in the park, older again, held samples of wood and greenery between his fingers, crushed a leaf against his palm, opened its flesh to half its depth with his thumbnail, squeezed. He inhaled its faint scent, and at once, faster than he could resist, smelled lemon. He feared he was recalling more than he was smelling, because how could this leaf in Cumberland contain a wisp of lemon? He had drawn and studied this leaf before, he was almost certain, and it had not then smelled at all of a distant joy.

He dropped the leaf to the ground as if burned, rubbed his palms, and moved away into the wood. He sat heavily on a fallen tree, and the rotted branch yielded a little under his weight.

The mushrooms and toadstools, the logs in the wood that bore them: Why did God teach every rabbit and squirrel which of them were nutritive and which were venomous, so that a hare might pass two identical offerings before nibbling at a third that was, but for a faint tinge to a rib along its stalk or a blush across the velvet of its dome, perfectly the same? Why did God instruct beasts but allow men to ingest blindly and now and again writhe in tortures or die outright, unless a student of nature watched those rabbits first, sketched those tinged stalks and blushing domes, wrote and advised the cooks which mushrooms to avoid? Matthew Thatcher, in his first year at the hall, had drawn and written guides for the cooks and boys, so that all the baron's people were, with much effort, brought up to the level of knowledge equal to that of a juvenile squirrel. God did not bother much for His humans. Or He expected men to do it for Him.

If one erred, then one died, and God looked to the healthy hare instead. And if one knew the secret laws of the forest but glanced away when gathering the mushrooms, forgot to pay heavenly attention, or if one drank strong drink before gathering them, or simply looked up and enjoyed the sky that God offered (and knew that one was gazing gratefully upon), and then pulled those deadly caps without checking their stalks and domes—

Or, Thatcher allowed himself to think further (or Satan caused him to think), what if one simply pretended not to know the difference, never to have learned it, and took the flesh of the blushing dome into his mouth and let fall away from this life all that he clung to with such effort and exhaustion? Thatcher might then avoid that cannon God had aimed against self-slaughter, as the man onstage had warned, and let go these memories and costumes, these lies and lost worlds, the child growing up without him, the wife, caressed and pressed by other hands, who'd long since forgotten him as he had fought to force her burning image from his own memory. He could simply eat the venomed mushrooms until sleep overtook him forever, and the smell of lemons would be the last scent he knew.

What god would care? The god of squirrels and rabbits? The god who secreted his venom here but not there? Why can I not eat as if I were a hare too old to care any longer, or a boy who had never bothered to ask the necessary questions, and then I could let drop, like so many heavy bags, all the years lost, all the pork and wine consumed under all those suspicious eyes all those years, the brutally heavy years dragging behind me, until I am there again, in the garden atop the hill, the scent of fig blossoms and lemon and the swaying blue below as bright and transparent as all the domed blue above, all of which persists, despite my efforts.

I have not used God's proper name. God's name could not matter, not truly. Why would He care what I call Him? Does He not know my real heart always, whatever my lips say? The Jews will not say any name, will not write it, but they do not forget it. And if they did? Still they fear and love and worship Him, even if none could recall the word they've been taught never to utter. When they washed me Christian, they asked me to forget the true name of God. And so I have never said it since, not in front of others, and have not for many years even heard it in my head. I cannot recall the last time I heard His name within my quiet mind. But did I forget it?

Atop the hill, above the sea, there is a house with a tree with fruit. The boy, whose name I will not think or say, loves that fruit. The fruit has a name, but I will not— She, the boy's mother, who gave the boy to me, the mother of the boy whose name I will not think, she said it was a good place for a tree like that, with the round fruit that should not be thought of, since it was gone and therefore should be forgotten.

The boy, the boy's mother, the roots and leaves, the round fruit. I knew their names but would not say them and cause myself pain, because I am a coward. He knows my real heart, and He deems me damnable.

Those mushrooms, each with a name, each with their God-given taste and purpose, and some might end all this.

2

MATTHEW THATCHER TOOK his meals, usually seated alone, at a trestle more or less close to the high table in the hall. He slept for many years in that same hall with other servants on rushes, though none slept near him, from rumor or fear of his old name ("Did they cut the end off you when you were a boy?"). He had fallen from Turkey to Elizabeth's Turkey carpets and Turkish acrobat to this floor, straw mixed with herbs he suggested to cover smells of food and bodies and other things. He lived like this until Moresby, in growing dependence, demanded Thatcher sleep on a pallet at the foot of his lordship's bed.

The household dined mostly in silence but for serving men and dishes. Some nights, especially after her ladyship had died, the baron might rage against Thatcher's incompetence, unjustly on the whole. Tonight, Baron Moresby pulled a fur more tightly around his frail limbs and in the process spilled his wine. Dr. Thatcher saw the lord's anger even as men mopped away the mess and refilled his cup, watched for the hand to tremble, which it did, in a manner that told Thatcher how much time remained until the flailing would begin. His labors tonight would be more than usual, or at least no less than what had become common in recent months. None of the herbs held the man steady longer than a day or two anymore, and small angers only narrowed the time between his fits.

Salted pork again. It no longer had any effect on Thatcher, no longer seemed to be aimed at him in any way, neither taunt nor test. There was a pig to kill and eat, salted and served again and again. The baron demanded it, though Thatcher had suggested, somewhat meekly, careful not to be taken for a crypto-proselytizer, that pork was possibly an instigator of the baron's fits. But the lord demanded pork more and more often since the pox had carried away his wife (and several serving people), and perhaps each slaughtered pig was an effort to slaughter himself, believing his doctor's counsel.

The first pork? A great hall, the stewards and ushers, the trenchers set with slabs of pig. Eyes on Thatcher for his reaction, comic or revelatory as treasonous. Someone's cruel, probing politeness: "Dr. Thatcher, if the meal offends . . ." The hall's silence spread thick to receive his reply: "Your generosity and kindness are exemplary to us all, and I am well contented to eat what all Christian men at your table are fortunate enough to be given."

Thatcher had, of course, been fed pork hundreds of times since his conversion and his years with the baron, and invariably when visiting a new home or when someone who had heard his story first met him. It no longer made him gag, did not even cause the tightening of the throat he could hide from those next to him at table. There was a time when he told himself that Matthew Thatcher ate the pork but it never touched the lips of Mahmoud Ezzedine. He could recall that trick of the mind, these years later, but could not remember if he had ever truly believed it.

He had also told himself that Allah might transform the pork, so that a true man who desired not to offend but whose circumstance reduced him to this might swallow the flesh and know that, before it touched his lips, Allah had made it clean. This of course was quite close to Christian transubstantiation, for which belief good Protestant Dr. Thatcher should fervently hope that Catholics might burn for their last minutes on earth and then infinitely in the hereafter. It was also not far from the story he had told every member of the embassy, believed by none and gratefully accepted by all: It was not wine but bull's blood. In the years since, Dr. Thatcher had viewed the wine and ale as the necessary antidote to the island's persistent English melancholy, though keener eyes than his (or his own eyes when he was younger) might have guessed they were no antidote but cause.

"It's coming," slurred the baron, the knife falling from his hand with a clatter, but Dr. Thatcher had been watching its approach for some time and was already in place. He caught his ever-lighter lord in his arms, lowered him to the ground, turned his head, fought the curved wooden implement between his remaining teeth, held his weakened limbs tight against the palsies that would one day, even quite soon, seize his heart, beyond Matthew Thatcher's ability to press it back to iambic life.

In 1591 Baron Moresby had for the first time returned to his senses to face a Turk. He awoke to himself first and then, after only a moment's clearing of mist, to horror. A turbaned Turk leaned over him and inquired, "You are quiet again inside your body and head? No pain? No lights?" Another wretched palsy, and this Turk had seen it. Moresby foolishly tried to sit up on the cushioned bench in an annex where he had been carried, away from the queen's presence, but he moved too quickly. The Turk caught him across the chest and steadied him. The pages remained in the corners of the room. "It is not the first time you have suffered such a crisis, my lord?" The Turk wizard knew that as well? He waved the pages out of the room.

"Did everyone witness it?"

Mahmoud Ezzedine paused, confused by the question. "Have they not seen it before in you?"

"Never."

"But was this the first? It did not seem to me that it could have been."

The Turk's questions, his knowledge, his tone: He knew all this? "I sense its approach. I know its fuse. I am always alone and away before anyone can see."

"To what end?" Ezzedine asked. "You are in no danger *except* if alone. Yours is not a fatal palsy, I do not believe. You have suffered this since you were a boy, I presume."

"How can you know all this?"

Ezzedine lightly, shyly, shrugged, as if the knowledge were not Moresby's carefully hoarded secret, suppressed, bribed over, killed for, over years of worry and caution.

"Since I was a young man. But the events have become more frequent these months. And the time between the warning and the fit is briefer. Today I did not have enough time even to leave Her Majesty's presence, it seems."

Ezzedine studied the man's face in confusion.

"What is it? What are you staring at?"

"I apologize. Please excuse my ignorance. But what matter if all the world should know of your sufferings? It is of no moment to your ability or your wisdom in council."

There was only silence in reply as the baron finally gathered the strength to stand. He stared in open wonderment at the Mahometan physician, his head slowly draining of its excess noise and motion. "You have seen my affliction before? In your land?"

"Of course."

"It is not viewed as fearful?"

"Why would it be?"

"But Turks are savages."

Moresby still thought them so, even when the queen's new physician began treating him for his afflictions. The baron's reliance on him became obvious enough that the doctor was called before the queen: "Dr. Thatcher. My lord Moresby has for so many years been one of the wisest councillors of my realm." The queen examined the line of her recently Christian doctor's newly beardless face. "His loyalty to us in all matters is exemplary. His sufferings, however, do tax his spirit and our own, and we are moved in love by his most piteous state. And by your loving care of him, which we did view, and which has brought you to our care in turn."

"My lord is, Your Majesty, in no danger to himself. His ailment is an anomaly of the humors and only an inconvenience to him, nothing more."

"You relieve our mind, though still we fear for him. Answer me true, sir: Would he not *benefit* by being far from the noise and unease of Whitehall and London, in air that is not noxious? He is very brave and would resist us in fulfilling this desire. And so we free him of responsibilities here and allow him to enjoy a life . . ." The queen continued on, generously releasing her fitful baron from attendance upon her, overriding his bold attempts to be of service despite dangerous illness. That the baron was not present for this discussion confused Thatcher slightly, until he recognized the ceremony as quite exactly what had been done to him some months earlier, though he was not astute enough to hear within her words the accompanying loss of land, wealth, patents, and privilege that his patient was suffering under the guise of medical care, nor did he know what crimes of faith or tongue or merely flirtation the baron had committed. "And as you were so wise in your attendance upon him these months, Dr. Thatcher, and as we wish to show our love for him and gratitude to him, we are granting him another boon from us, so that should he need your wisdom . . ."

So it was that Matthew Thatcher, never truly trusted in Elizabeth's court, despite his protective and strategic conversion, was for a second time in four months converted from a man into a gift. He was asked in the first occasion to surrender his name and religion, his family and home, and was in the second asked to give up nothing but the hope he had carried that somehow, by remaining in close quarters to the queen and submitting to the expectation of conversion, he might someday soon find a way back to Constantinople, forgiven, safe, and even honored for his uncomplaining service to the sultan (the conversion never to be discussed, of course, with anyone).

But no: A large measure of that hope was now extracted, brutally, and he moved north. He watched Whitehall and then London recede behind him with the anguish of a woman who, having lost a child, curses God more loudly when she then loses her cat.

The gift was carried to a place called Cumberland, an unwanted gift to an untrusted nobleman. Matthew Thatcher became an unimaginable foreigner in a small household, still carrying that stench of suspicion around him, not merely for worshipping incorrectly to their deity (as he was suspected of in London) but also for being the obvious spy of a hated queen who had tyrannically relieved Baron Moresby of a town home on the Thames and a lucrative license to import a particular sweet wine and exiled him to his only remaining property, Moresby Hall, scarcely more than a small house amid the lakes and becks, nearly falling into the Irish Sea. Matthew Thatcher was the man who daily bore witness to a humiliated lord's frailty, the very frailty the queen had used to destroy the luckless, shaking man.

And so Matthew Thatcher was cast farther still from home, farther into this befogged island. Its villagers and country people were even more frightened than London's courtiers of his accent and his reputation, which arrived either far ahead of him or speedily soon after.

His baptism in London had been a necessity. Not forced at sword's edge, it must be admitted, and blessedly not performed until after any potential Turk witness had returned to Constantinople, but it was clearly required if he was to be allowed to remain in Elizabeth's court, where any hope of return would be found. Now, banished from London even as a Christian, he felt hope dying and despair growing and his Christian costume more necessary than ever.

For many months, the doctor from Constantinople attempted to remember and secretly preserve himself as Mahmoud Ezzedine when alone and to portray only as deeply and frequently as necessary in company the Christian English Matthew Thatcher. What circumstances demanded, he would pay, but he would not become an abomination, even if fate dictated that he never left the damp and gray in which he had been abandoned, the stage upon which he must perform forever, this earthly limbo, like the underworld where Christians allowed decent pagans to roam with unborn infants.

He could still make his prayers to Allah when alone. The door to his small chamber locked, the keyhole covered, and even then the bed between him and the door, he placed himself in the corner, pressed against the wall so as to be invisible from the one window, and he attempted to stand and kneel, bow and stand, cross his arms and touch the floor. It took many months before he did not attempt it five times in a day, only a few more months after that before twice seemed in itself to prove sufficient dedication, and then many years before the words became difficult to recall or, worse, went unrecalled and unremarked in their absence, lines of prayer crossing and reblending, days passing without addressing God by His proper name.

As hope died, memory became unbearable, and so he began a program of forgetting. He might walk through the halls of his home in Constantinople, but he would keep his eyes on the ceiling, notice nothing and no one as he walked. He might sit in the courtyard or on the hill above the sea and permit himself to smell the air or the lemon tree, but he would studiously remain alone.

He managed his protective forgetfulness even into sleep, with great effort, waking himself from the most pleasant dreams when he realized they had been tricks to make him long for what God had made unattainable.

Even after he had not dreamed of home for months, he was shocked to remember those long-ago dreams; these, too, would have to be forgotten somehow—memories of remembering, absurd, were no less painful. He could remember how he felt, waking in deep feeling, still able to smell his wife's hair, able to feel the heat of the stone in the morning under his bare feet, just outside his house. For a long time he would crash awake from dreams as if dropped from the sky, as if he had been elevated to paradise only to be shoved backward off a cliff. In his sleep he used to approach Constantinople with such speed, across the water, French ships and pirate corsairs beneath him, flying like a bird or a thought, and the waves would rise from his feet, cutting through the water like the fin of a porpoise, if a porpoise could sail with such grace on this side of the water as beneath it. He would soar at the coast of the Bosporus, only to be deflected from the shore as if an invisible wall had been lying in wait, beyond which his wife and child could hear nothing of his cries.

Baron Moresby was an old man of more than fifty now. More than once a week the lord was seized in his predicament's jaws and thrown about like a rabbit clutched by a pocket beagle, teeth pushing past fur, past skin, past blood vessel, muscle, tooth touching bone. The baron's memory holes gaped wider now, swallowing not only the seizure but several hours before it. The resulting anger at each loss of time grew worse. The warnings that a seizure was coming were now almost nonexistent or were so blended into his usual demeanor that everything, or nothing, seemed a warning, and again he woke, the sick on his face being wiped away by the patient and quiet doctor, so that at times Moresby could almost laugh at another repetition of the slowly aging scene.

Dr. Thatcher ministered to the baron's convulsions and insisted upon the natural explanations of his suffering, to their mutual benefit and protection. (A popular guide to witch-hunting identified seizures as a simple and obvious proof of possession, which could have led to the baron's execution, were he a man of lesser rank or a woman of any rank.) In Cumberland, Thatcher attended to nothing else and to no one else. The baroness had her preferred physician and curatives, until her death, and she would not allow her children or her few ladies to be touched or even spoken to by the (probably unwavering) Mahometan. Were it not for the baron's dependence upon him, Dr. Thatcher would have found himself turned out of the hall, a masterless man in a strange country, without home or friends or work.

But the baron most definitely did need him. Elizabeth's loving banishment of Henry Fairleigh, Baron Moresby, from court, from the heat and press and fumes of London, should have resulted—by the doctor's own reckoning—in fewer attacks, and yet they struck only more frequently in the country and with less warning. It was increasingly difficult for their victim to hide his ailment, and soon he no longer cared even to try. He demanded his doctor stay by his side more often, even at prayer, which resulted in the odd sight of the baron attending holy services (lightly Catholic here in the north, far from London's reformation fashions) supported arm in arm by a Turk.

Moresby could not free himself of his need for that Turk (evidence enough of unnatural possession, in the eyes of many in Moresby Hall). At times the baron believed the doctor must have been Elizabeth's spy, or Cecil's. Still, after a seizure, when Moresby would come to himself in a room away from company, cleansed of the sick he had been waking in since his thirteenth year, his head cooling with water and balsamo, a sweet-breath leaf dissolving in his mouth, the nobleman could even feel some affection for this pagan physician whose witchcraft, or treachery, or twisted loyalties, or what have you, did not matter at moments like this. Moresby felt something, the name of which eluded him, for no word had been coined for a man in his situation.

Beneath this dependence, however, bubbled inevitable disgust and shame. This Turk, converted though he may have been, was the symbol of all Moresby had lost, and it would have been odd if the baron were able to view the man who treated his downfall, the man from a foreign land, the man sent by the queen who destroyed him, as anything other than a wretch. More, it would have been very odd if such open scorn in the baron's manner and words were not imitated by the dependents in the household, who sought in action and attitude to win their lord's favor, and so Dr. Thatcher was both free and abused, respected and repellent, judged by the highest and the lowest of the household as vaguely rotten, a judgment that from there fluttered by report and gossips' tongues to villagers and peasants and tradesmen, until everyone within a few miles of Moresby Hall knew Matthew Thatcher as a Mahometan in Christian clothing, a wizard, protected by his enchantment-subdued lord for reasons no one could quite understand (unless they had heard of the lord's seizures, and then it was clear that the Turk held his Christian slave in thrall only through violent magic).

But Thatcher was no more a Turk these many years on, and sometimes he shouted at them, the peasants and whispering ladies, the cooks who spoke when they knew he could hear. He shouted at them that he had given everything up and was no more a Turk than they. But this was a drama he shouted only for himself, in silence.

A long decade later he no longer felt, I am posing among them, trying to look like them, an evil act. Instead, he often—for days at a time—simply felt as if he had always lived on this island and always would. And when the realization came—that he had been for days walking blindly, forgetting to remember that he was a man of the one true God, the servant of the sultan—he no longer even felt the pain he once had. He could, with exercise of will, hold memories away from his mind. To survive required forgetting, submission, the murder of pointless hope.

Tonight, amid the remnants of supper, the servants hardly even stared anymore, though several did cross themselves to guard against demonic contagion. Dishes were cleared; the pork was preserved for another day. The baron drew his legs into his chest against the cold that only he felt. Dr. Thatcher wrapped him in the fur and, with an attendant, lifted the bundle to a couch, where the nobleman pressed himself to his doctor like an infant to its mother, his fists drawn tight to his chin. Through clenched teeth, with his jaw still locked in spasm, as sleep struggled across his face and limbs, Henry Fairleigh, 3rd Baron Moresby, whispered, "Please don't leave me, Matthew." And he slept, suffering and contorted, in his doctor's arms.

Thatcher woke in the dark, still on the couch, his arms numb from the weight of Moresby's brittle, unmoving body. A large man, dusty from riding, stood above him, studying this tableau. He held a candle, and a curious stableman stood behind him with another. The two lights lit only the lower halves of the men's faces. The large man moved the candle closer to Thatcher, obscuring himself.

"Dr. Ezzedine? Do you remember me?"

3

GEOFFREY BELLOC STOOD watching, unnoticed, as Matthew Thatcher considered the Solway Firth, a finger of the Irish Sea probing into England, curling, scraping, picking away sand and soil, carrying it off. The Turk doctor's hair battled the wind, and his cloak billowed up until the Mahometan pulled it close against the cold and indecisive rain.

"Are you hungry? I have something rare." The doctor turned to find the baron's guest, the imposing Mr. Leveret, removing from his bag a ball of cloth. Leveret shook it, and the cloths fell away as he drew a knife from his belt. As often happened, the sight of a knife provoked in Thatcher the image, even the desire, of throwing himself onto the blade or merely sighing in acceptance as its bearer drove it into his chest.

"I remember you being taken by the queen's orchard," said Leveret.

Thatcher bent himself backward to hold his gaze on the face above him, a moment longer before looking down to see that the giant's hand held a pomegranate. The sight was confusing, as if Thatcher had conjured the fruit from out of his own memories, as if staring at the sea until his eyes watered, longing for a far-off garden, could produce one of its blossoms.

"Do you? Remember me? Remind me, Mr. Leveret, please, where we met. I thought it was last evening with your arrival."

The doctor spoke English quite well, much better than a decade earlier, but with the same strange intonations, the scratched noises that carried Geoff back to the summer of 1591, all those Ottoman voices and smells that filled the court those months when even a man's glances were foreign and difficult to translate.

But if, for a moment, it seemed like no time had passed since those days, looking at Thatcher corrected Geoff's chronology: Ten years in the north had aged the Turk, and Belloc wondered if he ought to go elsewhere and begin again, tell Cecil and Beale he had miscalculated, but that would be a costly, perhaps fatal, delay.

The doctor was fatter in a few places but leaner nearly everywhere else, his head and shoulders pulled toward the earth and the inevitable, his hair white and coarse, the eyes retreating into grottoes of bone and skin. Perhaps his age would make him easier to control and easier to insert into the play. Old men walk onto stage unnoticed and unresisted; audiences instinctively feel they perform no action, only comment; what harm can they do? Important characters just keep speaking around them as if they are deaf, until finally they are acknowledged with an exasperated "Well, what is it *you* wanted?"

David Leveret described their shared scenes precisely enough: the baron thrashing on the floor of the Presence Chamber, his fists drawn to his cheek; the lady's cry of demonic possession; the tool the doctor had used to protect Moresby's tongue; and a strange detail that Thatcher himself had never forgotten—Queen Elizabeth's slippered foot appearing, just its jeweled tip, from under her gold and red gown as she leaned forward for an avid look at her baron's convulsions.

With the tip of his dagger, Leveret pushed a few swollen red seeds from their waxy bed onto the Turk's white palm. The rain prickled, blowing diagonally, and the fruit glistened with beaded water and pale, clouded light. "I don't suppose that the English variety is as good," said Leveret. "The queen's father planted the first one in England, so they are still news. I suppose the Turkish ones are far sweeter, from your hot sun."

Thatcher let the seeds sit on his tongue, firm and pregnant, watched the crosshatched sky brighten as the sun yellowed the ceiling of gray, and the rain stopped, almost stopped in place, glowing and suspended. Ten years had vanished since last he had tasted a pomegranate, outside of dreams and carefully framed recollection. He bit, pressing the ruby until it burst. The cold red release of juice was almost audible in his skull.

Leveret fed him more, watched from above (where it was easy to keep his glance disguised, as if he, too, were considering only the sea and cliffs, James's kingdom at the arse of the world just beyond the firth). "A gift to me from a friend at court," Leveret said, a little pride in his voice. "That's probably one of England's five hundred this year. No more than that."

"You are very fortunate," said Thatcher, a tint of red touching the white of the whiskers at his lip (pomegranate juice or the last of his own coloring).

"Rather more common in Turkey, I think? I imagine them falling into the streets, growing wild."

"Something close to that, in places. Like sour apples here."

"Enviable. Have some more. Are there fruits there that we in England do not have at all?"

"There are. Flavors difficult to describe."

"But easy to remember, I would guess. Something about the memories of earliest life, the smells and tastes that one can still summon, even years later." Leveret cut another few seeds free, watched the man take them greedily. "Please, have the whole thing. A gift."

Thatcher laughed a little, looking up to Leveret and then nodding. "That is most kind. I cannot even politely pretend I do not want it. It is extraordinary. Like a child, to want to make oneself a glutton without a thought for what price gluttony."

The giant laughed. "No price. Truly, just a gift." He offered his knife, but Thatcher declined and unearthed the seeds with a deft thumb instead. "Yes, I do remember you, quite clearly, Doctor. And, of course, you were much discussed, celebrated even."

"It was only one day. It was only what physicians do."

"Oh, not just that. Your fame lived on behind you in London. Really? You don't know the rest?"

Belloc watched and waited, would not speak again until Thatcher admitted curiosity, expressing his first *need* for Belloc, having already suspected he was falling into debt. The doctor chewed, slow to reply or make any expression at all to the puzzling statement—a skill he had learned in his years as a foreigner in England. One never knew when an accusation was being made or a trap laid. Belloc watched the man's natural protections and was pleased. That would do very well.

"My fame?"

"There are not so many Turks who became Christian as we once expected. There was one fellow back in '85 or '86, I recall. He was going to be the first of thousands; we were all certain of it. But then nothing for a while, until . . . you. London talked about it for some time. A man who chose England and Christ and Elizabeth, left behind the sultan and the wealth of Turkey. Were you married, sir?"

"I suppose that I still am, if she lives. Surely God will accept a marriage made between heathens."

"And this, too, you left behind. A child as well, I am told."

Thatcher only nodded slightly—the giant asked questions but already knew the answers. He examined the fruit, now heavy in his hands, felt the tips of the seeds cut and stick between his teeth. Belloc watched him bend a little, the crown of his head drawn just an inch closer to the earth as the rain began again.

"There was a play about you." That did it, shocked an unguarded expression onto the man's face at last; Belloc would know from this point forward what sincere surprise looked like on Matthew Thatcher's face. "Your name was changed, but it ran a few performances. They added a fair piece, of course. A love plot, and another Turk, wicked, tried to stop you from being baptized, at the altar."

The doctor moved his lips but didn't seem to know what might emerge until, finally, "A play?"

"*The Turk's Revenge*. Double meaning was nice. Your revenge was to become Christian, but then the other Turk took revenge, too. Bit of a tragic ending. Bunch of makers punched it together. Munday and Chettle did the bulk, I think," he added offhand, as if Mr. Leveret were not at all sure of Thatcher's interest in all this. He could see that it was a bit too much still for Dr. Thatcher, whether he was going to be drawn into such details as to what happened at the end of the play or how it could be that a play ever existed or who this man was or what he had come all the way from London to say, or if he had even come expressly to find Thatcher. "Was it very different for you? Your baptism, I mean. As an adult. Did you feel the waters wash away your superstitions, I wonder? An infant feels nothing but a bath, I would guess. But you, a man . . ."

"I had studied Christian law and scripture with Dr. Dee. He prepared me for my conversion, for the men who examined me."

"But the baptism itself, Dr. Thatcher. Did it feel—what's the word—did it feel . . . right? Certain?"

"It has not washed away in the years since," said Dr. Thatcher.

"And up here, in the north, do you feel the pull of the old ways?"

"Why would I feel more Mahometan in the north?"

Belloc laughed with release and relief, tilted his face up to the renewed rain. "No, my friend, do you feel the pull of the *Catholics*?"

"Sir, I am not sure I have ever met a Catholic. Would I know them by their appearance?"

"By their actions and words."

"I did not come to England until 1591. I understood the Catholics to be eradicated by then."

"Easier to rid the island of rats, Doctor. You arrived only three years after the Armada."

"People spoke of this to me. Do you mind if we go to the bench? I need to sit awhile."

Belloc watched the man move slowly toward the stone bench set under an alder tree. He guessed there was pain in the knees. Even this seemed promising. Everything about the Turk was now unthreatening. He was interesting without being dangerous in any way. He would walk onstage perfectly. As he sat heavily on the wet stone, he rubbed his face, pressing the collected mist from his thick eyebrows toward his damp temples.

"Are you in pain? Your legs?"

"Nothing to complain about. You are young still, I think, Mr. Leveret? The day comes when, like a river changing direction, every day we try to lose as little as possible."

"Would you like to read it?"

"Read what?"

"The play. *The Turk's Revenge*. I have a copy back in my things at the hall. Went up for sale in St. Paul's this month."

Thatcher pulled a pomegranate seed from its bed. A man he could not recall meeting had come all the way from London with exotic fruit and a copy of a play inspired by his life.

"You are a celebrated and pious man, Dr. Thatcher. Celebrated for your piety and your loyalty to the queen."

"I would like to read it, if that doesn't strike you as immodest. How does it end?"

4

"SHE WOULD TAKE even this from me?" asked Moresby.

"My lord, her generosity to you is demonstrated every day." Leveret pointed through the narrow window to the small chapel behind the house, in service to the family since the Conquest, with never a change to its content or fashion. He had forced the chapel door open the night he arrived, half a penny to the stabler to look away: the silver candlesticks, the carved crucifix, the painted statue of weeping Mary, the Latin Bible, the rood screen, the little box with splinters of wood and someone's black fingernails, the wall painting of hell, paradise, purgatory, limbo.

Moresby's sort of Catholicism was still common up north—Cumberland, Northumberland, Lancashire, the Scottish borderlands. Far from London, the old lies lingered, hellish embers in basements and chapels, old priests muttering superstitions, awaiting a savior king with Rome's blessing. Things just wouldn't stay quite clean up here in the northern mud, like a floor that needs regular scrubbing. Age-old families, whose wiser members prayed right and well in the queen's company, dressed their house priests up north in surplices, elevated the host to transubstantiate it into the living Flesh, used the old mass books, baked their paste God wafers in the old kitchen. Elizabeth knew. She left them in mumbling recusant peace, if they had the good sense to keep quiet and not take up arms. Moresby should have been kneeling to her in gratitude for every day he wasn't slit open.

And the baron had been careful enough. Enough of Cecil's intelligencers—some previously Belloc's—had come and gone through this house, stewards and poets and washerwomen, listening to table talk, fabricating what they hadn't heard so as to have something to report, for which the men in London might pay a penny.

"You were Walsingham's man, back in London," moaned Moresby. "Tell me true."

"I was."

"And have you had men here? In my service."

"I have."

"Was the Turk one?"

"No. He served you from love and duty, I would say."

When the day came—if the day came—that King James proceeded south to London, he would need a route that carried him from supporter to supporter, collecting strength as he descended. A chain must stretch from Edinburgh to Whitehall, and the first links must be found here, in the north, where Moresby's land nestled up to the Scottish marches, where the old religion of popes and Bloody Mary and traitors had yielded hardly at all to cleaner ways. If James VI came to take the throne, he'd need to walk through these lands or sail past them. If James were to find love here, it would be because the northern lords thought he would be a friend: tolerant at least, a true Catholic at best. If he was Catholic, he'd raise in a day an army waiting to walk him the rest of the way south. Belloc could almost, with a squint, see James's difficulty: The whole world was shouting at him to lie loudly, while pleading for him to whisper the truth to them alone. But that, too, fit Geoff's desires elegantly: Moresby now had every reason to please the man he took to be his future king.

"Give me that rug," Moresby commanded hoarsely. The man called Leveret obliged. Even reduced to this condition, the littlest baron possessed this magnification of strength, a simple lever, to

shove a man twice his size across the room. Geoff felt the old reflexive readiness in himself to obey the noble voice, to be shoved. He
draped the fur around the old man's shoulders.

When Geoff had last seen the baron, seized and shaken on the
gleaming herringbone floor of the Presence Chamber, he was not
precisely young, and Geoff himself had been two or three stone
leaner, but this ruined old man, stooped and trembling under the
weight of the rug he needed, could have been the father of the man
Elizabeth banished north.

That famous gift, of a Turk doctor to the baron, an insult, perhaps, to both at the time, had become a comfort in the baron's old
age and polite exile. The implications of the gift, though, vibrated,
and Belloc sensed these vibrations coming from the Turk, wherever
in the house he was, vibrations like rings around a silver salmon
that, an instant before, had descended under the river's black surface
when one was looking elsewhere and heard only the slivering of the
waters.

"Her generosity?" The word had been burning Moresby these
silent moments, until he couldn't hold it in his mouth another instant. "Generosity? After my treatment by her? The attainment of
my patents and precedents, the fees and escheatment of my land, my
house in London, sent here, in this state." He'd been holding these
angers warm for a decade. His rage was stronger than the body that
contained it; it made him cough. Mr. Leveret watched: another
performance of the slow surrender to the inevitable. He waited,
and here it was, the next step in the dance: "Why should I?"

"Why should you obey your sovereign?" Leveret asked quietly.
Moresby turned his head away, a pouting child. "Do you demand
more cause than to know she asks it of you?"

"So say you. Why doesn't Her Majesty make the damned gift
herself? I can't stop her."

"She wishes you and James to be loving friends. She asks that *you*
make this gift yourself." Moresby, even in his anger, seemed not far
from sleep. "And I say this, better this, my lord: You do *yourself*
want James's favor. She is generous in this, too, allowing you the

glory of James's pleasure from your kindness. You must know how they speak in London."

Aroused from near sleep now, but just short of coughing, Moresby's anger pitched precisely: "How they speak in London? How would I know such matters, Mr. Leveret? Tell me that, why don't you."

"They say that he is next, so in your generosity, you do your queen and future king both service at once. He wants to know who along the line is his lover and who his obstacle. Much thought has been expended on this matter. You might make this particular gift to the King of Scotland so that he knows your love. You might write a letter, phrased according to certain suggestions I bear from London. I think it best if you address it to the king, in care of Mr. Nicolson."

"But of all I might offer . . ."

"This is what the queen would have you give, from your own heart, with no mention of her."

"Mr. Leveret." And here it was! Even here, with a baron! You would have thought their nobility bought them something, but no: Even here, the moment arrived when the voice tightened, turned wheedling, and the Walsingham-trained eye could see the frightened mind begin to bargain from a feeble position as the pincers closed around him. Like a man who owed the spurrier more than he could pay, like a mass-mongering priest caught in a hiding hole, like a conspirator at the sharp moment when he realizes all his co-conspirators have been only feigning all along and waiting for his blunder, counting up and writing down all his nasty thoughts these many months: that same skid of the voice, the slide upward, the wet-eyed smile, the sickly showing of teeth. "Mr. Leveret, you must understand," pleaded the little old knight. And with those words Geoffrey Belloc knew it would be settled to his taste. He never even had to threaten violence.

5

D<small>R. T</small><small>HATCHER AMONG</small> his mushrooms, on his hands and knees, peering at the log, sniffing caps, his fingers pressing lightly on the springing speckled velvet stools. The children of the house laughed and imitated him; he did not mind, if he even noticed anymore. Today, to exercise the faculties he sometimes feared might escape him, he forced himself to recite the names of every mushroom and tree and herb in the baron's wood, over and over, in English, Latin, Arabic. Again, faster. He walked back into the open park, his bag heavy. He rubbed a paste of his invention across the burning cords of his knees. And now for exercise—memory here, to avoid memory there—he recited the names of Moresby's household: the steward, the steward's wife, the steward's children, this many grooms, that many ushers, plain serving men, seamstress, stabler, kennel-man and -boy. The rooms of the house: Upon the marble bench under the alder beside the inlet of the firth, he closed his eyes and walked from room to room, up and down each stair, picked up and placed back down an object in each room, saw the plan of the house as clearly as on paper, and when he reopened his eyes, there stood in front of him one of those impatient serving boys—page and servant at table both, an economy—whose name Thatcher had just rehearsed.

"He wants you now," said the boy, gazing at the man who had just been sitting, muttering strange magic words in strange tongues to himself from behind closed eyes—a spell to capture Christian souls most definitely—but the boy was not afraid (he was very much afraid but planned to retell all this to the other boys, if he survived this commission, and he would say he had been ready to battle the wizard).

"Is he well or stricken?" asked the doctor.

"He said to come now. Don't ask me why. Don't know."

Thatcher arrived to find his master wrapped in still more rugs and furs, close by the fire. Henry Fairleigh, Baron Moresby, would not look at him. "There is an apothecary in the village. Tell him everything you do for me and how you know the signs before the fits. Teach him quickly. But he is not clever."

His thin arm appeared from under the rugs, grabbed the poker, and stabbed weakly against the logs. Still Moresby would not look at his doctor. Again the weakened voice, but now even quieter, some other note besides feebleness: "And then pack up all your rightful possessions. Nothing that isn't yours by right or custom!"

"My lord?"

"You're leaving in the morning."

"My lord?"

"Take what is yours, nothing that is not."

"For how long shall I be gone?"

"Forever. I have no further need of you."

The third time that the doctor learned he was going to be made into a gift, he thought of a few things to say, but each of them was wrong.

"That Leveret's servant will come in the morning to fetch you."

The baron gathered his furs tightly around himself, doubling in size, and stood, walking to the fire. He had almost no hair remaining, and his skin was thin nearly to translucence. Thatcher stepped forward to offer his hand, but Henry Fairleigh turned away, spitting words that there would be a payment of some pounds in the morning; the auditor would send someone with the money.

"My lord," Dr. Thatcher attempted again, but that was all there was to be.

6.

MATTHEW THATCHER, WITH no other option but to be obedient, arrived in Edinburgh. He stabled the last mare who'd
borne him and took a bed at a particular inn behind a leather tannery. He was slow to accustom himself to that extraordinary stink
and surprised to realize that he was mourning the loss of the relative
luxury of Moresby Hall. His circumstances had been comically reduced yet again. From the Palace of Felicity to the air behind a tannery. Hope had fled years ago; memories were to be fought off, like
invaders carrying despair. But now in Edinburgh, Matthew was left
yet more alone, by his new masters and all his gods, to study and
learn acceptance, while memory resurged, strong and painful. The
Koran called him Ayyub; the Bible, Job.

While Thatcher supped alone in the inn's main room, an ex-
tremely small man, almost a half man, wrestled his way onto a stool
before him and opened a bottle of sugared wine. "Drink with me?"
he asked, uninvited and unencouraged. A man of easy mirth, this
Gideon poured generously for Thatcher and himself but grew no
more confused and no less chatty for the cups he drained. He was a
player, he told Thatcher, and his company would perform *The Sultan's Seraglio* the next afternoon in a courtyard nearby.

"I have traveled all this island's height and breadth, and jigged with Irish, too, but never have I traveled among the savage and god-less Turks, to my disgrace."

"I was one of them," said the doctor finally.

"Good, then. You're the fellow for me. Tomorrow, near here, there's a house with a sign of a swan, and up the stairs a room where you'll be waited for. It's got no windows. Make your way there be-fore twelve o'clock. Your friend will be there. And you drink with-out getting drunk. That's quite good. Do you know how to look behind yourself? And see if anyone is walking in your footsteps?"

"And why would anyone follow mine?" Thatcher meant it as a joke; a foreigner, he felt himself followed and observed all the time, unless he sat alone in woods. The dwarf began to explain a few methods of invisibility and evasion. The doctor laughed: It was ex-actly a game he'd played with Ismail so long ago.

And the next day in that windowless room of the Swan waited the giant David Leveret, who greeted Dr. Thatcher with the smiles and embraces of an old friend, as if their long-guarded fondness could only be expressed now at last, here in Scotland. "My doctor, my doctor," Leveret nearly sang. "The hero of the story. Gideon found you; I'm glad. He can be tiresome, but as a drinker he wants nothing. You can always trust him as my messenger, always. You will see a lot of him. He is your one certain friend in Edinburgh, aside from me, but you and I cannot be seen together, so Gideon will bring you messages or take you to me. But I am ahead of my-self. We have much to discuss. Are you hungry?"

This would be the moment for a lesser man to lose his temper, demand explanations of the events beyond his control, the sudden shift of every loyalty and duty. But for all of Belloc's opaque good humor and conversational wandering, Thatcher did not flash any anger at all, and Belloc felt a rejuvenating satisfaction at his choice of Matthew Thatcher.

"So I am now a gift to you, Mr. Leveret."

"Only briefly. And that is our secret, yours and mine, Doctor. What will you eat?"

The Turk wanted no food and no drink, perhaps finally learning to be wary of taking anything before confirming its cost. Belloc considered his approach to the man's heart, felt the prey's surprising complexity, wondered how Beale or Walsingham would have stalked it.

"If I am only briefly Baron Moresby's gift to you, then what am I?"

Praise first: "Moresby holds you dearly—a 'cherished prize,' he called you. You have made an estimable life in England, Doctor. You have a reputation for piety and wisdom. You are renowned as a great healer. You are treasured."

"I am, I suppose, not a slave, because I take payment, but my lord Moresby took me as a gift from a queen to whom I was given as a gift. And now he gives me to you. No one thinks of me but as a gift." Belloc discerned a note of self-pity. "Mr. Leveret, a gift does not take pride in being a gift, I assure you. It only serves."

"Some Mahometan axiom, I assume, but whatever the mood of Moresby's gift, your value must have doubled in your years with him if you are now to be two gifts in one."

Thatcher bowed his head in submission, waited.

"And the other recipient awaits you. Moresby has already sent word of your approach. He has written, as I showed him to do, of your great skill and knowledge. Has he told you who your new master will be?" Thatcher shook his head, showed no serious interest in the matter. "Well, then, I have some extraordinary news for you. You are, for all eyes to see, the gift of your lord Moresby to James the Sixth, the King of Scotland." The doctor seemed indifferent. Belloc pressed on: "You will go up to the castle tomorrow. If you and I agree on the matter."

"My consent, then, is necessary?"

"Of course."

"Then please speak to me plainly. I am Lord Moresby's gift to you or to the Scottish king?"

"To me, in truth, though none shall see it. And to the king, for all to see, but only for a spell, and only at my secret pleasure and your secret agreement. For different eyes, different performances. But both gifts are the will of Queen Elizabeth."

Thatcher looked at his hands on the table while Leveret let his new creature consider his situation. In the face of Thatcher's continued silence, Leveret walked to the door. "I would really be happier if you ate and drank something. Life will be easy in James's palaces, but I would do my best to be a host until then." He called down the stairs for another bowl and cup. He closed the door and leaned against it. "Doctor, all of your loyalties and all of your duties are aligned: sultan to queen to Moresby to queen and to, I hope, your friend: me. This will be very simple. And at the end of your service you may ask a boon of me, of Moresby, of the queen, and it shall be given to you."

"But not from the King of Scotland."

"Perhaps from him as well. He may be grateful to you. And you may choose to stay with him forever. But"—the giant smiled at Thatcher with the promise of something remarkable—"I think better things are possible for you."

The doctor nodded as if this were all as clear and simple as Mr. Leveret proposed. Leveret laughed, a sound like a hunting dog's bark of delight. "We have come to you because we need a man of medicine. I—the queen—need your certain diagnosis of James's condition. That is all."

They were all illegible, these English. Each in a different way was a liar or a clown, amused at their own paradoxes and parables. "What disease do you fear he carries?"

"A deadly one, and damnably contagious. The same as his mother and father carried. One that would cause endless suffering in England. Will you help me prevent this infection, Doctor? You will save more lives than in the rest of your entire career. I am not exaggerating in the slightest. If saving lives is your role on God's green earth, then He is offering you the opportunity to be the greatest physician who ever lived."

7

THE NEXT DAY, Gideon came to Thatcher's room at the inn behind the tannery and instructed the doctor (as he pissed in the
doctor's pot) to hurry himself along to a particular fishmonger's
store at the very edge of the town. The doctor was to walk right
past its front and around to its back courtyard, where a stair would
lead him to a room with no windows, and there, again:

"Matthew, my friend. Our conversation continues."

Edinburgh was no less pungent today, and Dr. Thatcher tried to
concentrate on his lessons and the willful mysteries of David Leveret, his peculiar friend, who was explaining why Mary (James's
mother), the Spanish Armada, the northern families, the pope, the
Prince of Portugal, and the French Catholics were all part of the
same war, massed forces of evil with the destruction of England as
their shared goal, and how the great and urgent mystery of the
world was the true nature and loyalty of James of Scotland.

"Has no man in England seen the king?" Thatcher asked.

"He has never been to England. A man who was once my master
met him, on a mission of diplomacy. He said James was childish,
difficult, had tantrums like an infant. The family is mad, you know.
His father murdered his mother's lover. She in turn murdered his
father. She also of course attempted to murder our queen, to which

James raised not a peep of protest. And now the king spends half his time with male consorts in his bed, all agents of the pope."

If Belloc expected wonder or even amusement on Thatcher's face, some willingness to laugh at James Stuart and thereby make the Turk's task easier and his loyalty to Leveret more plain, then the Englishman was disappointed. "Perhaps people in the sultan's palaces carry on like this all the time?"

"Have you a portrait of him?" asked the unimpressed doctor. "So I will recognize him."

"He'll be the fellow wearing a crown, I imagine."

"Of course. I apologize."

"I was only jesting, Matt."

"Is it such a horror as this? Are Christians truly so varied? Elizabeth's father was Catholic, was he not? And every king and queen before him? And did he not also have her mother killed?"

Thatcher was, as nearly as Belloc could tell, asking in all sincerity. There was something amusing, and reassuring, in his foreign perspective: He was unlikely to be led astray by emotional confusions. "Well, those were quite different circumstances. Listen, my good doctor, I sometimes thought the same, back in the very hot days. I thought, Could the Catholics really be as horrible as this? As you say, my grandfather was, it must be said, Catholic, like everyone else. Is there not some peaceful way to come to terms? But I have seen them. And there isn't. They would burn you alive for thinking one thing about Jesus, or slice you to bits if you wondered if their wafer were merely bread baked by the same baker you always knew, or if the priest who murmured Latin and told you that you were damned unless you confessed to him and that your mother was in hell unless you paid him to release her were just the younger brother of the boy whose ass you kicked every day when you were both children. The Catholics, I promise you, were crueler than we were, and still are. I would think, Really, why this fuss? Why burn hundreds of people just because we want to hear the word of God spoken in a language we understand? You Mahometans don't wrap your stories in some foreign tongue, do you? Only preach it in Greek? No. When I tell you that James cannot be Catholic *and* king, it is not because I care about the small questions of theology that university men debate. What do I know of limbo?"

"Do not the Protestants kill and torture Catholics in their turn?"

"Comparing methods without comparing causes."

"You say the causes are a distinction too fine for some men to see."

"True. So then what remains? Them and their fires, or us with ours. I pick us." Belloc rather hoped the doctor would laugh at that. "No, in seriousness, I tell you we cannot ever have a Catholic king, because we have finally stopped being divided on this in England. We are settled now. We can live at peace. We are English, and we are Protestant, and the two words are one and the same. That's Elizabeth's greatest good work. But if a Catholic comes to rule us, London will bleed like Paris bled. They will get back to burning men alive down to the very dust or slicing them open to look for God's love in their steaming entrails. If that is not bringing ill health to a nation, I don't know what is. And a man who heals, Doctor, can prevent all that, with a timely diagnosis." Leveret sat back, breathed deeply, and looked at his man to measure what had penetrated.

Thatcher nodded. "What distinguishing marks have they? How does one know them?"

"Know what, man?"

"Catholics."

"That would make my job easy, Doctor. They look just the same. Perhaps this distinction makes no sense to you," he said in a calmer voice. "Perhaps there is nothing comparable in your religion."

"In my religion? Still I am a Mussulman to you? I have spent so long trying to be one of you, fearing I would be nothing if I could not at least be you. But no one ever has believed it, not truly. It is . . . frustrating. You wish me to hate Catholics? Very well, I hate them."

8.

A T LEAST, AT their next meeting, the smell was tolerable. Gideon the dwarf instructed Thatcher to roam for an hour, then, as if by merest chance, find himself behind a baker's and climb up yet another back staircase to yet another windowless room, where David Leveret waited yet again, now with warm bread and meat.

"Last matters today. George Nicolson, the English emissary to James, is not your friend. Nor are the agents of the French, the Spanish, the pope, who are sure to be there, too, and will do whatever they can to insinuate themselves with you. Everyone will be watching, at first, to understand if you are who you say you are. Assume that you are watched. Always. You are a player in a drama: the innocent and good doctor. Do you ever go to the theater? Good. But you are friendless once inside the palace walls. There is no one else. You are simply the physician, given with love by Moresby. You expect to spend the rest of your days doing whatever King James would ask of you. In truth, you have no friends but me—certainly the one most able to do for you whatever good you might desire in this life."

Belloc waited for something—resistance, gratitude, resentment, negotiation, rage—anything other than this calm submission.

"Anything you write, even in Turk, even ciphered, will be opened and read before it leaves Edinburgh, no matter who claims to carry it for you. Seals upon letters are not real; they can be broken and replaced, with none the wiser. Do not write anything you do not want read by the King of Scotland or the pope. There are certain phrases, watchwords, I want you to commit to memory now, and if those are spoken to you, then you know you are speaking to one of my trusted friends."

"How many phrases?"

Belloc watched the doctor sip his wine and eat his new bread and close his eyes, not from exhaustion but in a sort of waiting restfulness that seemed the most foreign thing about him. He could simply pause and wait, without expending any energy in curiosity or emotion.

"I understand that I am asking you to perform strange and difficult tasks," Leveret said. "And they may not all be necessary. We can let events dictate our decisions. We will talk, you and I, before any final choice is made."

The doctor didn't reply for a long moment, and then said, "I will examine the king's conscience as best I can. But if I'm unable to, then the other . . . Is it not against any God, what you would ask?"

"If the reason is just, then what we do is just."

"But do you not hear the voice of conscience arguing against it?"

"Yes, of course I do. Loudly. But that is the highest sacrifice we can make for justice: Even our conscience must suffer. We are prepared to cause ourselves this pain, because we do what is just."

"Will God not punish us for the act?"

"No. If my faith is strong, He will not judge me except for my faith. And what stronger sign of my faith can I exhibit than my willingness to make my conscience ache in His service? If I cannot sleep for the howling of my conscience, what a gift I have given my God."

The Englishman was waiting, it seemed, for Thatcher's approval of his logic, and so Thatcher nodded, a little, and held himself silent again.

That quiet submission again. It was not enough. Belloc had

Gideon watching the doctor's room every night, but the Turk never left the inn, never snuck to the stables to consider a horse and a fast escape. He seemed ready to do Belloc's will out of duty, obligation, submission, the lack of other options. But there had to be more: If the pinch came, Geoff wanted the Turk's innermost heart, and Belloc felt certain that he could make the Turk *desire* something that only Belloc could give him.

Leveret said, "Put that aside, and let us instead turn to something more pleasing: the matter of your reward. I have friends at court in London who love me well. They would be glad to do me or friends of mine a turn of kindness. You are a man of great knowledge and value. Would you wish to return to London to live? After this task is complete? In wealth and comfort at court? Or in a house of your own? With a stipend."

"I need no such thing."

"Does earthly wealth not impress your pagan mind, Matt?"

"I want no more than I need. And I need little."

"But you suffer from a thirst for endless knowledge, I think. A room of roots? A team of men to bring you samples taken from the queen's own planting houses?"

"I need no bribe, Mr. Leveret, but will do your bidding from the debt I owe." The Turk only shrugged, as if he had no interest at all in the question.

And so Belloc offered the great prize he had been holding in reserve until this last moment. "If I could arrange for your transport even farther away?" At first, Thatcher seemed not to understand his meaning. "I know our ambassador there, Henry Lello." Silence. Silence. "You do want to return, don't you?"

Belloc saw he had somehow angered him, even though the doctor replied softly, "I will die in England, Mr. Leveret. Or Scotland."

"Would you not return to Turkey, if you could?"

The doctor's face twisted and aged for a moment before relaxing again with obvious effort. "It is an impossibility. I long ago tried to erase that desire. It is of no use to think on such things."

"The effort not to think must have been great."

"Whatever it was, it was an exertion I would not wish to have been in vain."

"I see." Geoffrey Belloc at last did see, understood the Turk's submission and this one moment of anger. Up in the palace, at the moment of crisis, or in relative safety at James's side, the obligated man might hesitate, might listen too long to conscience's arguments or simply surrender himself and the mission to a royal court's luxury. But the man who was hungering for home would do neither. Matthew Thatcher must dream of Constantinople. "I would not hold out to you things I could not deliver. I would not ask you to hope without reason. After your service to me, to the queen, we will reward you. It can be done."

"And the sultan would have me back?" That anger again, a little sharper. "I was a gift in his name and now I am returned? A horse sent back lame?"

Belloc rolled a bit of bread into a ball, collected dirt off the table with it, flicked it across the room, tore a larger piece for himself. "I suppose you don't hear much news in Cumberland, Matt, but the sultan you knew has died. His son is sultan now. Am I saying this right? Mehmed? Mehmet? Mehmet the Third, I hear. Why is that funny?"

"I treated him. He was a boy. He had a— It's of no matter."

"You were a trusted man. You loved your work there, I would imagine."

"I did not complain."

"When did you know you were a gift of the sultan? It was a surprise, I think. So what then? You wanted to be English and a Christian? I don't think so. You submitted. That's what a good Turk does, yes? They said stay behind, so you stayed. If you say no, what happens to you? Or maybe to someone back there? Maybe you were protecting them."

"Mr. Leveret, let us leave these matters, please."

"Well, there you are, then. I never had a wife myself, Matt. Something about having someone around all the time, watching me. I don't like it. And then what? They get sick or old, and then you feel that loss, too? Not for me. But you: I think you seem a fellow who'd appreciate a woman looking after you. Might be fond of her, take care of her in turn. Look, am I wrong to see you as a man who has accepted his fate out of excessive virtue? Loyalty, patience, duty: That's you, yes? A man who might, let's say, wonder if somehow he could return to wife and child, carry with him whatever treasure that might show the Turks he merits a warm welcome. We could provide you with something, to make your return even more valuable to them. Maybe you stole something of value from the queen, learned some great secret at court. As I say, we could write our ambassador, set the stage. No one needs to hear about the baptism. That wouldn't do at all back home, would it? And you'd be home. Where the pomegranates grow." Silence. The Turk sat still, except his fingers tore bits of bread. "As a start, we could have the ambassador ask after someone, if you wanted to know first. What's her name, Matt?"

But Thatcher, attacked and exposed after these days in the strange spy's company, refused to play. Leveret had arrived at this moment of offering him an impossibility, teasing him with a place that might no longer exist, might no longer be populated by anyone he knew or only by a dead wife or one who might wish him dead or never think of him at all, by a boy who might not know him if he saw him. He had spent a decade wringing desire and hope from his heart, a treatment as scarring as fire, and only possible in the isolation of Cumberland, where no rumor reached him, where no memory could be triggered by a face or a word, where even the hope of a letter in either direction was ridiculous. Matthew Thatcher had committed the slow murder of hope or, indistinguishably, watched in helpless torments as it committed suicide. But at last it was done. Hope lay at his feet, unmoving.

Until he was poisoned, slowly, by pomegranate seeds.

So now he fumbled for some other conversation, clumsily repeating questions as if he had forgotten the answers he had studied these past three days: "Tell me again, please, how one perceives the difference between men of the true religion and the superstitions of papistry."

But David Leveret stood up and took him by the shoulders, knew he had him: "Tell me true now, Matt. It's all a joke to you, isn't it? It never took ten years ago, right? You're still a Mahometan under the skin."

"And if I were? I heard what became of the queen's Jewish doctor when they thought his conversion had failed."

"Different case, I'd say. Matt, I wouldn't care a whit if you bow down to Mohammed. I would think it logical and all the more reason to send you home after this is all finished."

"If I were a Mahometan still, seeing it was safe at last to speak the truth to you now, Mr. Leveret, then I would confess that all you Christians are madmen. Stunted in all things. What better proves Allah and Mohammed's truth but this: The Christian medicine is incomplete. Your ability to reason, to observe, to calculate, to comprehend creation—all incomplete. This is proof enough, I suppose I would say, except that Christian ideas are also incomplete, without the conclusion of Mohammed's truth, and so you fight one another. And now, to distinguish between Christian madmen? This one is confused because he kneels or does not, or reads Latin or does not, or trusts his priest to perform the magic bread spell or does not. Therefore, this fellow or that one must be burned alive. And if their *king* is confused! Then *every* man, woman, and child in England is condemned to burn in Satan's hell and must rise up and kill the confused monarch. All Christian madness, and if only you would embrace the truth, you would all know not only peace but contentment and all the fruits of knowledge therefrom: medicine, astronomy, mathematics, poetry. Listen, please, Mr. Leveret, listen to what masters have been produced from this truth: Averroes, Algazeles, Abu-Becet, Al-Farabius, Abu Ma'shar, Alkindi, al-Majusti, Abu Bakr al-Hassar, Al-Karaji, Avicenna, Geber, Alhazen. I can continue for hours." The names flowed from Thatcher's tongue, and his accent grew more Turkish with each syllable, both men noticed at once. He stopped. "This is how a Mahometan would address you,

Mr. Leveret, and your strange request of service. But I will not do so."

"Will you not?"

"No. Because it is not a game to me. I am grateful to England and to the True Church, to the beauty I never knew existed for far too long in my life. I am a Protestant Christian Englishman."

"You do not long to return to Constantinople."

"I do not."

"You have no one there who longs to see you again?"

"I have not."

"So your wife and boy stay there and you stay here to die? This cannot be what you desire most."

"What I desire most?" His voice almost wavered, but he held the line against this renewed assault on his last line of defense, his mined and counter-countermined walls and moats, and he threw back at his attacker all that remained of his armory, to defend the corpse he had acquired at such cost over a decade: "Loyalty to the sultan demanded that I serve the queen, who did in turn ask that I serve my lord Moresby. And he now gives me to you, to whom I owe all my loyalties amassed so far: to him, to the queen, to the sultan. I owe all to you now, David Leveret of London, and so desire nothing more than to acquit myself to your satisfaction."

Belloc watched the man's face. He was angry, no question. It would do. "Matt, I think you're a liar, at the very least, and that's fine. Because one thing I can be sure of: You're not a Catholic. You'll do just fine up in James's castle."

PART FOUR

MATTHEW THATCHER and JAMES STUART, 1602

. . . .

If God should take her Majestie, the succession being not established, I know not what shall become of myself, my wife, my children, landes, goodes, friendes, or cuntrie, for in truth noe man doth know what . . . I tell you, Mr. Speaker, that I speake for all England.

—A poore member of this House [of Commons]

1

With Baron Moresby's letter as his passport, Dr. Thatcher was given a small room to himself in Edinburgh Castle for sleeping. At Leveret's suggestion he also requested and was granted a second room to work in, to be useful, to serve as an apothecary of sorts, cut and cook his herbs, offer such medicine as he could to other members of the household. A kindly under-steward saw the logic in this request, even took pity on the man, sent here to be a doctor, unrequested, unexpected, likely undesired, surely never to be welcome.

When Thatcher had laid his few possessions upon a low bed in his room of stone, as inhospitable as the sky and air of Scotland, he inspected his chamber according to Leveret and Gideon's instructions.

You will assume in solitude that you are at all times regarded.

He had already been in this castle for some time, forgetting that he was being invisibly observed. He wondered if he had done or said something foolish in his inattention. Leveret had taught him to stand upon a table and touch the highest board of the wall and the ceiling, to lie down upon the floor and peer against the boards that touch it. *Have you a lens?*

There was a table by the narrow window and three chairs of three different designs, as if he might have companions come to visit. He considered moving the table into the corner, standing upon it, and examining the ceiling and walls as he was taught, but surely if he was observed as closely as Leveret had predicted, what possible explanation could he have for standing on movables, feeling the walls, using a lens to find the listening holes? Let them listen, let them watch. Let them observe all his normal behavior while he seemed inattentive; that at least appealed to his true nature.

Even if James should embrace you as his brother or confessor, there are embassies and legates from Catholic lands, and they will be watching you. There will be other English there, but they are not your friends, nor are they to be trusted. They will have already decided to support James in his expectations, no matter his heart, or have chosen someone else and will view you as a threat to their ambitions, even if you show yourself to be entirely without interest in any matter but plants and animals and ointments, as you naturally seem. Mr. Nicolson, Mr. Villiers, Mr. Green, Mr. Byam, and Mr. Shaw—all of these Englishmen will watch you and test you and lie to you. Your only friends are those who speak our watchwords to you.

Thatcher labored to perform as Leveret instructed. But days passed and he was ignored: fed, left in peace, ignored. He inquired when he might be introduced to the king and was daily ignored.

"Dr. Craig will take you in hand," said a steward when the nature of Thatcher's existence became clear to someone higher in authority. But John Craig, physician to King James and Queen Anna, was unable to pronounce even a single word to Thatcher when they met. Thatcher's politeness—"Dr. Craig, sir, I am honored to assist you however I might"—was met with a mere squinting of one eye and silent motion of lips. Thatcher feared the man was on the threshold of a tremendous apoplexy; his face's contortions resembled one of Baron Moresby's preambles. Craig nodded several times, too many times to signify any assent to anything, just a speechless furious attack. And then he turned and walked slowly off. There would be no collegial sharing of herbs and medicaments, no exchanges in Latin or shy invitations to draw astrological charts.

Thatcher laid himself upon the bed, the effort to pull his legs up off the floor almost overwhelming, almost audible. The strain upon his limbs and veins to be alert at all times, to be careful of every word and every glance, left him with scarcely the vigor to rise from sleep or lower himself into it. He must collect the information, make his crucial diagnosis at once. *The urgency cannot be overstated, Matt.* His eyes closing for just a moment, he recalled: *All of your correspondence will be read.*

There were spoken codes painstakingly taught behind the fishmonger's, above the baker's, ciphers he was meant to commit to memory, but he was sleepy now: *If you bring books, on nature, or of a religious sort, or of anything else, they will be read.*

He would go into the fields and write about what he found in Scottish nature, cleverly hiding his observations of the unnatural Scottish king within them. *If you make notes, your observations of plants will be read.*

He was very tired. There was a task he was to perform according to Leveret's specifications before he slept, though he had said nobody's name was certain or meant to last an entire lifetime anymore. James VI wished to change his name to James I. *That was a jest, Matt.* Someone was to be observed and communicated to, they would announce themselves, if they said Mr. Thatcher then they were Leveret's friend if they said Dr. Thatcher if they said Dr. Ezzedine, but this friend must be met as quickly—

If you walk alone, you will be observed. If you speak with the king, you will be observed. You will not know if someone is observing you. You will not know if someone is following in your steps.

Thatcher had asked: "Then how are we to come to our much-desired Clarity? Is the king not also aware of this? Will he not reply to my questions with the knowledge that others are listening, so that he may be addressing a lie to them while I believe he is responding to me truthfully?"

Had Thatcher spoken aloud? He opened his eyes; his eyes opened. He attempted to sit up in the wooden bed but felt himself unable to. He was sweating despite the cold draft from the closed pane. Had he shouted? Had he revealed himself already, in these first days? *Matt, I want you to think about succeeding. About what you might ask of me.*

About what the queen might grant you in her generosity and gratitude. About what our men in Constantinople might be able to discover on your behalf. Give free rein to your natural curiosity.

Suddenly he was able to move quickly, like a younger man, like a man who would fight for his own cause and fate: He floated to the ceiling without having to move the table and without being seen. He found eyes peering at him and quickly hid from them any sign of his false intentions. He found ears beneath the floorboards and filled them with lies. Mr. Leveret and his dwarf appeared and told him again that there is no instant in which he is not observed. "But remind me, please, Mr. Leveret: This idea that we are always observed—this is what Catholics believe or English Protestants?" Thatcher asked. "It is what the spy who will live another day believes," said Leveret.

As he floated above the table and chairs, Thatcher used a lens and found a section of ceiling through which he could propel himself, as if swimming through the baths in the New Palace, and so with a deep inhalation Ezzedine swam through the ceiling and emerged wet and warm in those very baths. It was the matter of a moment to leap from the baths and dry himself, pay his obeisance to the sultan and Allah, and fly to his home, to his wife and son. One was older than when he had left for England; one younger. This was to be expected, considering the number of years he had been stranded, but he was surprised to find that both were blind, with milky eyes, unmoving clouds behind rapid lashes. The pounding of his heart, of thunder, and then of Christian cannon against the city walls startled him, but he recovered himself and led his stumbling family to safety, a few miles ahead of David Leveret and the Queen of England.

2

AFTER ENOUGH DRINK to make their apparent friendship convincing to anyone who cared to watch, Gideon the drunken
dwarf led the drunken doctor through the noisy tavern, out through
the courtyard, and behind the stable, where Leveret awaited him, in
shadow and in silence. "Matt, it's a relief to see you. I worry about
you, you know. So tell me the news. What's your progress these
weeks?"

"I have made myself available. They have given me a room.
Rooms. I am gathering herbs in the fields. I am awaiting my intro-
duction to the king. I ask every day."

Gideon barked, "Are you playing a game, Turk? These *weeks*?"

"I'm sorry if that is a poor report. I feel I have only been there a
few days. I haven't been introduced. I haven't even seen the king."

Belloc calmed Gideon down with a glance, and they were both
silent as Dr. Thatcher explained the difficulty, the indifference to
his presence, the days of waiting. Belloc was not angry, nor was he
ready to feign anger to control his man, but he felt something not
far from panic. "Matt. Things in London are worrisome, do you
see? I need you to be a bit less meek for me. I need you to get close
to your patient with a subtle urgency. If he had a quatrain fever,
you wouldn't wait to be invited, would you, Doctor?"

Two days after leaving Leveret and the darkly moody, disappointed dwarf, Thatcher discovered that he had been wrong: He *had* seen James VI, without knowing it; the King of Scotland hadn't been wearing a crown after all.

Dr. Thatcher had, in his days of awaiting acknowledgment, wandered in the gardens and woods of the castle and had nearly walked into two men in a fevered embrace behind a stand of trees. Thatcher stopped in his path, unnoticed. The man with blond hair could not have seen him, or anything else, as he was kneeling in the pine needles, his face pressed into the standing man's groin, the standing man's fingers tightly wound in the blond hair. And the standing man, his own black hair in curls falling over a crimson jacket, turned his head toward the frozen Thatcher, but his eyes were tightly shut, and Dr. Thatcher walked quietly backward and out of the wood.

Two days after meeting Leveret and Gideon, in a hall asking again for admission to the Presence Chamber, wondering how to exhibit subtle urgency, Dr. Thatcher saw the black curls, the crimson jacket, the eyes now open but shadowed and sleepy, as they passed. And now he wore a crown. So that, then, was James, King of Scotland.

The king did not acknowledge Thatcher's low bow, if he noticed it. He passed in quiet conversation with an older man easily a head taller. Thatcher rose and watched the receding pair: The king looking up to his stooped, skeletal councillor, whose beard dwindled up his cheeks as plants do when stones begin to dominate a landscape. James's head tilted upward generously to hear the whispered comments of his adviser. The king seemed a young man still, not yet arrived at the frosty, solitary heights of forty. But he was as troubled by the Scottish cold as Thatcher was and pointed his chin toward a boy holding a fur, which soon was lifted and lowered upon the royal shoulders. The king revealed to Thatcher's eye a limp, or something less than a limp, something halting in the royal step, discomfort in the simple motion of walking. Though He had made James king, God had then denied His anointed child this natural ease He granted many lesser men.

James was the doctor's third potentate. God had set Thatcher upon such a strange path, such as few men might ever walk. What was Matthew Thatcher that he should travel among kings and queens? In another court he stood, able to observe yet another man placed high above all others. Three royal courts he'd lived in. The progression from grand to shabby, from trusted to irrelevant, had been like separating himself from paradise in leaps.

He considered his task for David Leveret and wondered if chance had not already carried him to its conclusion. He may have inadvertently found an honest answer already: Did the king's behavior with the blond man in the wood perhaps prove James to be either Catholic or Protestant? He would tell Gideon the dwarf to carry the news to Leveret. If the men's embrace when they thought themselves unobserved was definitively diagnostic, Thatcher might leave Edinburgh already. He might leave Scotland. He would return to Moresby, if the baron would have him back.

The rest of what Leveret offered was impossible, a lie, and Thatcher would be wretched if he allowed himself to imagine it otherwise. It was cruel even to have hinted at it.

Two mornings later, Thatcher was woken before the sun, his twenty-third morning on the wooden bed in a small closet in Edinburgh Castle. "This morning, Doctor, in the Presence Chamber," said the boy, for the twelfth time, sent from the steward who had told Thatcher upon his arrival and after reading the letter from Baron Moresby, "I'll send a boy to fetch you for your presentation in the morning." Eleven times the doctor had presented himself, been led to an antechamber and told to wait. Eleven times he was taken out of it, only to be led back to his own room with no explanation.

The twelfth time, this twenty-third morning, the doctor waited again for hours, again in a small annex again still decorated with only a painting of the king's mother, Mary. The identity of the painting's sitter, and not much else, the boy had told him. The same room in Elizabeth's court would have had ten paintings, and in Murad's court (Mehmed's court now, he corrected himself) drapes, divans, bowls of food, carafes of sweet water, windows open onto gardens, fountains, music, *warmth*. But today, in a room of brick and a poorly paned window, under the painted eye of the woman who meant to murder Elizabeth but lost her head, Matthew Thatcher waited for more hours, his thoughts contained, by habit and force, to formulae and the functions of herbs, organized by land of origin, pages of Avicenna coming effortlessly to mind and rolling memory: "Calamint, calamus, calx, calcii hydras, chamomile . . ." He was able to produce the pages in his mind in Arabic, Latin, or English. "Mace, maidenhair, marsh mallow . . ." His expertise glowed inside him, lit the dismal room and the painting of the murderous queen: "Orders of fungus (saprophytic, parasitic, nonpathogenic, sub-pathogenic, pathogenic) in various types of soil or landscape . . ." He had been able to commit these pages to memory more than thirty years ago, after scarcely more than a single reading, and not a word of it was lost! He began to recite to himself the names of first-degree compounds of materia medica—but then stopped: He had been imagining himself teaching the list to his child. And he had been forming the words audibly.

He began again, staring at the painting of Mary to banish from mind the image of his son, careful now not to make a noise, and soon his flow of thoughts had rolled into his task, the details of which he rehearsed over and over, for fear they would wander the moment he needed them: *Master Leveret requires for the safety of his country my sworn witness to any inarguable proofs that James is a Protestant or a Catholic. Such empirical behaviors would include the formation of a sign of the cross, the demand that Latin mass be spoken in secrecy, the taking of confession, the raising of the host above the priest's head during mass, the presence of crucifixes in the royal chapel, and the priest's wardrobe, including chasuble and not merely cope or surplice. Roods, murals, vestments, popish books, holy water, censers: All of these were to be counted, cataloged, and seen in use by the king himself.*

A noise from outside the window. Dr. Thatcher rose and stepped upon a chair with tufts of yellowed horsehair so that he could see below. He watched as the guards lifted the gate for a group of twenty horsemen, at the center of which rode, far more comfortably than he walked, that same small man, the King of Scots. The troop of them—the king's gold-circuited black curls within their heart—burst forth across the bridge to the road beyond. Thatcher, high above, saw James VI ride off for an afternoon's hunt or to process to his other palace, a mile away. Thatcher was going to wait in this dark and bricked room forever, with none but a dour Mary, Queen of Scots, for company.

All it would have required was for Elizabeth to force herself to love a man or, even less, merely to allow a man to wed her, to cover her, to create a child. If that had happened, then Thatcher would at least be lying tonight in Moresby Hall. But Elizabeth's father cut off the head of Elizabeth's mother for her sexual disloyalty, and that may have been the moment after which Elizabeth would never trust a man. It may, too, have been when Matthew Thatcher's life (which had not yet even begun in Beirut) was written to its end in the tiny rump of mountainous land called Scotland.

Too candid when young, too loyal to oaths he made to those who cared nothing for loyalty except that which was due to them—he could begin to think this about himself, to compile his complaints and prepare the indictment against all those who had hurt him, but it was too kind to himself. No, he was a criminal at heart. He could imagine himself wronged—by Cafer, by the ambassador, by his sultan, by Queen Elizabeth, by Baron Moresby, by David Leveret—but who among them had bowed his head to the loss of his life and family? Who had then so lightly cast aside his true religion merely to protect himself in a foreign land? None. None had turned his back on his family and on God as swiftly and slowly, as gradually and completely, as the man born Mahmoud Ezzedine, the forgotten of Allah. And Leveret, one of the island's many professional liars, lightly promised that he could restore it all to him.

Again, in this darkening closet, waiting to be told he was free to return to his other dark room, he practiced the gestures of Protestants and Catholics, securing their distinctive arcs in his body's memory.

GEOFFREY BELLOC HAD a message from London: Elizabeth was out of bed and taking some bites of food again, had sat for audiences but fallen asleep on her throne almost at once. Not exactly clarifying, but it surely meant that time was limited. He sat with Gideon the dwarf and wondered. They drank, and Belloc reminisced. "I think of him up in that castle, and I remember what it feels like. Living in the hot water, there is a strange and persistent small panic. You try to settle it with rituals and caution. But the mood you live with as a constant, as the foundation stone for all other moods, is fear. Potential catastrophe is coming up the stairs for you *right now*. Some of the fellows and all the women spies I ever knew just lived with it and accepted it: They were constantly sorting through lists of things to do in their heads; they're looking at everyone and everything, always assessing. Lists to do. Lies to tell. People to distract or frame to take the punishment for what you yourself are doing. Don't forget what you said to him; subtly push her attention the other way.

"But then I knew, too, some of them—only men, this kind— that go the opposite way. They pretend that fear and worry isn't there at all. The mask of unconcern. They might even believe it, that they're calmly above it all, like they have pure soul or God's goodwill or some fitness, all proven by easy sleep and a quiet beating heart and steady voice. But it doesn't last, you know." He topped up the tiny man's cup. "They always break worst of all. There are some geniuses in the game, but genius is no more common among spies than in any other trade."

He looked at the ceiling, then asked Gideon, "Do you think I picked the wrong man?"

3

"YOUR MAJESTY," CROAKED out an old man in a cloak of mottled, patchy fur. "The English lord of Moresby doth send to you his devoted love."

"It is welcome. He is a near neighbor to us here. We do hope to grant him our presence before too many years have passed." How politely a man could imagine the death of God's chosen Queen Elizabeth when he lived on the far side of the borderlands and had everything to gain by her decease. "His lands lie between the Liddel and Solway Firth, do they not?"

"You are precise in your geography, Majesty. The baron invites you whensoever it should please you and hopes it will be soon. He sends to Your Majesty as well a gift, with all his worshipful love." The old herald read from the letter, adjusting it from first to third person, reciting the lines Belloc had dictated for Moresby to write. "He sends to you, O King, Dr. Matthew Thatcher, his most trusted and wisest physician, one upon whom he relies for the very extension of his days and what comfort he is able to find on this earth. He hopes that Dr. Thatcher might carry and deliver all his vast knowledge and wisdom of God's healing ways to the throne and court of Scotland and forge with his powers the longest, most glorious reign for you."

The king, draped across a throne, his legs kicked over its arm, placed his hand atop that of the blond man, who stood beside him, caressing the royal shoulder. "It is a loving gift. And would this doctor enter into service to us? I would not take him from his master's home unwilling if he should prefer it there, in green and warm-aired England."

"Generously considered, but he is here, Your Majesty, and might assert his will freely before all the court now."

"Is he? Shall our Dr. Craig question him in his knowledge, to determine if he is wise enough to remain with us? Or is this to look at a gift without gratitude? What says the Church, Mr. Spottis-woode?"

The gaunt and gray man, taller than the king, bowed low and spoke quietly, and the king and his friend both laughed at his whispered words. Mr. Spottiswoode, crossing his arms to cradle his elbows in his hands, squeezing them fitfully as if to warm himself, turned to the herald. "Say again his name, this doctor's name," demanded the man all in black.

"Matthew Thatcher," replied the old herald in old fur.

"I know this name. Is he here? Bring him to us," ordered Spottiswoode.

The king, annoyed, dropped his friend's hand. "I have already instructed this, sir. The Church need not show such excessive love as to repeat my every word."

Spottiswoode retreated a step and dropped his head.

But, of course, Thatcher had been in full view of every man, woman, and boy in the chamber throughout this entire conversation. They could have seen him and asked anything they wished of him at any time. He had simply been invisible, even absent, until the moment King James said, "I know this story, too, John. The Turk." The king turned at once to face Thatcher. "You are Matthew Thatcher? The doctor from Arabia?"

"I am Matthew Thatcher, your doctor to command, Your Majesty. I come, most recently, from Cumberland."

"I do not believe that Matthew is a Saracen name, is it?"

As Thatcher shimmered into visibility under the king's attentions, he felt all eyes on him—some score of men and women, ambassadors and legates, thanes and ladies, all poorer in dress and manner than those in Elizabeth's court. There was silence but for a single musician, somewhere distant and discreet in the hall. "I am honored that Your Majesty knows anything of my humble life. That he has taken any interest in my poor story. But, yes, when I was taken out of my blindness and blessed with the gift of God's one true faith, I was granted the privilege of selecting my name. I was sponsored at my baptism by John Dee and a man named Matthew, and I chose to call myself after him and Saint Matthew, who is so wise and beloved that even in my former country he is respected, though there he is called Matta. His life of faith and knowledge is one I hope to emulate."

The king stood and walked toward him, uneasily, favoring his right leg, and Thatcher wondered if he had once sustained a fall from a horse. James studied Thatcher, and Thatcher lowered his gaze to the floor but first saw stains and bits of food on the royal tunic. The blond boy still at the throne watched with his hand over his mouth. The king said, "Mr. Spottiswoode, did you ken that the Mahometans spoke of our saints in this fashion? That they know of the true faith in such detail?"

The man in Geneva black pulled the corners of his mouth down, as far as they could extend, before replying, "They do study it, Majesty, but only from their particular madness: They think to better it. As our Lord Jesus did surpass and supersede the law and scripture of the Hebrews, so do Mohammed's people believe their book completes and countermands, improves upon, the Gospels of Matthew, Mark, Luke, and John."

"Do they? Do they really?" The king was astonished and then began to laugh loudly, and many joined him in hilarity. "But do they *really*? Dr. Thatcher, is this so? I cannot think Spottiswoode is correct."

"I regret that it is so, Your Majesty. A nation confounded by false teachings, prisoners of ignorance."

The king stopped laughing, seemed at once to be pained by this hideous information. "This must be set to rights. The very moment I am king of all Britain, we will set to chastising and correcting this madness."

It was, after a moment's examination of one another's eyes and posture, the consensus of those present that the king was in earnest and not making some complex play of wit, and so there was no laughter but only nodding and solemn agreement. "Yes, yes," said the blond boy in his golden jacket. He had an accent Thatcher could not identify, and the youth asked the king directly, "How will you begin? What to learn to them first?"

James—energized in conversation about his future power, the uncountable English armies he expected to command—seemed much younger than Thatcher had first guessed. The king in turn examined his new physician carefully. "Dr. Thatcher, you and I will speak together about this, and I will learn from you what manner of thought guides the Mahometan."

"It shall be my honor, Majesty, to share my humble knowledge with you, that I might aid in your efforts to bring light to a benighted nation."

"Mr. Spottiswoode is my realm's most learned man of God and a great mind within our kirk. So, Mr. Spottiswoode, tell us, please, how many do they number, the nation of Mohammed?"

Spottiswoode did not hesitate or clear his throat but asserted at once, "Scarce three millions, my king. Far fewer than the kingdom of the righteous, even if we take not into our count the papists."

"In every land? Arabia, Turkey, the Moors? So few as this? Why, then, it is no matter to—and why has no sovereign in Christendom taken upon himself the task of correcting them these many centuries?"

Thatcher felt a wave of dizziness, an uncertainty of how and where he stood. Were they all silently laughing at him? Had they been preparing, these many weeks of waiting, some sharp wit he did not understand? If this king and his whole court were mocking him, then he had already failed Leveret's task, and his fate would soon be determined. Or could he have lost track of the world in his years of exile? Did this little king know something that Thatcher himself had never learned? Perhaps, in these ten years, the world had been turned on its head. Ezzedine had left a land that dwarfed Christendom, that laughed at histories of perpetually lost but viciously cruel Crusaders. But now the king's certainty that this tiny island—far less, just this poor tiny topmost ornament of the tiny island—could somehow convert a people whose numbers, as any man who had seen some of this world would know, extended uncountably . . . The doctor's thoughts came to an end of words, and only images proceeded to his mind: his garden, the sultan's shoulders, the blades of a janissary troop in formation, ants along the side of a table leg—

"What think you, Doctor? As you are the first we have ever known who has corrected himself from what he knew as a child, what can you teach us about the nations of Mohammed and their children, so that we might replicate your great conversion in vast numbers and at great speed?"

"I shall give it all consideration, Majesty."

"And I shall give you all attention. We will discuss this matter together. It shall be a task of highest import when I am in London."

Thatcher bowed deeply and, if they were not mocking him, then he had, perhaps, taken the most difficult step Leveret had assigned. If he were soon to sit and discuss religion in privacy with this young man, it did not seem impossible that James might describe the manner in which the Christian God revealed Himself to the King of Scots. It could be as simple as that, and no more-desperate actions need be taken.

The future, if it can be said to exist at all, is surely shaped in part by imagining it. That night, alone in the small chamber, Thatcher allowed himself to imagine—for the first time in years—what might happen to him next. He lay down upon his bed and closed his eyes. He turned his head to snare the echo of a distant noise, and years of discipline and painful habit melted away. He allowed himself to see his return, a vision waiting these many years for Thatcher to weaken. . . .

The water and the bridge, the stones in front of his home that warmed until late in the day, when they held their heat even after the sun descended and moisture gathered upon them in beads. He laid his palms across his closed eyes, to savor what was happening behind his eyelids, to seal in the visions before they seeped away, before his strength returned and he banished all these pictures as the work of temptress devils.

4

MATTHEW THATCHER WAITED for the royal invitation, his commission to become the king's confidant on matters of theology, in which consultations he would extract the one-word answer
that Mr. Leveret urgently required: "Catholic" or "Protestant." As
long as there was Clarity, as long as he could deliver Mr. Leveret
certainty, it did not matter which word he spoke. The word itself
would launch Mahmoud Ezzedine to Constantinople.

He could not quite believe it, though, even as he toyed with the
story for his own pleasure, a pleasure he knew to be dangerous, a
pleasure that would kill him if the story never became real.

And, of course, the king's whimsical invitation to the Ottoman
did not become manifest. Thatcher passed still more days and then
weeks alone, ignored. The same suspicions that had drifted around
him for years in Moresby Hall now wafted behind him as he passed
through the halls of Edinburgh Castle and, when he and the household moved a mile away, the halls of Holyroodhouse Palace. As he
did in Cumberland, he walked alone for relief, now on the grounds
of Holyroodhouse and the land outside the city gates. He ate alone,
in the fields or in his room. He walked under the windows where he
thought the king might be, in hopes James would see him and summon him. Instead, two more weeks passed with nothing to write

and nothing to tell Mr. Leveret nor any messenger whispering secret watchwords appearing to surprise him.

There had been three sets of secret words trained into him in one of their upstairs rooms. He couldn't recall them just then. Leveret had said there was a way they would be said, not only the order of the words but their tone, something abnormal that would confirm the identity of anyone who presented themselves to Thatcher with this phrase as livery, but they were slipping from him now.

And then, finally, after these additional weeks of silence and forgetfulness, Thatcher was summoned.

He would move quickly in conversation. He would have his single word.

But he found in the small chamber to which he was led not the king but a tall, thin young man with freckles and blazing red hair. A seal hung from a tin chain around his neck, over black clothes decorated here and there with fur and colored pieces. The page who had led Thatcher to the room backed out of it and closed the door behind him at once. The red-haired man bowed deeply to Thatcher, who bowed in return, and the two men, left alone, stared at each other, waiting for something to happen.

Finally the young man withdrew a document of several pages from within a stiffened and stained parchment case. "Will His Majesty be joining us here for my report? Or shall ye lead me to him?"

With some effort, Thatcher learned that this man was the coroner of Edinburgh, new this year to the role, after his father's death, and that he had come to make his office's annual presentation to the crown. For this occasion, the coroner had dressed himself in his finest garments (within the limits of sumptuary legality) and had reasonably hoped to be seen by James himself, as his father had been twice received by Mary, James's mother. Thatcher shyly made inquiries to the page outside the door, who carried the questions to authorities unspecified, and after some long time ambled back lazily with instructions: Matthew Thatcher was to receive the coroner's report, orally and on paper, as a royal councillor for disease, newly appointed. "From whom did this appointment and assignment come?" asked Thatcher, but the page had no answer but a shrug and a vague history: He had asked outside another door of another page, who had disappeared and returned with the words this page had just recited and was prepared to recite again if the Turk needed to hear them again.

So Thatcher returned to Adam Strathquin, coroner for Edinburgh, stifling an urge to apologize and mustering instead an effort to make the young and nervous man feel welcome and important: "It would be my honor to receive your report on behalf of His Majesty, James, sixth of his name, *rex Scottorum*."

The words settled inside Adam Strathquin's ears. His disappointment was unmistakable, and Dr. Thatcher wished again to apologize. "If you please, sir, begin at once. The king is waiting impatiently for me to bring him your reports," commanded Thatcher generously.

The young man took a deep breath, and with a practiced, theatrical gesture suitable for a full and attentive chamber of courtiers and royalty, he paced back and forth, now raising his hand to the sky, now to the far wall of the chamber, all as a young actor had taught him earlier that week, and he recited Edinburgh's enumerated losses, studied and carefully inserted into his memory, trained since boyhood for precisely this catalog: "The city in the past twelvemonth has not been swept to sea nor overrun by witches nor monsters. Neither have we been depopulated by plague, despite its efforts in taking 997. Further: 320 abortive and stillborn; 6 affrighted to death; 556 aged to their reward, like wine, or cheese; 10 to apoplexy; 2 burst or ruptured; 443 to a carnosity of any variety; 209 to violence of medicines; 1,229 to consumption; some 115 mothers in childbed; 3 to fallen jaws; 44 from the rising of the lights . . ."

Later, Thatcher stood alone beside the guard gate through which the king's hunting party had left some hours earlier. He tried to create an excuse for what he was doing, as if he had any real business in this corner of the grounds. He sat, tired beyond measure, his back against an outer wall, and he must have slept, because next he knew it was darker, and he was being spoken to, though the sounds did not at first register as clear words: *ye—ken—throu—pa-al*. Thatcher had not seen the man in some weeks. Fat and tightly encased in his velvets, his beard forked and waxed into points, Dr. Craig was (again, or still) angry at Thatcher. After a moment of being awake, Thatcher could perceive some of the words below the man's accent, as when a spring breeze removes last season's dead leaves: ". . . yer days of lurking aboot. We nae need ya. Nor need any damnable other Turk physic, ye see. He's in health and will remain so by God and my hand. So back to Moresby, the wise way, eh?"

"You are the king's most excellent physician, Dr. Craig. I have heard tell of your skill and wisdom. He is most fortunate to have you."

The man stared, let his jaw open and shove forward, pulling the rest of his head behind it. He half-closed his eyes under their thick red hedges. "Am I? Aye, and ye're a Turk, and enough of ye now." Or something like this, Thatcher later thought, still trying to sift meaning from the doctor's furious brogue.

The gate rose with a shriek, and hooves rang the stones, and Thatcher realized he had been hearing them coming up the steep path to the castle for some time and so had provoked Craig to keep him talking, an excellent excuse to stand in wait. The king was through the gate first, his friend in gold riding behind him upon the same horse, his arms around the king's middle. In front of the king's leg hung a saddlebag embossed with the arms of Scotland, and within it a miniature hound showed just its brown head and soft ears, made slightly translucent by a beam of lingering sun. The dog squinted its greenish eyes in the light. Some prey had left a little blood on its snout. The king walked his horse past the low-bowing doctors, their napes and backs all that were exposed to his height. He slowed his mount and shouted to them as they straightened, "My doctors! In consultation! Excellent!" He brought his impatient horse around to face them. "Do you hunt, Dr. Thatcher?"

"No, Majesty. I do not ride well."

"Then what do the people of your nation do when hours stretch before them?"

"The ordinary people, my king? Or people of your greatness, such as the sultan?"

"Oh, now! And do you know the habits of the sultan of the Turks, Matthew? This is an extraordinary claim." The king's friend laughed behind him, clinging to James tightly, despite the horse's obedient stillness.

"I do, Your Majesty, for I was once his trusted and private physician. And from the time I was a boy, I was his competitor at chess. Though he was a far greater player than I."

"You played chess with the sultan of the Turks, Dr. Thatcher?"

5

"TELL ME OF his palace."

"The sultan's New Palace, like Your Majesty's castle, sits atop a great hill, visible from every direction."

"And his court," the king began, but made himself appear busy by studiously centering his pieces within their starting squares, assuring himself of precise distances between each. "His court, is it . . ." Thatcher knew the young man wanted to ask something and hoped to hear a particular answer to the question. He reminded Thatcher of his own son at that moment, of Ismail, as preposterous as such a resemblance must have been, but something in the gesture or the face: Like a young boy, the king feared an answer but couldn't help flitting toward the question like a moth. "Does the sultan's palace exceed those of Elizabeth?" James finally managed in a rush of words, with a child's show of indifference. "I have heard that Nonsuch, for example, is the queen's favorite."

Thatcher could not afford to be blunt in his reply, but even Ezzedine would have been polite. Beyond a spy's policy or a physician's kindness, Thatcher's tact was improved by some uncertainty after a decade of studious forgetting. "Things are different in different places. For example, there are different animals and birds within the sultan's court. Where I have seen dogs in Elizabeth's court and yours, Your Majesty, there would be no dogs in the sultan's palace. Instead, he does allow peacocks to strut."

The king looked up from straightening his pieces: that same childlike face, but mischievous now. "How many cocks hath the sultan?"

"Beyond count, Your Majesty."

The king laughed like a boy, and Thatcher was puzzled. From within the groups of people walking about in circles, trying to look busy but merely needing to be in the same air as the king, one man in black and gold velvet drew a chair close to watch the chess game begin. His face had been stomped and ruined in the familiar patterns of smallpox. "Your Majesty," he said in an accent Thatcher recognized as Spanish or French, "I hope to learn much from watching your game."

James ignored the man. He licked his fingers and pushed forward a pawn. "I am curious what sort of player the sultan is. Bold? Reckless? Cautious?"

Thatcher said, "I felt often that he had foreseen my mistakes and helped me to arrive at them quickly." The doctor felt the spy's difficulty in ranking his lies: to probe the king for his religion, to protect the man from the truth that his realm (and the realm he hoped to inherit and find rich) were embarrassingly poor compared with the sultan's, to compliment the king on the novelty of playing chess with the sultan's chess player while complimenting him on being a better player than the sultan or his doctor.

"Surely this is not a bishop in your country?" asked the king, and Thatcher heard the old challenge to prove himself.

"England was my country. And now Scotland, Majesty."

The king waved at the words with annoyance. "Enough of that now, man. What do the Turks call this piece?"

"It would be a war elephant. Though I have met men who traveled in the deserts of the Arabs, and there it is known as a camel."

"Remarkable. And yet they all move the same, as a bishop does?"

"They do, on only the incline and the decline."

"And your horsemen? Do they wield curved blades like Saracens?"

"Some do, Majesty, resemble the mounted warriors of the desert or the Turkish janissary."

"And do they ride recognizably Arabian horses in the carvings?"

"That I could not say. I know very little of horsemanship, I fear. Do these pieces resemble Scotch horses? I thought them all small breed."

"Not at all," said the king with renewed enthusiasm. "We have a surprising range in our horses. Most surprising. But the other pieces are the same? This is the king? Or do you say the sultan?"

"The shah, Majesty. And the very word 'checkmate'—*shah mat*—comes from Persia: 'The king is helpless.'"

"Oh? 'Checkmate' is your word? Very cleverly done. That is one in favor of the Mahometans, I confess."

"But other pieces are different. Your queen, I am afraid to tell you, is no queen among the Mahometans. A woman has no place on the board. They prefer to call this piece the vizier or the councillor. The secretary, you might say. Like Mr. Spottiswoode? And I cannot see why we of Scotland call this a castle when it moves so swiftly. Surely those Turks know something when they make this piece a war chariot instead, dashing forward or rapidly moving sideways to protect the shah."

The king licked his fingers and considered his next move. "I wonder that the game is the same game across the vast expanse of continents but such small things alter for the people of the desert or in Scotland."

Thatcher moved his piece and replied, "Stranger variations I have seen across the world. In other countries, men believe themselves to be the creation of gods we know to be false."

"An interesting comparison, Doctor. Or do they simply call God by a false name? And with some correction would they learn to address Him accurately?"

The wind shifted and a mist of rain drifted across the arcade to intrude upon the royal game. The spray wet the king's red pieces, raising tiny blisters down only one side of them, and Thatcher remembered being hurriedly brought to treat a little boy in Constantinople one night, the minute pustules covering every inch of the future emperor's roughly rouged skin. The beaded Scottish rain broke and streamed down the doomed king's red crown, but James made no motion to retreat farther inside.

"I was corrected as you describe, Majesty, some ten years ago. I have often wondered at the very question you have asked. Do the Catholics of Rome not know the true nature of God? Do they imagine a God who does not exist? Are they confused or are they malevolent in how they choose to address the one true God? As the Arab thinks the bishop is a camel, he calls it a camel."

"But, Dr. Thatcher, examine more closely: The piece of his game *is* shaped like a camel, though it moves like a bishop. In this, he is not wrong. He does touch a camel in his country, and were he to call it a bishop, he would be a madman. I think of witches, for another example. I have written a philosophical book extending man's knowledge of witchcraft unto the furthest reaches."

"I know nothing of this subject, I am sorry to confess."

"My book is a work of natural philosophy, like your philosophers' study of herbs and medicines. Following precisely the same conceits of evidence, proof and so forth, I have inarguably demonstrated the falsity of long-held beliefs. Allow me now. Here. Close your eyes, Doctor. Good. Now, conceive in your mind, if it please and not frighten you, a witch. Be not afraid to think of it. Have you done so? Well, allow me to speculate that you have imagined an old woman."

"I have indeed done so. Was I in error, Majesty?"

The king clapped his hands once and held his two index fingers up to the sky. "Dr. Thatcher, the witch does *not* uniquely take the shape of an old woman! This is commonly held but is a dangerous belief, for it lulls us into thinking the danger entirely circumscribed to this one type. In fact, we have recorded episodes of witchcraft emanating from every conceivable human form. But what your conversation reminded me, and what is often remarkable about the women who do practice witchcraft, is this: their apparently sincere claim that they are doing nothing of the kind, even when they are caught in the act of dark enchantment. I have been present at several interrogations of witches and have seen them tortured. It is an elucidating experience, Doctor. When the woman who is guilty of the charge is submitted to bodily pain . . ."

Thatcher's efforts to discuss Catholicism further would have to wait, for the king's interest in witchcraft so strongly held him that he ignored the (losing) game before him. He was still eager to talk about black sorcery the following night at chess again.

6.

You're a mountain *of a man, aren't you, brother?*
    Belloc knew well (and accounted for in his planning) the necessarily circuitous route of intelligence: from an under-steward to a serving girl to a deliveryman to Gideon to Belloc: The doctor had begun regularly playing chess with James Stuart, nearly every day and sometimes more than once a day. It was the first good news in weeks, and Belloc slept well at last that night, and he dreamed of James's mother, and he woke thinking again of nearly the last time he had seen her.

Mary had asked that the small room in Chartley Manor be emptied of everyone except for Geoffrey Belloc, who made her laugh, who made her feel safe by his size, who made her feel worthy by his Catholic piety, who made her feel well and lovely by his shy and adoring gaze. "You're a mountain of a man, aren't you, brother?" When she was satisfied they were alone, she took his giant hand in her tiny one. "Lean forward now, brother, and kiss my cheek." Geoffrey did as the exiled, imprisoned Queen of Scotland asked. "Now you may touch my face. With both your hands." Drawing him close enough to hear her quietest words, she told him to kiss her mouth and let his hands descend into the front of her dress and there find a treasure she had hidden just for him, this mountain of

English boy who would do anything for Mary of Scotland or Mary of Nazareth, indistinguishable.

His fingers crept between the hard board of her dress front and the soft flesh of her breast until they touched a tiny folded square of paper, felt the unicorns on the seal that held the packet tight. "Your Majesty's favors are within my grasp," growled her favorite. She allowed herself the normal human joy of one more kiss, one more moment of his fingers' stroll, and she shivered before shouting, "Off me, dog!" and swatting at her attacker's face and shoulders. "Away from my sight at once!" Bowing low in apology, Geoffrey backed out of the room, and any of Elizabeth's men who held Mary in house arrest at Chartley would have thought the Scottish harlot had decided to tease one of her followers from the sheer boredom of her endless predicament.

Belloc carried the letter to the kitchens. There, in one of the empty beer barrels awaiting return to the brewer's for refilling, he pressed his thumb against the corner of a lightly stained section of a hoop and sprung open a small, dry space to wedge the paper. Mary's correspondence would continue its journey: The barrel would go to the brewer's; the letter would be retrieved by the brewer, who would see that it reached its intended recipient, Sir Anthony Babington, who would break its seal and decipher its contents. Only later did Geoff learn that in this particular letter, Mary encouraged Babington's plan to coordinate an invasion of foreign Catholic powers with an uprising of Catholic Englishmen to support the assassination of Elizabeth and the placing of Mary on the English throne.

Geoff learned this because the brewer, too, was an agent of Francis Walsingham. Before delivering the sealed letter to a trusted messenger chosen by one of Mary's English confederates, the brewer would hand it to Arthur Gregory, waiting patiently at his side in the brewery, sharpening and warming his blades. Gregory was one of the few men on earth who could undetectably break a seal. Having copied the enciphered letter and undetectably resealed it, he returned the original to the brewer, and Mary's fatal letter continued on its intended path. The copy, meanwhile, was taken to Tom Phe-lippes, waiting at an inn less than a mile away, polishing his specta-cles and studying his cipher sheets. He would decode it, having easily broken Mary's system weeks before, and send the deciphered plain text on to Walsingham in London by fast rider. The principal secretary would be reading Mary's letter before it even reached the doomed Anthony Babington, and nearly before Geoff was back in Chartley Manor, gazing like a boy at the splendid beauties of the Scottish queen.

The last time he saw Mary the Queen, she looked him in the eye not sixty seconds before her head was cut from her in a single swing. She did not look like the embodiment of evil. The sight of Geoff in the gallery below her caused her lips to stop shaking for a moment, surprise taking command, for an instant, of fear and sadness, and Geoff recalled the feeling of those lips against his own, and the flesh of her breasts against the backs of his fingers, before he could re-mind himself of the murders she had gleefully assented to.

7

THATCHER WAS WOKEN in darkness by a familiar page boy, and when he could at last open his eyes, the impatient child simply said: "Chess."

A few minutes later, seated at the board and setting the pieces, plates of lamb and bread next to them, the doctor watched the sleepless king warm himself at the fireplace. "I could not find rest tonight. Do you know many English people?" asked James, again pacing with his peculiar step, bending forward at the waist with nearly every motion of his leg. He was dressed for sleep, and his favorite young man dozed upon a couch in the corner, his face turned away from the candles and fire.

A door opened, and the same man who had already watched several of their games from close quarters entered, somehow alerted that a midnight board was being prepared. He, too, was unkempt, and sleep still fogged him. "Majesty," he said, bowing, "I understand that you, too, are up in the night watches. I have come to offer company." James grunted and waved him away with scarcely a glance. The man bowed again and dragged his disappointment out the door.

"Spain's pest," said the king. "The sultan can play chess at any hour without interruption from the ambassador from Madrid, I imagine. But do you know many English, I asked."

"I have known a number, my king," replied Thatcher, watching the king's gait. "May I ask, Majesty, if your legs give you pain?"

"Never on horse, do you know?" He took a drink from a serving man. "In the saddle, at once I am comfortable. Do you hunt, Doctor? No, I've asked you before and you said no. But, truly, it is the finest thing." The king, tired in his eyes and awkward of pace, nervous in his manner even when exerting himself to be regal, became briefly another, happier, still younger man when talk turned to horse and hunt, and Thatcher felt again a sort of father's affection for him. Or it was no more than an older man's pity at a young man not yet aware of how irrelevant so many things are. Thatcher had the odd sensation of seeing beyond James's title and crown to see a man, and then one not terribly impressive. He had never had this experience with the sultan. It was impossible to separate that man—even as Ezzedine salved his cuts and burst his blisters—from the terrible power of his role. Murad had been a sultan in his blood, in his bowels, in the hairs that fell from his head at a young age and in the whiskers that were gray before he was thirty. Murad the Third was an emperor in his sleep, upon the stool, under Ezzedine's bandaging or cutting hand. Even Elizabeth, goggle-throated, her gullet hanging low, melancholy and yellow-toothed, might once have been—*must* once have been—a queen of great beauty and strength, and she preserved that within her somehow. She alone—a *woman*—rallied troops when the bloodthirsty Spanish were just off the coast. But this one, this misshapen boy, the stains of food upon his nightshirt, who—Leveret had told him—cried out when thunder jarred his sleep: He was a man first, second, third, and treated as a king for lack of better candidates anywhere in this barren land.

"You must see my horses, Doctor. I will show you the most noble beasts after our game. Tell me now, you do love horses, though you do not ride them? The Arabians, I am told, are great horsemen. But I was asking you, and you did not reply: You have lived among the English," the king said as Thatcher finished setting the pieces. James was not quite accusing in his tone; it was like a boy's demand for one more story, or it was only a statement of wonder: Even this

Turk had done something the king had not, for he had lived among the English.

But then the Queen of Scotland passed through the chamber at its far end, curious about her missing husband, and there was bowing and delay, ceremonial standing and sitting and kissing of hands until she and her ladies had passed out of sight again, and the king with relief slumped into the chair across from his doctor and took a piece of moist lamb between his fingers. He examined Thatcher. "Doctor, is Queen Anna more or less lovely than my cousin queen?"

Thatcher wiped his tired eyes and attempted an expression of knowing appreciation of female forms on this island of hideous women. The difficulty lay in soothing the king's husbandly pride even as a French boy in golden clothing came to stroke the royal cheek now that the queen was out of the room, in praising the future Queen of England without insulting the current one, while ears circled the enviable chess game at closer and farther distance, ears in thrall to Spain, to Rome, to London's factions and rival futures.

And in his nervousness, Thatcher found he had mislaid the name of the current Queen of England. "Majesty, your queen is not surpassed by any woman's beauty."

"Not even by . . ." prompted the king, and his young man laughed. James seemed to wish to hear a specific formula.

"Not even. Not even Queen . . . the queen . . . your cousin in London."

James laughed at the discomfort he thought he had provoked in his opponent. He licked his fingers and moved a pawn. "One must not allow oneself to be flustered by the enemy! Surely the sultan knows that, my doctor."

Thatcher bowed his head in good spirits at the king's wit. The word "Elizabeth" leisurely arrived in his mind.

"But what sort of men are they?" the king demanded yet again. "The English, I mean." The persistent question seemed to be a test, for surely the king of all Scots must have known from his agents and diplomats what sort of men the English were. He was therefore asking not what sort of men the English were but what sort of man

Thatcher was, though he was asking in some coded way that the doctor strained to understand. He must, he knew, be honest with this king, except, of course, for why he was here, who he was, how he became this other version of himself, and how well he could play chess (or, at least, used to be able to play chess: He found himself having to close his eyes to recall old patterns of attack and then opening his eyes to avoid executing them against the weak but necessarily triumphant King of Scotland).

"Your Majesty has surely known Englishmen, though? They travel to you, pay tribute, bear messages?"

"Men such as Mr. Nicolson and all the little men who scurry about his feet, who come to pry and prowl for that woman in London or beg for my favor. The men who come and stay too long and grow confused in their loyalties, men who regard their future gains when weighing their present words. Jews of men. They know that I will be their king and so cannot speak to me honestly of anything. They portray her weaker than she may be, so that I might number my days by hoping, like a spaniel. Perhaps in portraying her as weak, they weaken her. Or they flatter me, so that when I do descend to London, I will bring them with me, make them thanes of this or that."

"The English are, Majesty, if I may boldly speak, merely men. They seem to me not far different from what I have seen of the Scots. But I come from a far-distant place, where men are very different, and so I may be blind to all the important distinctions between your people and the English."

The king smiled broadly now and clapped his hands together, stood, and walked, halt-limbed but pleased. "Yes! Aye, sir, this is what I feel to be true. We are, in truth, *one* people, and a man from a foreign land like you sees it at once. We are all the *British* people. I feel this. From Julius Caesar's day until this very moment, the rest has been mere confusion and faction. 'English' and 'Scottish' are merely words, like 'north' or 'south.'"

"I have seen no reason to think otherwise. My friend in London, Dr. Dee, spoke of a British empire."

The king stopped, checked his enthusiasm. He returned to the table and, still standing, considered the board, picking idly at his beard, drawing stray long hairs of his mustache tips between his teeth, smelled something on his fingertips then licked them clean of lamb juices. He moved a bishop, licked his fingertips again, and Thatcher saw at once in the reckless bishop's advance the king's childish and impatient hopes for his opponent to make a mistake. "There may, however, be one distinction that cannot be overlooked," said the king. "An Englishman may simply be defined as a Briton who proudly thinks he is not a Scotsman."

"To be certain, such English do exist."

"Have you known some like this? Do they predominate?"

Dr. Thatcher puzzled over the board, debated whether to make the wise move and avoid the rather obvious trap or to step into it and watch it sprung to please the king's vanity, unless the king had laid such an obvious snare to test Thatcher's skill as a chess player or, even more likely, to test his honesty as a man: Would this new companion be yet another foreigner who would flatter the king's weakest efforts? How maddening to be the king, when men hide the best of themselves for fear of offending and hide their worst from shame, and a king is only allowed to see, for all his power, the bland smile and nodding praise of men at their dullest and most dishonest.

Thatcher avoided the trap and captured the king's horseman.

"By God, you're a clever one," said the King of Scots.

8

MATTHEW THATCHER WALKED out from Edinburgh Castle, past the gate guardsmen in the courtyard, still sometimes unintelligible in their stop-and-start singsong brogue. He suspected they were able to turn intelligibility on and off, as one should be prudent speaking near an Arab sorcerer.

He passed through the gate onto the streets of the Royal Mile. Having explored the king's small gardens in his first weeks, cataloged what remained of his collection of roots and salves carried with him from Moresby Hall, and counted those seeds that had descended from gifts of Dr. Dee, by late winter Thatcher felt increasingly naked, his herbal stocks depleting.

He walked out of the city, left its walls behind, chose a direction at random. Snow dusted the hill named after King Arthur, some two miles from the castle. The frost in the early morning silvered the brown grass. It crackled under his step. Hares and fox kept their distance from him but pursued their morning tasks. He watched them, noted what they took and what they rejected, guidance in the winter herbs and roots so far north.

He carried no money, nothing of value, only his knife and bag. At Moresby's, he had always been within a mile of town or house. But Scotland was different, and soon he was not only out of sight of the city, hidden as it was behind hills, but uncertain even of the direction whence he had come. Would a Scots brigand lose interest in a man without money and leave him unharmed? Or slit him for the pleasure of it, just from the boredom of Scottish life? Thatcher could almost see another unintelligible Scot, smelling of beef and his own shit, drawing a blade and demanding the doctor's submission, as if Mahmoud Ezzedine had not submitted enough yet. Perhaps Thatcher this time would finally not submit but would fight, even though he had nothing worth the battle, would fight only to stand and not submit. He did not like pain, but maybe if the brigand knew his work well, it would not hurt terribly.

An end. He dies, in a flash of steel and a wet ripping sound, lowered onto the cold stones and damp brown earth. There must be an end, so why not that one. The difference between imagining it, fearing it, and longing for it vanished for a moment, and Mahmoud Ezzedine and Matthew Thatcher died upon the Scottish heath, the blood from his throat staining his collar.

Man's empire quickly receded, and Thatcher felt God's earth restore itself beneath his feet. This is what it felt like to be a liar and a coward and to walk along the earth a liar. He had long told himself that his submission saved his wife's and child's lives, but he had simply been a coward. He had been. The conviction was unappealable. How many parts of earth had he trod upon as a liar? Far more than as an honest man. He had last been an honest man in London. Then he pretended to save his family and pretended to forsake his God, and that was the end of him, though he had been allowed to breathe these many years since and to forget his past joys, his many crimes, his vows and sorrows, the words and correct ways.

Until he was asked to tell new lies, and then he would remember how far he had stumbled in his criminality, every lie he had fallen into, been forced into, accepted, leapt into, each slightly worse than the last: pretend to be a Christian, pretend to be English, pretend to be a gift, pretend to be faithful to your new lord, pretend to admire a king while trying to steal from him his secrets, and if he would not dislodge them, then there would be further lies to enact, written by professional liars. And all of it began when the coward had pretended that his cowardice was for the benefit of his wife and son.

He climbed the sloping paths of the Arthur hill, and the hesitant sun wiped the snow away, revealed flat black slabs merely cold and treacherously slippery, another death he deserved as a treacherous and slippery man.

He roamed yet another country, still farther from where he was exiled, still colder, still wetter, still stonier. Stonier than London, stonier than Cumberland, browner, inconceivably, impossibly ever browner. He walked slowly, bent forward to examine whatever was hardy enough to push stubbornly between the rocks. There was little of value here, even among what he could recognize. Some of the ground had been burned not long ago. He clipped some purple leaf from a thick green stem.

On his knees, hunched over the tiny shoots he was cutting and laying in his bag, he spied a rabbit and then a second and then a con-stellation of them, either newly gathering or visible only now that his eyes were adjusting to the planes of brown as the sheets of mist retreated. Thatcher remained still as the creature nearest him stood guard, watching him sideways as the others grazed the same land the doctor had come to graze. The beast rapidly calculated the dis-tance, the terrain, and Thatcher's age, and determined that there was no immediate danger. Passing greener choices, the rabbit, with one eye still on the kneeling man, pulled small, jagged-edged brown leaves from a branch. A second rabbit joined the first in tasting this unlikely choice. And so Thatcher stood and walked slowly to the branch they rapidly fled, tasted a leaf himself. It resisted his bite and then yielded with a slight bitterness. He gathered as much as he could find, annoying the creatures who had taught him of its im-portance.

He sat and waited for them to grow accustomed to him again. They of all creatures could see that he was no danger.

And if rabbits could, then surely Allah saw into his heart, even if Thatcher no longer could. Surely all was well there, where Allah alone could peer. God was great and knew that Thatcher had feigned this curiosity in Christian ways, this habit of dressing and shaving his face like them, of praying like them, only because . . . because . . .

As often happened as winter became spring, Matthew Thatcher told himself, again, the story of how he had come to stand upon this ground. The story changed often. Sometimes it seemed true, sometimes even as if it had happened to him, that he had made choices that led him here, and that things could not be any different than they were, so one might as well carry on. Other times, though, he could scarcely recall the faces of Cafer bin Ibrahim, or Queen Elizabeth, the ambassador, Dr. Dee, and the priest who bathed him into the Christian faith, or the sound of the crowd that day cheering the coming conquest of Catholicism by an army of converted Mussulmen like the new Christian, Thatcher. And then Saruca and Ismail would threaten to appear, and Thatcher would open his eyes, find something to distract himself.

Enough. Work. The task. Mr. Leveret had said it might be done. One step first. Mr. Leveret had promised, if such a man's word could mean anything.

He stood in the field, the rabbits all at a distance, the clouds thickening down upon him, and peered about to see if he was observed. "The Catholic," he recited, just audibly enough that he would further etch the annoying details into his memory, and so that he could compare the words as he heard them with the words as Leveret had spoken them. "The Catholic kneels to receive his magic bread, crosses himself, closes his eyes, and believes the bread to be transubstantiated into a slice of the prophet Issa's flesh. The proper Englishman, however—"

Thatcher stopped. Surely Leveret had not referred to Jesus Christ as "the prophet Issa." No. Again. He closed his eyes, stood swaying in the cloud-darkening field, and organized once more the sounds of Leveret's explanations last fall, the tap of Leveret's hands upon the table as he reiterated each point. And Leveret's voice, higher than his deep, broad body would suggest, quieter but somehow expanding the threat of his size rather than reducing it: "The prophet Issa," he said again in Thatcher's memory. He could hear that voice, high and menacing, say, "The prophet Issa," but knew that it could never have been, would never have been.

"The correct and honorable and pious English reformed will make no sign of the cross upon himself and never will touch an image of the Lord or bow before any symbol or image except a cross. A Catholic, filthy and superstitious, will believe in any relic kept in a church's crypt—a saint's nail clippings, a piece of the True Cross, a dish or coffer touched by saint or apostle or even the prophet Issa . . ."

Leveret's voice had somehow braided itself onto that of an old man in Constantinople, discussing Koran with his old friend as Ezzedine had walked past them, nodding his greetings. That old man was discussing the prophet Issa as Ezzedine had walked past them, easily fifteen years before. There was nothing memorable about the event, but here it was, on this Scottish plain, demanding Thatcher's attention, disguising itself as instruction from his secret master. The sounds of a Constantinople road. Here.

He knelt, made the sign of the cross upon his face and chest. He bowed his head, "as Catholics often do, but not universally, nor exclusively," then raised his head to the sky "as the blessed of Christian England should do when humbly begging confirmation of their salvation." He brought his fingers to his lips, and the smell of the jagged brown leaves, beloved of the rabbits, expanded into his nose, reminded him of something: A food? A sauce? A spice upon a chicken he had not eaten in a dozen years, across continents from where he now stood alone?

He kissed his fingertips, tried to keep the scent alive, as some Catholics bring beads or a cross or a painted image to their lips in defiance of all holiness in London (or Constantinople), in violation of the holy commandments.

If the King of Scotland did this and then became the King of England, there would be war, and England would burn: The men and women and children would, on their inevitable plummet into the pitch of hell, first seize up in war on earth, a nation in a fit, like the baron in one of his spasms.

But if James did no such thing, kissed no tokens, scoffed at relics, ate no singing cakes, then his soul was clean by English standards and peace would follow, in this world and in paradise hereafter.

Or all of this arcane knowledge would be of no use. Perhaps James's soiled and tattered soul was so well hidden that it would be impossible to discern through veils of caution and deceit. Said Leveret, "You are not released from vigilance or your obligation to report to me because you find no evidence of Catholic sentiment. The absence of evidence is insufficient to reassure us. Rather, we will await your certain statement that the King of Scots harbors no popish feeling and is sincere."

A task set by a madman. Or a quest that would drive a man mad. Thatcher was sent here to scour for the invisible. Or to hunt to the death a nonexistent prey. Perhaps the answer London so desperately needed to know was not merely as yet unknown but literally unknowable. Or shrouded by countless other veils of deceit, without any end, so screened that it was only theoretically discoverable, as a particular and specific grain of sand at the bottom of a black Scottish lake could, in principle, be discovered with sufficient effort. Does that single grain exist? Yes. "Then do fetch it back to London, please, Doctor, that one grain alone, no others, and be quick! The kingdom depends upon it!" One may as well be dispatched to this filthy, damp kingdom of fog and stone and be told to bring back God Himself. What is this strange little man's religion? How many grains does a soul weigh? "Dr. Thatcher, hasten yourself to Scotland, sir, and straightaway measure the weight of the mad king's soul. Account, please, the number of angels in heaven. Trim at once the hairs on the devil's backside and weave from the barbed shavings a nosegay to delight the queen when seated upon her privy stool and ornament the royal farts. And if you return and we deem your labors unimpressive, then we shall begin at once to disembowel you upon a stage before a crowd baying for the blood of a Mahometan sorcerer. How would that suit you?"

James was not a fool. He was odd, and often stupid and childish, but he was not a child. There would be no chess game so enthralling that the king, distracted, would reveal his manner of Christian faith for Thatcher to scoop up from the table like a captured bishop.

Dr. Thatcher hated this tiny kingdom far to the north of everything. How much, by compare, even the baron's lands, only 130 miles to the south of where Thatcher scraped leaves from the brown earth in redoubled efforts not to think of Constantinople, seemed gentle, green, and fat. Scotland's stones and dirt, unsuited for anything, stood a single and fatal mile too far from all Constantinople's shades of blue, and the distance chewed on him, weakened his resolve not to think of family and home, more than it had in many years. He hated his task, he hated Scotland, he hated all the brown, he longed for color, the blue of sky, the blue of sea, the blue of the dome some 130 paces from his front door, the door behind which his wife and child waited.

And it broke, it broke. Willful efforts not to recall would no longer restrain the need to see them, to know what became of them, to try—even if futilely—to explain why he had not returned nor sent them any word. How he had thought he was protecting them. The first images that roared back were so strangely prosaic: a cut on her hand, from cooking, and Ezzedine tells her to stay still so he can wash the blood away. She shows her teeth to him in her pain. And that . . . her pain . . .

He dipped cloths in hot water and then pulled them out of the water with a stick, let them cool just enough that he could wring them. He pushed back his wife's gown, away from her stomach, her skin tight as a girl's, and he laid the warm, damp cloths across Saruca's belly, and she sighed. "Does it help?"

"You know it does. Do I have to sing your praises every time? I am the most fortunate of women to have you."

"You only remember that once a month."

"Tell me true now, and do not lie." Saruca held his hand over the warming towels and her furious, cramping belly. "Does he have you treat the concubines for this? Do you lay warm towels on twenty angry bellies? All of them sighing and saying you are the greatest of all wise healing men? Because if you do, I will have to make you a eunuch. And I will." She smiled and then nearly laughed along with him, despite her pain. Ezzedine hoped, a little, that she boasted to her friends of the care he gave her, hoped they were jealous, a little.

Perhaps he could return. Perhaps she was still young enough to suffer those monthly aches and would be glad to have him again. And Mahmoud Ezzedine rolled on his side, alone in a field, and wept with the misery of lost years and the burning, flooding return of vicious hope, the rebirth of it in his cramping gut.

9

T HE COOL AND distant sun had hidden itself again, a curtain of cloud drawn across the sky with the speed of a skein of birds in autumn. The chill was sudden and too potent for his cloak, too piercing for his bones. Yet still he knelt, as Catholics do, and then he bowed as only the Mahometan does, bowed his face to the stone and furze, the thorn and weed. With no sun to guide him, no recollection of where it had last shimmered, he had no ability to say where east would be found, and he kissed the ground and presented himself humbly to Allah while facing Dublin.

He returned to the city, to the mile of road between James's palace and castle. He stopped where a street performer had gathered a crowd in one of Edinburgh's dark alleys. He thought of Constantinople's jugglers and swordsmen, the magicians of fire, the gamesmen with their chestnuts and cups. Even Elizabeth had had a Turkish tumbler, those months when Ezzedine had served the Ottoman embassy.

But this performer today on an Edinburgh back road was different, and the sight of him troubled Thatcher.

The doctor moved around and through the crowd (with its inevitable Scottish stink, slightly different than the English stink, more meaty, but even these years later so unlike the sweet aromas of Constantinople and its people). From a raised wooden platform beside the road, the man was levitating. He flew. He floated three or four feet above the platform, not as if he stood upon some hidden second platform but wavering, sometimes nearly falling, as though fickle winds from below were only just strong enough to sustain his weight. If there were ropes holding him (as one day a rope would surely hold by the neck a man such as this), they should have caused the children gathered close to him (and those leaning out of a window above him) to shout out and reveal his trickery. But none of the children was less than delighted to see a man fly, as they had one and all dreamed of flying.

The magician drifted in the air, up and down, forward and back, before he slowly rolled into a somersault. Children began to turn their own on the stony street, possibly the first painful step to learning his skills. One boy above had both of his legs outside a window and was about to throw himself forward into nothingness, expecting fully to float as this demon floated just out of reach. A woman seized him by the shoulders and drew him back inside as he shrieked.

By then the man, upside down, allowed his shirt to fall over his dangling arms. He played the clown a bit, spun like a board back toward upright with a look of horror, ashamed at his errant clothing. "Would anyone be kind enough to give me a coin?" he pleaded. "I mean to buy myself a better-tailored garment."

Coins jingled onto the platform below him, and as he bent forward to collect them, there was a great sound of ripping. The man returned to fully upright, embarrassed. He exerted himself to see the cause of the sound behind him, but only turned in a circle, revealing to the crowd he had torn his slops, and his hairy backside was protruding. The clown turned again to face the laughing crowd but seemed not to understand.

"Is your bag made of calf's leather?" a young woman asked Thatcher. "It's a bonny handsome bag."

Thatcher instinctively pulled the bag close to his side, expecting a cutpurse or snipping pony to seize it, but the woman was apparently alone and earnestly praising his possession. She held her own basket and looked him in the eye and asked again. "Is it made of calf's leather?"

"I suppose it is," he replied. "I don't know, I confess. I bought it at a market. In Cumberland."

The woman was troubled by his answer and seemed frightened by his voice. He knew her expression, like that of some country girl afraid of a Mahometan, speaking to him only to prove her courage. She waited a moment, then turned away, said, "God be with you."

"And with you as well," Matthew Thatcher answered, turning back to the performer.

But then his bag was complimented again by another woman, the second time in an hour. It was just a simple leather bag, dyed but faded after these years of use. The second young woman found him a quarter mile away from the first, touched him lightly on the wrist, and said, "Is your bag made of calf's leather? It's bonny handsome."

Unquestionably this was some method of thievery. Why else would pretty girls speak to him at all and use—no. "Oh, oh!" said Thatcher. "Yes. Of course. No, it's not of calf or of horse but of simple leather, English." The oft-practiced words fell out in the correct order but hurried in his excitement.

"Why did you deny her before? Did you have reason to fear? Was someone watching you?" she asked.

"Yes," he said. "That's it exactly. I thought I saw someone looking."

She led him, from a distance, into a public house and up a flight of stairs, delivered him over to Leveret and Gideon with a sigh and a shrug. "Thought he was observed. I didn't see anyone, Mr. Leveret."

"Then be quick, Matt. I must have your report. You have been too long silent. Give me news from the chess table."

"I don't know yet. The answer. The man . . . you know who I mean? The man? You understand?"

"Yes, yes, my God. I know who we're discussing."

"Well, the man is not clearly one thing or the other to me. Sometimes it seems that he's the one, but then other times he seems to be more the other."

The woman stood with her back to the door and laughed loudly. Gideon was incredulous: "That's all? After all this time? From a dozen games of chess?"

"You know of the chess? How? I thought you would be pleased that I have won that audience."

"I am, Matt. Very pleased. Now, have you been inside his sleeping chambers?"

"No. Dr. Craig is allowed within, but I am not."

"Have you seen his private chapel? Or Queen Anna's?"

"No. I worship with the rest of the household on Sunday and holy days. The king worships alone with Mr. Spottiswoode, or in view of the others, and it is, I believe, completely Protestant."

The dwarf pulled himself up and onto the table while Leveret closed his eyes in thought. Gideon reached out and grabbed Thatcher's nose, hard enough to water Thatcher's eyes. "Mr. Leveret wants Clarity. Total transparent, perfect knowledge. A soap bubble. You, my Turkish friend, my son of Mohammed, you must"—pinch of nose—"do"—twist of nose—"better." Slap to the cheek from the tiny hand.

"Enough, Gid, enough," said Leveret, opening his eyes. "Matt, please. Tell me what worries you."

"He does not speak of God with me. Witches, yes. Mohammed and the sultan, yes. His certainty of becoming King of England, yes, but no talk of Rome, pope, communion wafers. I cannot—"

"You can. You will." Leveret stopped. "Matt. We have arrived, I think, by your own description, at a turn in the road." Leveret said to the woman who had brought Thatcher, "Step outside now." He waved even Gideon out as well. They complied at once, and Leveret told the doctor: "The answer is still uncertain. I don't blame you for this, but it is. So there's nothing to be done but to proceed as we discussed." Thatcher looked at his hands on the table. "Can it be done, do you think?"

"I suppose it can."

"And are you still opposed to doing it?"

The warm damp cloths upon Saruca's belly, the warmth of the stones outside his door. He would not abandon her again out of fear or conscience; he would not be a coward.

He looked David Leveret in the eye. "Can you really return me safely? All the way?"

"I can." Leveret took his intelligencer's hand. "I can, Matthew."

Thatcher returned to the field where he had seen the rabbits. And when he had sat long enough and quietly enough, it was dark. He returned to the castle gate and was made to bow and press his face against stones again because the guards could only lift the gate two or three feet off the ground. "It's caught, sir," said one. They made enormous and noisy effort, lifting and pulling, wrestling with thick chains, but "It's no good, sir, broken at the pivot wheel, I think." So Dr. Thatcher had to lie upon the ground and squirm under the portcullis's dripping teeth while the guards laughed themselves to aching. He pushed his bag through first, squeezing it tightly shut so that the rabbit he had snared could not escape.

Upstairs, from his workroom window, soothing the rabbit in his arms, he watched the gate open smoothly for a cart piled high with boxes and food.

Time being short, certain steps were undertaken simultaneously that should have been performed sequentially and corrected at the first hum of error, in the order he had discussed with Leveret in their talk at the fishmonger's when the doctor still resisted the giant's scheme. A plot born half-formed and monstrous from drunken speculation upon a stage in an empty theater in London was, in the performance, far clumsier than in its rough and maculate conception. Simple causes and effects were jumbled. Questions drifted past, unanswered. Punishments came before crimes. Precautions were developed at the same time that risks were taken, or after. Precise measurements were impossible, always vital and always impossible.

And so Matthew Thatcher sat on the floor of his workroom, holding a rabbit on his lap that would not breathe, whose heart would not beat, no matter the manipulations.

And so Matthew Thatcher, unsure of his own weight in precise numbers, uncertain of the strength of these northern herbs, knelt upon thawing fields out of sight of the city, wandered unguided like a Protestant, knelt like a Catholic, bowed to the ground like a Mahometan, muttered and heaved and vomited like the damned.

And so Matthew Thatcher made such notes and observations as he could and proceeded, half-blind, upon his hands and knees, through a lethal wilderness of ignorance.

"**I** HAVE DISGRACEFULLY LITTLE to offer you, Majesty, as token of my gratitude for my welcome in your court and for my joy in your company these months. I am a poor man. I have medical knowledge but nothing, I fear, that Dr. Craig does not possess in superfluity. And yet I do have this, carried with me these many years, and while its poverty embarrasses me as a gift, still it would honor me beyond measure if you would accept it from me."

Thatcher bowed before the curious king, a boy again, delighted at a coming surprise. Thatcher drew from his bag a carved box. It opened on a silent hinge of smooth wooden pegs. "You showed an interest in the differences the first time we played. I have since debated whether it is suitable for a king."

James peered inside the case at the small war chariots and viziers, the elephants and shahs and janissaries with their curved bows and curved blades, a few of the bows broken in the years since Mahmoud Ezzedine had packed the beloved set and gone to sea on a French ship from Constantinople.

James handled each piece in turn, placing them on the board between them after brushing away the pieces of his usual set. When the board was full, the king looked at his doctor and said, "They are excellent, Matthew of Turkey. We will use this set exclusively now, you and I, only for us. White will always be my army."

"I will set them so myself every time you desire a game, Majesty."

"Don Diego, regard, please, the gift I receive from my humble doctor. Handsome, no?"

"Indeed, Your Majesty. Would you like a set from King Felipe? I will write to him at once."

"No, you ape. I want you to admire *this* lovely set, which is newly given to me."

"It is most intriguing, Your Majesty."

Don Diego, not to be outdone, and inspired, without knowing it, by the king's anger, presented James with his own gift a week later: a small monkey in black and gold velvet, to match the Spanish ambassador's usual garb.

Not many games later, King James was looking at the board with a frown, as if disappointed by his predicament, as if he didn't remember any of the moves that had led to this moment. Dr. Thatcher watched the royal face. The frowning was a show, but it did not seem to hide any strategic wisdom, as proven by his next unstructured attacks and retreats. James again reminded Thatcher of his son, making a face trying to look serious, and Thatcher, madly, nearly mentioned Ismail.

The king's monkey had rapidly learned to imitate his royal liege: He tilted his head to consider the board, just as James did. He pressed his front paws together like hands and held them under his chin while he pondered. He even had remnants of food on his little jacket. He licked his paw and picked up a piece, nodded thoughtfully in a perfect impression of the king. James and Thatcher both laughed, and the monkey seemed pleased with himself. He did it again. James fed it a grape while Thatcher restored the pieces to their *status ante simia*.

"How delightful, how droll, when animals ape us and aspire to behave like us!" said the king of all Scots.

"The problem comes later," said Thatcher, "when we, engaged in our usual tasks alone, realize we have come to resemble them and seem less like men for it. We tilt our heads and peer at our chess-boards, and it appears we may be no more aware of ourselves, no more intelligent, than a monkey on a lead."

King James VI of Scotland licked his fingers and pushed his shah into the protective shadow of his war chariot's far side. "There are, without question, false reports," he said, returning to the talk of several minutes earlier. "Not every claim of sorcery or witchcraft is honestly or correctly made. Each report must be investigated cautiously. Calmly. Using all the reason that God has given us. One must even say *humbly*. One has seen jealous neighbors accuse wealthier neighbors, in hopes of stealing property. One has seen fornicators eager to discard superfluous wives with a fierce accusation of the black arts.

"I think of my own mother. Her worst behavior, when seen in certain light, was ill-judged. I suppose some who accused her of witchcraft did so in good faith. I saw as a child no small amount of violence, often in her presence. At her instigation. And, too, men fell in love with her with great frequency. Enchantments can take many forms. None of this means she was a witch."

Thatcher slowly moved his elephant into the killing field and tentatively removed his hand, to warn the king to pay better attention. The monkey sat on the king's shoulder. James licked his fingers again and pushed his own elephant recklessly far across the board. "She killed my father, you know."

The doctor chose to take a janissary rather than a war chariot with his elephant. He feigned disappointment and self-reproach when the king, with moistened fingers, took vengeance on the offending piece. Thatcher was not particularly skilled at this performance of frustration, and he often forgot to perform it altogether. Worse, he sometimes forgot to make errors on James's behalf. But he also realized that self-sabotage often wasn't even necessary, because he no longer played the game as well as he had as a younger man. The board was more difficult to comprehend as a whole, as a frame for changing shapes. He knew he was losing the ability to see patterns, to see how the board would appear after decisions still to come.

When, after Thatcher's next move, the king made no answer, Thatcher looked up from the board. James was staring off at nothing, the monkey touching his ear. The king stood with a suddenness that startled Thatcher, a chess piece in one hand and wine in the other. The red wine splashed onto his jeweled fingers and his jacket and the board. The monkey leapt to a side table. "This king—I was but a babe and not birthed yet, still inside Queen Mary's womb. They had a blade to her swollen belly, with me just an inch or two from the cutting edge. You see, my father murdered her secretary, from jealousy. In anger, another man threatened to murder my mother, to lead a Protestant rebellion against her, as she was a Catholic. I heard it all, you see. I heard her find the words to escape our perilous situation. She charmed them all, my father first, won him back to her and to the Mother Church of Rome. I was jostled some, my leg injured, as you see it now. But I will never forget the power she had over them, her skill with words and tone of voice. A species of enchantment, but not witchcraft, I would insist to this day."

Dr. Thatcher sat still and silent, watching this recollection of events the king could at best have heard, not seen. He wondered if the king had to reenact these events with some regularity in order to not forget them or to draw from them some lesson, or if he was compelled to do so, gripped by the past and the events of his mother's life and death. The monkey, in all this tumult, voided his bladder onto the floor. James paid it no mind, spoke of witchcraft and his parents' violent and wavering Christianity.

"Of course, some might well argue that only a practitioner of witchcraft could have had such power. Or managed my father's murder not long after. I think," he said, calming a little, "that there are cases where simple human eloquence and charm is no witchcraft." The king, having again tried his mother and found her innocent, returned to his seat, with no sign of embarrassment at his agitation, no trouble at the monkey's filth. He licked the wine from his fingers. He dabbed at the chessboard with the cuff of his shirt and sucked the drops from the fabric, placed the piece he had held all this time back on the board without much thought to the game, on a space selected at random. "But, all this granted, one must seize upon the cases of unquestionable malevolence, the examples of Satan worship and unnatural crimes, of sacrilege and heresy. This is a matter of justice and safety, which it is my duty to administer. In London in equal measure. I will be the hammer of witchcraft there as I have been here."

"Your mother was Catholic, and your father, too, Majesty?"

"They were. It was the Mother Church, you see. And now, well, answer me this, Matthew the Turk."

"Majesty?"

"Do you think it wrong to hang witches by the neck until they are dead?"

"I am not expert in such questions, but if they might be corrected rather than punished, then I suppose hanging might be—"

"Yes! Exactly!" The king clapped his hands, and his monkey leapt into his arms, presented his little face to be kissed, and the king complied. "It is a gentle and loving thing, if they can be corrected, for the women to be hanged instead. It shows our mercy and approves their penitence, their *corrected* souls. Well said, Doctor. But for the other, unrepentant, incorrigible woman-devils, the fire."

Eⱼ ARLY ON AN April morning, Matthew Thatcher was summoned to the king's apartments. It was the first time he had received such an invitation, and he feared a medical disaster had arrived. He brought what medicaments he thought he might require but found, upon arriving, that Dr. Craig was already installed and treating nothing more urgent than a boil on the king's neck; Thatcher had been fetched only for conversation and chess while the surgery was carried on, with a dozen grooms scurrying pointlessly about.

Craig grunted with disgust at Thatcher's arrival and returned to peering at the globe sprouted just above the royal shoulder. The king's Spanish monkey sat in a chair, selecting from a silver plate of radishes. Dr. Craig proclaimed, "I will, with your permission, Majesty, now touch the inflamed flesh."

"That's why you're here, man! Don't be delicate about it. I'm not a lady."

"Of course not, Maj—"

"God of heaven! What are you doing to me?" James shrieked, and all in one instant the king stood, Craig stopped pressing upon the offending lump, a halberd-wielding guard burst into the chamber, and the king waved him away, embarrassed at the clamor he'd made. The monkey hurled its dish at Dr. Craig. The king muttered, "I mean to say—"

"I humbly apologize, my liege."

"I forgive you. I was thinking of the suffering of Jesus. Please. Proceed. Tell me, Matthew the Turk," said the king, exhaling slowly and gathering himself, "the source of your wisdom. Whence your natural knowledge and your scholarship of nature's illnesses?" Over the king's shoulder, Craig rolled his eyes at his pagan rival.

Thatcher finished laying the table for chess and was unsurprised by the king, licking his fingers, moving his accustomed opening pawn. "From teachers, from when I was a boy. From texts, both ancient and modern, of my people, of the Greeks and the Jews, who excelled in finding the secrets that God has hidden among plants and trees and within our bodies. From my own observations of health and disease. From my private studies of formulating salves from such herbs as I have witnessed animals consume when hurt, for their dumb wisdom is a blessing of the Almighty to instruct us."

"There now! At the end, at last, you speak of the Almighty. For it is He, first and last, who has endowed you with such wisdom as you possess."

"I do not debate this for an instant."

"For He has granted me similarly a power to heal men of certain ailments. Not so broad a knowledge of the humors as you possess"— Thatcher bowed his head low in thanks to the king's generous humility—"but still a power to heal. The scrofula. Can you heal it?"

"There are poultices I have attempted. Sometimes we cut away the vile areas. The removal of them in some cases discourages their continued growth. But it is a difficult malady."

"Well, I am able to cure it simply by touching the afflicted. Because I am God's anointed." He seemed to believe this, thought Thatcher. Or was it the same man who presented an implausibly weak chess game: Was he again asking Thatcher if he intended to be a flatterer, a man of no practical use to the King of Scotland? Thatcher looked at the doctor standing behind the seated king, but Craig peered solely and intently at the boil, his lips curling in worry.

"Have you cured many of their suffering, Majesty?"

"Not yet. I have never performed the act. It is done by sovereigns of England and France. We have never trucked with it in Scotland. It's perhaps a bit . . . popish." The king licked his fingers and moved his pieces farther into danger, from which Thatcher could not for much longer convincingly spare him. The king examined Thatcher with interest and asked again about which herbs best inhibit scrofula, the king's evil, then asked, replacing a janissary he had lifted and held but not moved, "D'ye think it too Catholic? It smacks of Romish superstition, no? To stand in church and place a hand upon the afflicted, make the sign of the cross over him, call down God's strength, then give the poor wretch a coin with an angel's image on it?"

"I do not claim to be any sort of theologian, Majesty. Surely Mr. Spottiswoode—"

"But you, somewhat uniquely in my experience, came to the faith by choice. To be a Protestant. Your soul is surely of the elect."

"If the kings and queens of England have performed the act, Majesty . . . But are miracles not viewed with suspicion, or is it not a miracle? I don't know. . . . Do they succeed? Truly? Men are truly healed by the royal touch?"

James's words were the words of provoked and angry certainty: "If the sovereign is chosen by God and sits in that throne by God's election, then, yes, Dr. Thatcher, men are truly and unquestionably healed by the royal touch." But then he hesitated. "Or they were, when there was no question as to the authority of the Mother Church or of its corruptions. . . ." Thatcher saw the quiver of uncertainty cross the unguarded royal face. One might well worry, upon achieving a second kingdom where one had never set foot, that sick men might leave such a ceremony exactly as afflicted as when they arrived. And so perhaps it was better never to try at all.

James wavered, even as he petulantly claimed his magic power. Perhaps it was due to this, or to his injured leg, his sloppiness, his love for the French boy who was hated by the rest of the court, or because he was wed to a queen who was scarcely present from day to day—whatever the reason, Thatcher pitied this young king and then liked him. It was never a question he would have asked himself in London or Constantinople—*liked or not liked?*—as if he *liked* a cloud or would trust this lion more than that lion. But this was a young man of uncertainties and unconvincingly declared certainties. That struck Thatcher with force, watching Craig lance and drain the king's shoulder into a silver basin: Leveret had sent him here to scrape until he found the king's hidden certainty, but James was uncertain of nearly everything, including his own hidden depths, strengths, convictions. He might in all honesty declare that he was a Catholic, and that statement would lead to whatever war Leveret feared, but the very next moment that same king might realize he felt no such Catholic certainty at all.

Thatcher recalled the feeling he often had in Ismail's company of wanting to donate his strength to someone younger and weaker, who needed it, to that fat little boy in a courtyard of stones with fig upon his face, figs taken without permission while Saruca pretended to be angry about it, or to this young nervous king with blood pouring down his shoulder from where Craig had cut with the competence of a butcher's boy on his first day at work.

Thatcher said, "Your Majesty, it seems to my ignorant mind that if the kings of England have performed the act successfully since the time that England left the Catholic Church, then the cure is proven not to be too Catholic a rite, since God continues to show His mercy and election of the monarch by curing men of scrofula."

As grooms dipped cloths in warm water to wash the royal shoulders, the king looked across the board and considered the older man, this physician who was not asked to practice any physic but who understood Christian thought so well.

"But, whatever its nature, is Your Majesty concerned that he not be seen in a rite that is deemed too Catholic?" attempted the clumsy spy.

"Answer me this, Dr. Thatcher. If you learned your skill from when you were a boy and in the land of the Turks, before you accepted Jesus Christ, why did the Almighty endow you with such wisdom? For you held yourself away from Him then, above Him in sinful pagan refusal."

The king's voice had grown slightly angry. He may have been imagining a young infidel, impudent in his hatred of a Christian God, or he was doubting that Thatcher was truly changed by his christening. Or he was naturally annoyed by what was being done to his own anointed flesh. Thatcher tried to provoke some Clarity for Leveret, prod the ambiguous monarch to take a half step toward London or Rome: "I would not presume to understand why God might allow such things. Perhaps He knew that I would grow to the light? Or He allows healing arts even among those who deny Him, so that His mercy might be manifest to them. Perhaps the suffering of any of His creation pains Him, even if that creation is in error. As so many who claim to love Him are in error."

The king smiled at the physician's flowerings of thought, and Clarity was perhaps only one simple question away, whatever that question was. . . . James kept his eye on Thatcher as Craig furiously daubed the ever-pouring royal blood, trying to hide his own confusion. "No. You, Dr. Thatcher, were *chosen* by Him for special knowledge."

"I was born and bred in a land where all of us—king, priests, mothers, and fathers—credit a holy book and holy word that you rightly call pagan. I did err in my ways, but from no evil heart. And so I believe God was willing to bless me with some glimmer of light, which to my good fortune has brought me to your realm and to Your Majesty." From over the royal shoulder, Craig looked at Thatcher with open worry, either asking for help in stanching the giant slash or concerned that Thatcher would say aloud the obvious: Craig had made a massacre of a simple boil-lancing.

"If Your Majesty believes that I am making some error in my understanding of Jesus, I am still a child, though I vastly outnumber Your Majesty's years, for it was but a few years ago that I was led to the Bible and enlightenment. . . . If you think I should be taught further by Mr. Spottiswoode, or . . ."

The king enjoyed some private amusement. "No, in truth, I would not change your soul or even gaze upon it. It is yours. I simply wonder why God rewarded you when you still scorned Him."

"It is a mystery, my king. We did not know. And that to me is a great wonder. For those who fall into error, they may not know they have strayed. Let us say, for I have heard it said in England, that the Spaniard or the pope is in error, damnably. But do they perhaps not realize it any more than I or my parents knew of our errors when I was a boy in Constantinople?"

"The pope's legate and the Spanish ambassador are here in court. Shall we ask them if they believe themselves to be in error? Stand behind me when we inquire."

But the king had lost interest in the conversation and snapped at Dr. Craig, "Are you finished yet with your intrusions into the royal body, sir? Have you left me any blood at all?"

13

NINE DAYS LATER, the king's monkey died after a brief and explosive illness, and Dr. Thatcher was called in to examine the poor beast, still wearing one of its several fine velvet jackets, though its matching cap had slipped onto the table upon which it had been laid. "I don't know what you hope that I might do," admitted the doctor quietly. "The creature is already dead."

The primate of Scotland, Spottiswoode, nodded, nervous, and drew one long bony hand through his rain-cloud-gray hair and the other across his mouth. The reverend churchman faced the discomfort of his coming task: "The king will be saddened. He will surely ask the reason for the animal's death. It was young, I am led to understand. His Majesty may look to blame the interference of dark practice for his untimely loss. If his enemies were able to strike so close to the royal body from a distance, then we would require defenses. And culprits, I suppose." The thought seemed to exhaust him. "If, on the other hand, it was a matter of natural distemper, which you, Dr. Thatcher, might explain as a tragic but unavoidable and commoner death, then we might be calmer for the king's safety. Your assessment of the cause of its demise would be most helpful. Dr. Craig confessed his ignorance. A natural explanation, if you can attest to one, would be most pacifying."

"I wish I had been summoned when the animal was first ill. I might have . . ." But no one said anything in reply, and Thatcher didn't quite know what he might have done.

Thatcher lifted the monkey. It was beginning to stiffen; its head and limbs drifted slightly downward from his hands, but slowly, as though through thick liquid. It weighed eight or ten pounds. "How much time passed, please, between its first symptoms and its decease?" Some grooms and page boys consulted before an answer could be found, though none seemed certain of it. "And when, precisely, did it first show signs of illness?" Thatcher calculated the weights, times, intervals. It seemed reasonable to ask, "What was its usual diet?"

Spottiswoode's impatience burned through his reserve. "Damn your hemming and hawing, Turk. Is it plague? Or an assassin's poison? Or is it witchcraft after all?"

"Surely those would not reassure you or the king," said the doctor quietly. "I think it best and most accurate to say that the king's companion suffered from a fever brought about by a dishevelment of the kidneys."

Spottiswoode nodded slowly, encouraging them both.

"Further, I would say that simian fevers of this sort are not contagious to humans."

Spottiswoode nearly smiled at this extra bit of good news.

"And, if it soothes the king's mind, we might also say that his pet did not suffer in his expiry. Unless His Majesty witnessed otherwise?"

At this there was a great satisfaction and gratitude to the doctor for his wisdom.

Thatcher then spent most of that afternoon in his working room, performing various calculations, some of which troubled him in their results, while others alarmed him in their incompleteness. The information he lacked weighed on him, as though an absence could press more heavily than a presence.

Those same calculations were examined and hurriedly copied,

while Thatcher was playing chess with the king, by a familiar page in the pay of the Spanish ambassador, but neither the page nor the ambassador could make sense of the scratched figures and letters. Even the copy sent to Madrid left the most acute cryptographic minds of the Spanish court unable to draw conclusions as to the Turk's intentions.

14

THATCHER WIPED CLEAN the chess pieces, indirectly licked so many times now by the King of Scotland. He laid them back into their case and washed his hands in a silver bowl with a crucifix etched into its deepest point. It had been in his room since his arrival. No one remarked upon it. Evidence of the king's Catholicism or merely his tolerance of the queen's? Or of the court's disdainful Protestantism, since this popish dish was left to a formerly Mahometan doctor to use to wash his hands in a room with three dead rabbits on the table?

"Mahmoud Ezzedine," says the man in his dream that night, after Thatcher had discarded the rabbits in the fields and fought back his own tidal nausea with a vial of white liquid. "Mahmoud Ezzedine," says the man, and it is himself, only far younger. He bows to the dreamer, young Ezzedine greeting old Thatcher. He is scarcely thirty-five, the age of the King of Scots. His hair is black and his muscles lean, his beard thick. Dreaming Thatcher tries to extend his hand to touch the young man's face. He is in Beirut, younger still, and a moment later older and back in Constantinople, his wife and son beside him. His mind is strong—Thatcher can see that from where he floats, or sits, high above the road on which Ezzedine walks the short distance from his home to the Sublime Porte. They want for nothing, his wife and son. Thatcher, awake, blinks in the

cold Scots night: They wanted for nothing because young Dr. Ezzedine could cure men of many ailments, and the sultan was pleased
to allow him to do so in the most wealthy and wondrous of places.

Thatcher sleeps again, and young Dr. Ezzedine has waited for
him, welcoming the dreamer back to Constantinople. The young
man is ambitious for his own glory, yes, and Allah's. And he will live
here forever, even if the man whom he hosts tonight will die in
Scotland. Dr. Ezzedine explains to Dr. Thatcher that his path will
rise in seniority among the sultan's physicians as he grows wiser and
wiser, never older, only infinitely swelling with more and more
wisdom of ointments and cures and anatomy and how men might
be restored. "All of this is going to happen, Dr. Thatcher," he says
to the older man, who struggles to stand in the heat of Constantinople. "Because I serve God and this greatest of all men. And now
the sultan has asked that I stay the night within the walls, to be sure
the young prince grows no more fevered in the darkest hours."

"You will succeed. I remember," says Dr. Thatcher, now forced
to sit in the shade of a yellow wall, unable to walk, his legs molten.
"You will save the prince, and then, after, the sultan himself—not a
messenger—*the sultan himself* will come to thank you and to say he
loves you."

The prince opens his little eyes in the darkest hours of the night,
slow to focus in his ebbing fevers, and he says to Dr. Thatcher, "You
are kind."

Ezzedine was once that boy's age, sleeping outside on the sand
alongside the Middle Sea in the Levant, far from his future glory.
Thatcher kicks that sleeping boy on the beach, kicks himself over
and over again, but he will not wake, just rolls in the sand, snoring
contentedly. Thatcher shouts at his younger sleeping self, "The
courtier, the chief of offices, the eunuch's voice, are not the sultan's
will. If one calls you and says you must serve the sultan's ambassador upon a ship to England, do not listen." But the boy refuses to
wake, intoxicating sleep too delicious to the young: *Just a few more
minutes, please.*

And sleep is too dry and exhausting and elusive to the old; he is nearly awake now: "You will be back among us, honored and loved by the sultan even more, in a single year, even less. We shall summon you," says the ambassador to Dr. Ezzedine, unaware or uninterested that Ezzedine would convert and place himself beyond honor, reassuring the unhappy doctor as the oars of the waiting ship slapped the water in unison with the sails thundered by the wind at Southampton.

Dr. Thatcher woke completely to the thunder, to the pounding door. The furs had all fallen from his pallet. The gray light of Scotland promised nothing. He knew precisely what the pounding signified: Clarity. He was prepared to do what was required.

But he was wrong. Instead, the boy in velvet clothes stood with his candle before Thatcher's dry eyes and said, "Quickly. She needs you this moment."

"She? Who?" Thatcher leaned against the door as vertigo spun him.

"The queen."

"But I am the king's to command." He knew it was foolish as soon as he spoke, having done nothing at the king's command but play chess, but his thoughts had rehearsed for so long how he would perform in bedridden James's presence on a night or morning like this, how he would cunningly plumb the depths of the royal soul until he struck doctrinal bedrock.

The page had heard of Thatcher's past and thought himself above the task of speaking to Ishmaelites. "Must you have it all explained? The king commands the queen. The queen commands you. And she commands me. And so I . . ." He considered "command" but left it unsaid. ". . . so I must bring you. Can you not simply do as you are told?" The boy turned his eyes skyward in exasperation, looking for Jesus to step in here and deal with this idiocy.

So Dr. Thatcher followed a Scottish child down multiplying halls and up wooden stairs to other halls lit only by small windows at their distant far ends and to a closed door halfway down yet another unlit corridor. He had never been in this part of the castle and suspected he would not be able to find his way back to his own room if left alone.

A lady in night dress waited outside the closed door with a single candle, and the page, his distasteful duty done, lifted his hands, as if to show the woman they were both clean and empty. He turned away to find some uncontaminated place, leaving Thatcher to her care.

"Thank you," said the woman. She had been weeping. "Thank you for coming. Dr. Craig refused. But I had heard you spoken of, and the queen gave me leave. She is suffering, though does not complain of it terribly much."

"The queen? Here?"

She didn't answer but opened the door and led him into a room low-ceilinged and dark, buttressed by slanted wooden beams that threatened the shins and head. The room was bare except for five straw pallets upon the floor; only one was occupied. The stench reached Thatcher before he saw her—another woman, around the same age as the lady who led him in, five and thirty, though it was difficult for Thatcher to judge precisely. He heard the door close behind him, and with obvious effort the suffering woman opened her eyes and turned her head slowly to look up at him: "Are you the magician?"

He sat beside her on her mat. There was a water jug on the floor beside her. He brought it to her broken and bloodied lips, the rest of her unmoving beneath a thin blanket. Her face shook from fever, her loose skin trembling, waves across a pool. The liquid fell from her unclosing and unclosable lips, and he dried her chin.

"I am not a magician." She seemed—as much as her face could express anything besides pain—disappointed, and he hurried to add, "I practice physic, knowledge any man might honorably gain from nature."

"Will you heal me?"

"I do not yet know what hurts you. What is your name?"

"Margaret. Why do you speak like that? Are you Spanish?"

"No, I have come from England, gentle Margaret."

"I am English, too."

"Ah. Well, a country sister, then. Please show me what is hurting you, Margaret. My name is Matthew."

She drew down the stained blanket and untied a string at her throat, pulled down the shirt that covered her breast. She showed no modesty or shame, only the same vibrating pain in every small movement. What remained of her beneath the shirt was wretched, torn, the source of the smell that now, unrestrained by blanket and clothing, rushed at Matthew. The skin could no longer close over the disease. In places the skin broke as an overstretched drum, as if wet and dried and heated and dried and wet and dried again in the full sun. Yet he leaned over her discoloring flesh, inhaled the foul smell deeply to distinguish the disease within it, a pox or cancer he had smelled before, eating away at the poor creature. He did this twice more until he found the smell he had suspected lurked. "Do you suffer terribly, Margaret?"

"Yes. I would weep, but I cannot."

"I see that. Your friend has been weeping for you, I think. Do you have many friends here?" He drew her shirt back up, tied it for her, drew the blanket back across her broken body. She even smiled a bit to answer him. "Are you making no water?" She shook her head once. "For how long?"

Behind him, the woman who had greeted him began again to cry softly. She had only now heard that her friend could not cry for herself.

Margaret said, "Do you promise to heal me?"

"I promise to try."

"Will I die?"

"That is for God, not me or you, to know," he said, though he had smelled God's unwavering answer.

"Are you a Jew?" she asked.

"Good heavens, no. Of course not. Why would you ask me this?"

Her gaze drifted away, almost unwillingly, but her will had little force.

"Have you family who may fetch you home, Margaret?"

"No."

He smoothed her hair and left his hand on her brow, caressed her, and her head turned to him, to absorb the touch.

"I can prepare some salves and a drink that will lessen your sufferings. I will return with them in only a very little time, Margaret. But you must try to drink more and to make water. It will help you feel better."

He stood in the corridor with the crying woman, who had waited for him, and asked her name: Annis.

"Annis, she is suffering terribly and will suffer more before the end."

"The end? Certainly?"

He nodded and took one of Annis's hands. "She is not contagious. It is not plague but cancer. The others who sleep here—are you one? You are. You are the bravest and stayed with her when the others left. But none of you is in danger."

Annis squeezed his hand and nodded, ashamed of the others and of herself. "She makes such terrible noises. And the smell. The rest found other places to sleep."

"I quite understand. But you are different. You will sit with her and give her peace until I return. I will give her something to help her sleep, but the end is near."

She nodded and wiped her eyes. He asked how he could find his chamber again, but something else troubled her: "If Margaret is certainly dying, she need confess her sins to a priest."

"Confess? Is she a Catholic, then?"

Annis nodded and reentered the room, closed the door behind her. Thatcher, trying to recall the path by which he had come, took a few steps in one direction, then went the other way, picturing on which side of the corridor Annis had been waiting when he arrived. His heart beat hard, and he was soon out of breath, though he had not done anything yet, and the woman's condition was certainly not the most fearful illness he had ever seen.

He faced at the end of the hall another of the wretched narrow windows, designed to allow only the minimal light and air for survival in a siege. He was debating which way to turn when the insolent page reappeared. "The queen wishes you wait upon her now."

"I must bring medicines to the girl. I have promised her relief at once."

The boy laughed at the Moor: "Meg will wait. The queen now."

"She is suffering. Margaret is suffering."

"Yes, yes, come along now, can't you?"

And so Thatcher was led down more endless corridors, which grew more well candled as he went, and then was bid to wait in a room bright with sconce and fire. He could not return to his room to fetch the one vial that would soothe Margaret in her pain. Instead, he stood and then sat in a small room with a cushioned bench and a tapestry of two unicorns, until a door opened, and some other page passed through, from one door to another, with no word nor even glance for Thatcher. And then the door opened again, and he was bid to follow another lady.

"I thank you for your care of our servant," said Queen Anna, when Thatcher was at last allowed to cross into her presence. Two other men, whom Thatcher had seen in court but never known by name, stood in the corner, and a guard lingered at the side, both alert and bored at once. "You are, I understand, from distant countries, as I am, Dr. Thatcher?"

"Madame, I was born in the land of the Turks but am now English, as I may hope pleases you and your royal husband."

"A pretty phrase! I am from Denmark and am as Scottish as others may hope me to be."

Dr. Thatcher bowed and waited. Somewhere, Margaret waited for him and his false promise to return. "Do you know, Doctor, that I came here with sixteen Danish ladies to attend me and, as the king slowly judged me more and more Scottish, they were returned to Denmark, one at a time, until, after Sofia left me, they had all gone because I was so perfectly Scottish at last."

"I would never have known that you were not, Majesty."

"But *you,* I believe, would still have several Turkish attendants with you, if you were queen. So, tell me, Doctor, was my little Meg not troubled to be looked upon in her nakedness by the fierce Saracen?"

"She seemed not at all to be frightened by me, Your Majesty. And, as there is no cause for any man or woman to fear me, this seems for the best."

The queen smiled.

"I hope to bring her some small further comfort tonight."

"And you shall. With our thanks and God's love, Doctor." He thought he was being dismissed, but as he began to bow and turn, she added, "Doctor, tell me, please, what do the women wear at my lord Moresby's this season? And you have been in London, before Elizabeth?"

"I have."

"And she? Tell me of her robes, please. Does she really wear one all of gold thread? With cuffs all gold that float though set with pearl?"

"Madame, I am sadly inexpert at remarking the details of clothing, I fear." He knew there were words he was supposed to say, to carve a phrase to exalt this Danish woman's beauty, but the needed words stumbled on their trip, fled from him. "Your dress will be very acceptable among the English."

"We are glad, Doctor." Her disappointment was perceptible.

He bowed for lack of anything else to say or do to prepare her for becoming Queen of England.

"Does our Meg suffer?" she asked.

"She does, Majesty, and I ought to return to her, with your permission."

"Very good. But tell us, please, will she die soon?"

He set himself and told the queen the truth: "I believe she will be called to heaven within a day or two, I am sorry to tell you."

"Then she must have my confessor." She turned to the insolent page for whom Thatcher had developed his first hatred of any creature in Scotland: "Bring Father Foyle to Margaret at once." The page bowed and ran.

As plain as this, the queen's confessor, by name. Father Foyle. The Queen of Scots openly declared her Catholicism, untroubled at all.

"I can be of more service to her, Majesty, if I may return to my rooms and prepare something for her."

"Then go at once. I only wished to thank you myself."

"I am at your service in this and all matters."

But instead, the queen commanded one of the silent men in the corner of the room, as if she had heard nothing Thatcher had said (nor indeed anything she had said to him): "My dear Mr. Nicolson, will you please lead our good and caring doctor to our king? He will be glad for a game of chess with his favorite adversary."

One of the two men Thatcher had recognized bowed to her and then to Thatcher himself. Mr. Nicolson, the man who stood with his hands clasped at his front, who now looked at Thatcher and performed the queen's errand, the man who heard the queen call for her own Catholic priest: This, then, was Queen Elizabeth's representative in the Scottish court, the man expected to report to London on all doings.

Thatcher bowed deeply and stumbled backward. (Even now, these many years later, he still felt he was insulting, almost treasonous, when he did not lower his head all the way to the very ground and touch his privileged lips to the celestial slipper of royalty.)

"Nicolson is not your friend," Leveret had taught again and again. "He's made his choice. If James is King of England, George Nicolson will be his most familiar Englishman. The longer he spends in Scotland, the fewer friends there are at Whitehall reserving a place for him in any other future."

"Dr. Thatcher, please," said George Nicolson, leading him out of the queen's apartments through corridors, past soldiers and ladies, knights and court lizards. "Your repute and past were much discussed here when news of your arrival first reached us."

"I thank you."

"Do you? You misunderstand me."

"Is the king expecting me for chess immediately? I really should return to my chamber and then to the serving woman who is suffer-ing." But Nicolson did not slow his pace. "Is it not—the queen asked for a Catholic priest. Is the king of her mind, then? Do they follow a different law than we do in England?"

"We?" Nicolson stopped walking. He took the edge of Thatch-er's coat, rubbed it between his fingers. They had stopped in the dark between pools of window gray and torch yellow. "We? I thought you, Doctor, were an unrepentant Mahometan who played at being English, and now you take deep interest in matters of Christian faith?" Nicolson was smiling, nearly laughing. "The queen is Catholic. The king tolerates her errors. This is no secret." Nicolson held Thatcher's collar tight now.

He leaned close to the smaller man's ear and hissed: "Go do what-ever you're here to do and get on with it, do you hear me? You're not here for the serving girls."

15

"Has Father Foyle come? The queen sent him herself."
"He came."

"And you have spoken to God? You feel that all is right now?"
"Yes."

"Margaret, I am so glad. Will you drink this? It will help you sleep."

"Please sit with me," Margaret said, almost inaudible. Annis sat in a chair by the door.

"Of course I will," said Matthew Thatcher. "As long as you like."

He sat on her pallet. He held her head on his lap. He lifted her head slightly, just enough to pour the greenish liquid between her lips and to push back into her the drops that spilled over. "I know that you hurt. I'm so sorry for you, Margaret. You are a good and lovely woman. You do not deserve this suffering. But you are not alone. God in His heaven loves you, and your queen loves you, and your friend Annis here loves you."

In the fields by King Arthur's mountain he had held snared rabbits in his lap, trying and failing, trying again. He felt their hearts trilling like rolling drums beneath the soft fur as they licked one greenish drop at a time from his fingers. Into late-afternoon cold he sat as heartbeats slowed, slowed, and the stones pressed into his fleshless calves and aching thighs. One drop more and the rabbit slept, or nearly so, under Thatcher's hands. It rained, and the wind blew the cold water into Thatcher's eyes and cheeks and across the rabbit's resistant fur. It spattered the nearly hairless skin inside the rabbit's ear and the backs of Thatcher's hands, and still the beast slept, its heart beating far more slowly than Thatcher's own, as other rabbits watched from shelter their colleague's mysterious fate.

Watching, too, was the second young woman who had so admired Thatcher's bag and led him to the dwarf Gideon. She walked out to him in the field, unnoticed, picking at something on the ground as she went, gathering ghostly wildflowers for the benefit of any watchers farther down the line of observation. The rain stopped. The sun did not appear, but the day lightened.

"Hello," she said, and he did not look up. The other vial now— cloudy-white drops counted out one at a time, aloud so he would not forget, "One . . . two . . . three," until the rabbit, its heart vibrating, was kicking so hard to escape the snare and the doctor's grasp that Thatcher could hardly restrain it and still keep his two little vials upright.

The rabbit sprinted off, then stumbled over, dead. A moment later it was up again and zagging for the cover of distant trees and the waiting, bobbing heads of its troop. Thatcher stood to face her.

"What has he said?" she asked.

"Very little about our question. He said that Scotland has more types of horses than one might imagine."

"This is interesting, though not part of your task."

"He asked me to describe Mahometan paradise."

"As if it were a real place? Or as your people imagined it?"

"Or as a way of misunderstanding the True Church?"

"Which is what to him?"

"I don't know yet. I am trying."

"Is all this"—she waved at the puzzled rabbits, the heath, the sky, the rain-drenched old man in front of her—"bringing us closer to what Mr. Leveret wants?"

"Yes. As I was instructed. But I am not ready yet."

"Then do it faster, or there will be an end." She said it sweetly, even as she turned to leave him. "Mr. Leveret says there is no more time to wait." She turned back: "And he told me to tell you something else. He's had a letter. Saruca and her boy are well."

As THE SUN rose, bright for once in Edinburgh, it made itself visible in Margaret and Annis's chamber, faintly and late. Annis slept on a pallet. Thatcher held the dead woman's head in his lap, felt the last of her heartbeats, and waited for her friend to waken, though he would not rouse her.

16

THE LOUDEST SOUND, after the hooves on the stones, was not the men shouting for Dr. Craig, nor the rattle of the chains and the creak of the gate rising, but the strange howling. The little dog in the king's saddlebag was raising an alarm and demanding immediate help as forcefully as any of the terrified men around him, each imagining the plague in their midst, or a country clumsily led by the king's infant son and foreign wife. The horror was dawning that everyone's life and peace might now depend upon Dr. Craig.

As James was lowered from his horse by four men, the dog leapt from his high perch and landed, stumbling, on the stones below. He at once rolled to his feet and began barking at the men carrying his master, plainly shouting commands. He was restrained by a kennel-boy with great difficulty as the king was lofted inside the castle, beyond his view but not his ability to smell. Of the few words James said between saddle and door, three distinctly were, "Hush, Pablo, soft." Later that night, Pablo (named by the king himself for a young and handsome Catholic priest who had been in the company of the Spanish embassy several years earlier, selected for that post for precisely his youth and attractiveness) attempted to escape from the kennel so persistently that the master of the hounds finally relented to the dog's unshakable demands and asked a page to lead him to the king's chambers. The dog had never been allowed inside the castle before, but he pulled at his lead to the point of choking himself and, by scent, led his tripping attendant to the royal apartments without making a single wrong turn.

17

THE SOUND OF running, the pounding on the doors, and somewhere a barking dog. From his window, Thatcher had seen the king carried into the castle, and he knew even from this high angle what symptoms had begun. Thatcher then sat, expectant, in an annex outside the royal apartments, waiting to be called, until he slowly realized they were not going to call him. He had never been viewed as a royal physician—or as anything more than a chess player and mortician of monkeys—despite Belloc's certainty that his man, conceived of on a London stage nine months before, would have wriggled himself into a position of medical trust.

Twice Thatcher sent word by a page, offering his prayers that his wisdom could be of use to His Majesty. The first message was received by Dr. Craig himself, who, still early in his inevitable failure, cheerfully scoffed at the impudence and turned the page back with a vicious retort. The second message, sent several hours later, triggered by Thatcher's internal calculations as to the illness's likely progression and by the sight of the troubled expression on a groom of the chamber as he hurried past, was delivered to Queen Anna. At this stage in the king's illness, she was kneeling at his bedside and had called Father Foyle to join her in prayerful vigil there. This time the page found a slightly more sympathetic ear. The queen could see that Craig was achieving nothing and growing more concerned for the king's (and his own) future, but she also recalled that Thatcher's last patient had died not long after he had begun caring for her. The queen did not blame the Turk for this, but she did feel a certain hesitancy or premonition that taking the same step twice would lead another affected party to the same destination. She asked Dr. Craig if another physician would be of use to him, and when he, unhappily but adamantly, replied that he needed no Turkish wizard's interference, she felt it for the best to send her loving rejection of Thatcher's second offer.

And so Dr. Thatcher, certain of what was happening in the king's apartments, paced, unsure what to do, then retreated to his chamber, unsure what to do, and sat on his bed, unsure what to do, until he fell into a thin and bristling sleep.

The sound of running, the pounding on doors, the distant then close then distant barking of a dog. Each time Thatcher woke, it was to the shocking certainty—new and piercing each time—that he had made errors of dosage or application, that someone else would touch the king's chess pieces, that he had not wiped them off properly or cleaned his own hands. He fell back into dreams indistinguishable from waking anxieties.

And then George Nicolson was at his door, speaking to him even as Thatcher was finding his uncertain and panting way back to wakefulness. Nicolson closed the door behind him and spoke with quiet urgency: "King James is taken quite ill, as you know. No one has called for you. In fact, they seem ready to let Craig fumble him into his royal grave. But I have come here to find you. Because I have great confidence in your special abilities. And I think they are necessary now or we will be too late. Your abilities in particular, Doctor."

Thatcher nodded and attempted to say what any healer free of guilt or fear would: "I hope I am able to be of help. To, to . . . to him."

Nicolson tilted his head and peered closely at Thatcher. "Do you know where you are, Doctor?" he asked.

"What? Yes, of course I do," said Thatcher, holding the door's frame to balance himself.

The English diplomat led Thatcher upstairs, through halls and, surprisingly, past the annex that had been his previous waiting room. The king had been moved to a different bed in another of his private chambers. The filth and excretions of the royal body had overwhelmed anyone's ability to keep the previous room clean enough.

Reverend Spottiswoode, grooms, gentlemen, valets and attendants, a few men-at-arms, Queen Anna and two ladies, Father Foyle, and Dr. Craig all stood about this smaller bedroom, unsure what to do or how best to present themselves. Pablo, the small dog, quiet now, sat on a bench near the bed, keeping an eye on all that passed. At Nicolson and Thatcher's arrival, Craig, damp and on the verge of panic, still moved to the door to prevent the insult of a Turkish invasion. Nicolson—taller, broader, and with more energy—simply pushed the doctor aside and led Thatcher in by the hand, delivering the physician to his patient's bedside. "You will have whatever you need. Please begin at once."

Nicolson then turned to the rest of the room and announced with authority, "Please leave the king and his physician alone. Your Majesty," he said to the queen in a quieter tone, "the doctor will require silence and solitude for his examination." Nicolson began the complex diplomatic and logistical process of moving resistant or obedient participants out of the closet through each of three available doors, sorting them according to his own methods.

As bystanders parted and yielded to Nicolson's command, Thatcher was able to see his victim-patient. The king was weakened almost to immobility, and at the sight of James's exhaustion and wretched misery—shaking despite blankets, filthy despite cleanings, gasping to speak—Thatcher felt misery of his own. The parched tip of the royal tongue shot out and about in search of moisture, and flecks of white appeared on his cracking lips, strings of something thicker than saliva beginning the work of suturing shut his mouth. "Your Majesty," Thatcher said.

He had to lean close to hear the king faintly reply, *"Shah mat."*

The young man's suffering in the emptying room, the pathos of the little dog watching in possessive worry, a few months of strange friendship between the Turkish convert and the Scottish king, and now these few words in Persian: All of this affected Thatcher, and he turned at once to Nicolson, who was nearly shoving the last resisters out the doors. Thatcher was desperate to end the young king's pain. "There is, I think, in my room, something I can try, some medicament, herbs. . . ."

The hard disappointment in Nicolson's face was unmistakable. "That's backward, man! Even I know that. You must make a certain diagnosis before choosing your treatment, Doctor," said the diplomat, nearly shouting the words: "Your certain diagnosis, sir."

"I do not know what to do," stammered Thatcher.

At that, Nicolson, who had now moved nearly everyone into one of the three neighboring rooms, turned and faced both king and doctor. "I am very sorry to ask, but, without some great wisdom, will the king die?"

"Certainly not," stammered damp Dr. Craig, still lingering, and Nicolson pushed him and his serving boy out of the room at once.

The king, with effort, moved his eyes to Thatcher. "Do I die, Turk?"

"Majesty, I fear . . . I fear . . ."

"Say it," commanded Nicolson.

"I fear it is your time," said Thatcher.

"Yes," said the king. "I feel it in my blood."

With that, Nicolson closed the doors to two of the three connecting rooms. "Dr. Thatcher. Look at me. Look at me, sir. Take a breath. Good. Now: Make a certain diagnosis, and act accordingly and swiftly to aid him as you see best. Can you do this?"

Thatcher nodded slightly, and Nicolson closed the third door after himself as he backed out, leaving only Thatcher, James, and the profoundly attentive dog. Nicolson had been thorough; it was the first time Thatcher had ever been completely unattended in the king's company.

"I am in your hands, Matthew," said the king, exhausting himself to make his words kind, as if by an instinct, beneath the trained skill of being kingly, to express courtesy when vulnerable.

"And God's, Majesty."

The king made the same noises that many other men make when they ail but cannot separate their lips and all sound is trapped in the throat and far behind the tongue. The king, Matthew Thatcher knew, had some few hours still to live in suffering before he met his Creator. He was stronger than a rabbit, larger than a monkey, healthier than poor cancerous Margaret. But time's impatience was clear as Thatcher counted the king's pulses, examined his tongue, smelled his breath, pressed an ear to the faint and slowing beats of the man's heart.

James murmured again, *"Shah mat."*

"My king." Thatcher felt his own voice thick and slow, his limbs delayed in their motions, as in a dream when motion requires more thought and strength than can be mustered.

"What says . . . a Mahometan . . . when death is near?"

"What matters that? You are no Turk but a king of Christendom."

"Does he confess to a holy man? Would the sultan?"

Thatcher thought of all the men and women and children he had seen die, the stoic, the frightened, the miserable, the mourning, the angry, the laughing. "No, King. There would be no priests there. Allah reads the righteous man's heart without any priest between." And finally, with that, Matthew Thatcher remembered and spoke the correct words: "Make peace, Majesty, howsoever you are moved by God to communicate to Him."

"Am I to die? Is it certain?"

"Yes. It is certain."

"I am ready."

"Do you wish me to fetch anyone?"

"No. Alone with God, we are naked. No priest. God has known my heart from birth. Faith, alone. By faith alone are . . . we saved. I am ready."

Matthew Thatcher held the hand of James Stuart, felt his weak grip fight to squeeze, and in that squeeze to ask for something, perhaps not life but a recognition that he deserved something. The king's eyes were closing, and the doctor cried out for help.

At once George Nicolson was back through the center door, closing it behind him. "Are you clear in your diagnosis?"

"Yes."

"With certainty?" Nicolson was nearly shouting now.

"Yes."

"Then what will you do now?"

"I have something in my workroom. I can give him some now and prepare more. It may . . . I don't know, but it may be of some . . ."

"Go now. Go!" Nicolson held open the door that led to the main passage and ordered a page to run the doctor to his rooms and back at once.

THE PAGE HURRIED down the hall with the Turk. Nicolson turned to the king, whose eyes were nearly closed, his breath slow.

Nicolson opened the far-left door and with a bow invited everyone he had shuffled into that closet to return. When they entered, the king woke, slightly, enough to cross himself with terrible effort, as Father Foyle began his final unction. Foyle was both mournful and satisfied at once, and Don Diego, the Spanish ambassador, closed his eyes and nodded slowly. James tried to speak: "I must confess all I have . . . all I have . . ." he stumbled, falling into Latin, and Father Foyle took his hands to hold him steady: "Yes, my son, fear nothing, speak no words but those that are in your heart. Be penitent, let God forgive you for your errors. Beg God in your silent heart that He accept your regret. Your good works upon His earth are plain for all to see."

The king crossed himself again: "God forgive me; God forgive my rashness and violence and lust." The Spanish ambassador knelt beside Father Foyle at the king's bed in a pool of murmuring Latin. The queen sat in the chair to the side, the little dog alert on her lap.

18.

D R. THATCHER RETURNED, sweating with the effort of running
both ways, in gathering up all that he had prepared in his
workroom and the herbs he needed to make more. He would not
leave James's side again until his recovery was certain. He swore it.
He was out of breath himself, and he resented his many years and
the cold of this island sunk permanently into his blood and bones.
Nicolson opened the door and led him within to the nearly empty
chamber: the king and queen, the pocket dog, and none other.

"Majesties." Thatcher bowed with effort.

"Please," said the queen, "use your magic to help our loving
lord." Her foreign accent was plainer than it had been the last time
she spoke to him, as if tonight she hadn't the strength needed to
keep it at bay and make herself Scottish. Thatcher approached the
bed. The king had deteriorated, it seemed, even in the time it had
taken Thatcher to run to his workroom and return. He touched the
king's brow.

James opened his eyes with effort. Despite the shortness of his
breath, the moisture of his face, the weakness of his grasp, the sor-
rowing smallness of his voice, still did James, King of Scots, sixth of
his name, attempt to command. "Is that it? Your Turkish philter?
Give it me." The regal manner was threadbare. His voice was so dry
and feeble that Thatcher feared he would cry in pity.

Thatcher offered to drink it first. "I cannot vouch that I have not made some error of calculation or selected grasses that may not be as potent—the season, the coldness of the soil so far north. Let us examine its effects on a healthy man."

"Enough. I need your courage. Give it me."

Thatcher's hands trembled as he poured all that he had concocted of the white syrup from the wooden bowl into a goblet beside the king's bed, a golden remnant of his wedding day to the Danish princess. The king blinked slowly and, with effort, tilted up his chin and pulled back his lips to receive the stream of liquid. Thatcher held the royal head. He asked for permission, but the king was too weak to grant or deny it.

With his fingertip, the doctor pushed the stray drops into the royal mouth before they could fall into his beard, never to be rescued. The king fell back against his cushion and clung to a single finger of his doctor's hand. He tried to smile: "In Elizabeth's England, poisoners are boiled."

Thatcher shrugged. "In Moorish lands they are blinded."

"Neither here, my friend," said James, though whether Scottish law was more merciful or more vicious was not clear. The king squeezed Matthew Thatcher's finger and fell back into a rattling sleep.

19

D R. THATCHER CUT all the herbs he had and boiled more syrup over the fire across from the king's bed, the beams of which had been carved with protective symbols to prevent Satan's agent-demons from attacking the king through the fireplace. He cooled the syrup with drops of water or wine or beer, as pages brought jugs, and poured all that he could make into the sleeping king's mouth as the night proceeded. In the darkest hours Matthew Thatcher lost all faith in the very mathematics that Mahmoud Ezzedine had once learned. As the king continued to sweat and sleep, ever deeper, as his heartbeat slowed, mathematics no longer seemed immutable. Perhaps all the algebra he had used had been wrong. He began to doubt that the thin legs of Arab numbers could be strong enough to support real life. Thatcher had given the king more syrup than should have been proportionally necessary to restore him, considering the amount he had given to the first (and only) surviving rabbit and to himself when he had been far less poisoned. He recalculated the body weights and quantities, and mathematics confidently prophesied the king's survival. And yet the king lay immobile, his heart lazy, his breath ever fouler.

Still more weight pressed down on the despairing, guilty doctor: If math were all that mattered, then Margaret's fatal and merciful dose, taken with gratitude and open eyes, was a slim, greenish fraction of what the king had likely licked from his fingers over dozens of chess games. And of course, even worse, the precise quantity of James's ingestion was unmeasurable, since he had not drunk it but consumed it in imprecise smears over weeks. The monkey, proportionate to his weight, was dead within days of his exposure and before Thatcher was ever called to examine him, so Thatcher had missed his most relevant opportunity to test the properties of the white curative. A little creature shaped like a human who had swallowed the venom in the same manner as the king might have generously settled all questions, confirmed all variables (and even survived as well). But Thatcher hadn't been called.

Instead, Thatcher, his failure ballooning by the minute, simply cut and cooked more and more, pouring dose after dose of pale syrup into the king's mouth with trembling hands while swallowing down his own bitter prescription of remorse and resignation and conscience-ache and—somewhere far beneath, diluted almost to inefficacy—hope, and hopes, and the aroma of something far away.

20

Nicolson woke Thatcher on a chair in the annex, where he had been sleeping sitting up, his fingers stained and a cracked surface of white around his lips testifying to his self-experimentation through the night. "He wants you," said the Englishman.

The king was propped up, attended to on all sides, being washed and shaved, his nails buffed to shine. He had lost a great deal of weight. The French boy was back, dressed in blue, as was the queen, in white. Thatcher rubbed his weary eyes, tried to smooth his own clothing, aware of the sharp smells from his own body as perfumes were sprayed around the chamber. The queen and the boy were on opposite sides of the king, but both looked at the doctor. It was the first time Thatcher could recall seeing those two so near each other and wondered at the peace among the three of them. The room buzzed with gentlemen attendants and pages.

Thatcher began to bow, but James stopped him: "Matthew Thatcher. Stand straight for your king."

"Your Majesty's strength and health are returning. God be praised. Your kingdom and your people are thankful."

"My life is God's, but you were surely His instrument. I know, Matthew, what you did."

Thatcher bowed his head. He could do nothing else. He waited. The silence of the room, the eyes of the room.

"I stood at the brink of death. You stood beside me."

The men-at-arms by the doors.

"At my moment of greatest peril, as if in battle, my most loyal man was there. I am told, though I do not remember, that you stayed beside me, never rested. Your cunning and white magic protected me."

"I am without words, Majesty. I am grateful to God for your health."

"Yes. Well, I think there was rather more to it than that. And you shall be rewarded handsomely, Matthew Thatcher. The day will come when I shall be king of all Britain: Scotland, England, Wales. And of Ireland, too. And my royal physician shall be the man of great wisdom who did not leave my side when I was in my darkest hour."

Thatcher felt tears come, foolishly. Hope would burst through his lungs, out his eyes. His chin shook.

"But there is another gift I wish to make first." The king looked at Mr. Nicolson. "I have been wisely counseled. When my health is fully restored, and no sooner, I wish to give to another prince what has been so generously given to me. When I believed my life would come to its end on this earth, I felt calm and peaceful to be cared for by such a man as Matthew Thatcher. There is a woman in London who, I fear, will be at a similar point before too much longer. I can think of no more-suited gift from her ever-loving cousin and heir than to allow her the same comfort at her end as I had when I thought I faced my own."

NICOLSON LED THATCHER back to his rooms and his own bed. "It was my idea," he said, "and I think it rather clever. A gift of such value as you—savior of kings, after all. The queen will be pleased with him, reminded in allegorical fashion how concerned he is for her welfare. His generosity will be clear in her mind as difficult decisions approach. You are, in your presence, in your very body, Doctor, a symbol of James's love for Elizabeth. She should gaze upon that symbol for the rest of her days. What's more, you might make yourself useful by hearing this or that conversation near the queen's dying body, how various men at court view matters. You can let me know that directly, can't you?"

Thatcher feared he would be removed to London before he could find Leveret. He nearly said, "But I am promised to be going to Constantinople."

"I will see you again in London someday, Doctor," said George Nicolson. "You shall be serving your sovereign king again, and I will join you in that service."

WHEN THE KING was well enough to be left under the care of the much reduced and miserable Dr. Craig, Matthew Thatcher again made his daily expeditions to the fields and heath, to the hills, and back again behind the city walls, until, carrying his bag, he received compliments on its qualities from a passing young woman. He told her that he had an answer of absolute certainty and unquestionable Clarity for Mr. Leveret.

21

GEOFFREY BELLOC TOOK Katharine's report behind the fish market at the farthest edge of Edinburgh. After he made the young woman repeat Thatcher's message twice more, he felt the blood tide of rising joy, the ecstasy of remembering—of *experiencing*—how his heart and limbs had felt as a much younger man. Younger now by twenty years, he rewarded Katharine with extra coin and then took her against a wall, fish scales reflecting sunlight at his feet, like jewels on a slipper beneath a gown, and the image of Queen Elizabeth, the very first time Geoffrey had ever seen her, visited him, as she often did in moments like this, and Geoffrey Belloc began to absorb into himself the glory of what he had achieved. Young Queen Elizabeth's face glowed before him as he clutched Katharine's haunches in his terminal pleasure. Afterward, uncommonly alert and still excited, he decided to postpone his return to London so that he could hear the intelligence all again directly from his agent, to be certain of the report but also to enjoy another heady dose of this intoxicant, this rejuvenant. The gentlemen in Whitehall never knew this feeling. They never lived in the teeth of the thing, as Geoff had done, as the doctor now had done. God bless that Turk. He saved us all.

It was evening when Matthew Thatcher was greeted at Moresby Hall by an unhappy porter, who was annoyed to be receiving again

the Saracen warlock whom the house had been rid of months earlier. Thatcher was told to wait and then was led not to the baron but
to David Leveret, standing alone by the fire in a side kitchen, so tall
he stooped slightly under the oaken beams.

Belloc, in his continuing youthful pleasure, wrapped his arms
around Thatcher and lifted him off the ground. The roaring embrace caused audible cracking. "My most wise doctor!"

"We may be seen together?" asked Thatcher, exhausted, sitting
on a wooden bench and drinking deeply from the wine the giant
offered.

Belloc noticed that every wrinkle and crevice of his intelligencer's face was stenciled in dirt and dust from the hard ride south, as if
he'd been painted to appear onstage as an old man, his years adver-
tised to the highest galleries. "For now we may. And I want to tell
you something: You may call me Geoffrey. It is my real name."

"In England you are not David Leveret?"

Belloc laughed. "I am not. We all have different names sometimes, don't we? Now tell me all, please, Matthew, my friend: James
is well recovered?"

"He is. I last saw him at the chess table. He was himself. He was
playing my old Turkish set. Cleaned, of course. He was generous in
his thanks. He is a good and kind king."

"And you are certain that he deserved the cure?"

"Did I not tell your woman in Edinburgh everything?" Thatcher
asked in all sincerity, but Belloc took his tone for irritable resistance, a common symptom in agents crossing back home, released
from plots, asked to repeat again and again what they had done
when all they desired was to enjoy their return, to find a woman, to
talk without fear of misstep, to spend on drink and love whatever
money they could finally now collect.

"Tell me again. Sometimes a detail comes in the retelling. Did he
know he was going to die?"

"He spoke to me in Persian. He said that he was helpless."

"In Persian? He spoke in the language of a Mahometan? A Mahometan king of England: This is a result I had not been prepared

for. Please be serious with me now, Doctor. He knew, beyond doubt, that he was dying?"

"I told her, your woman, from the beginning that—"

"That you would have thought you were dying."

"Yes. I would have. It was unmistakable."

"And if your physician told you that you were dying . . ."

"His physician did tell him. He repeated it back to me. He was certain of it. Because it was not a trick. The king *was* dying, Geoffrey, *and* he knew it. James was courageous."

"You like him. Very well, then. When he knew he was dying, what did he do? Did he cross himself? Ask to confess his sins in Latin?"

"I told her! He did none of these things. He suffered. He nodded to me that he understood my words. That he was doomed. And he prayed."

"Who else was in the chamber with you at that moment?"

"No one. Later Mr. Nicolson. Then the queen. Later there were grooms and pages and guards. Dr. Craig returned, the Catholic priest Foyle, the Protestant priest Spottiswoode, the Spanish ambassador, the king's French favorite. But that all came later. He and I were alone. Entirely. And a dog."

"Tell me when you knew our answer with certainty."

"I was certain almost at once. James declined a priest. I offered to get one, and he declined. He said, 'By faith alone.' I recognized this phrase as a proof. You taught me. Dr. Dee taught it to me. James said this, knowing he was certain to die. 'By faith alone.'"

Belloc could scarcely believe the precision of the result, the crystalline perfection of his secret work. He had designed this on a stage, and now it had been performed, perfectly, to a rapt audience of one. He had lifted a kingdom to safety upon the lever of a plot. There would be no war to prevent James's coming, nor civil war upon his arrival, nor inquisitions and burnings, no murders in the streets. All this Belloc had done.

True, it might have been more satisfying if James *had* been a Catholic and Ezzedine had been forced to finish him off, deny him the cure, but Clarity had been the prey, and Geoff Belloc had tracked and captured it. Robert Beale had died waiting for *Clarity,* so Geoff would deliver it to Cecil and to all those gentlemen who loved and trusted Beale. And their secret armies would stand down; the imagined battles and slaughters would never come; England was safe because Geoff proved it safe, and now Geoff would declare it safe.

He spoke more quickly now, closing off possible mistakes with a beating heart. "He was alone with you? No one else there for whom he might have been projecting these words?"

"Alone. Not a servant, not a groom. And not enough voice to reach even across the bed. The truth whispered in my ear alone."

"And certain of his death?"

"Again I tell you, he would have died that night without the cure. And his body knew it."

Belloc blinked. He moved his huge hands slowly over his thighs and knees in some rush of pleasure; he was unable to remain still. "You brought an anointed king to the cliff's edge, and he showed us his innermost heart. My God, what a thing you did, Doctor."

"Did I?"

"You have prevented war, Matthew. You. *You.* You have assured a country's peace. *You.* There has never been so successful a plat of intelligence. *You* have saved more lives in this than in all your years of healing. Children, women, men. *You* have saved them."

"Have I?" Thatcher seemed not shy or doubtful but surprised. He turned to warm his hands by the fire. "And are you not in danger now, Mr. Geoffrey? If he is Protestant, then he will be your king. Will he not look for those who were responsible for his mother's death?"

"He well might," said Geoff, shrugging. "And if he means to be vengeful, I may well be at the top of his list. But I think James a fellow who may leave all that behind. England's throne was worth it to him."

Matthew Thatcher was no longer listening, only recalling the scene, the smell, the panic he had felt at the moment. Had it been only slightly different, at that moment of fever and fear, when men enact what they were taught as children, when in terror they forget all they have learned in their long lives, when with cascading pain they squeal whatever magic words or whining pleas they think will hurry their God to save them: If at *that* moment the suffering young man James Stuart had begged for a Catholic priest or had crossed himself with no more thought than a hand recoils from flame, then Thatcher would have feigned ignorance and defeat, expressed his unfeigned shame and despair, and fed him more green poison disguised as impotent cure. The Scottish man, at last revealed in all his Catholicism (no matter how momentary or delible), would have died by Thatcher's hand, envenomed slowly in games of chess he had thought he won, the white cure now withheld by that same assassin's hand. The murderer Ezzedine, the bloody Thatcher: Both would have been sent back to Constantinople to live, all debts discharged and medical work complete—James dead, Moresby dying, Elizabeth dying. Such a great and gifted healer!

Perhaps, he thought now, looking at the fire dance in Moresby's kitchen hearth, the years would somehow bless him, purge him of fault, of his apostasies and deceptions and this regicide, this murder of a nervous young man. He would walk upon the paving stones of Qustantiniyya again, clean, and through the archway of his home. Ismail, a boy of nine or nineteen, awaiting him patiently, feeding orange slices to his birds in their wooden cages. Saruca stands beside the boy, afraid even to look up at her returned husband, lest she howl for joy and pain.

No, never: He could never have been clean enough for them if James had been a Catholic. He thanked God, by whatever name He wished to be known, for having pointed James's heart in the direction Leveret and his masters wanted, for having permitted Thatcher to cure him of the illness Thatcher had caused, thanks be to God by any name.

"Tell me now, Geoffrey, please, if you cannot do what you have promised. Be kind in this, please, and tell me now, not later."

"Easy, Matt. Easy now. I am off to London immediately. You

will follow in a few days, as James's gift to the queen, as I understand. When you and I meet next, my dear friend, we must again pretend not to know each other. But you will have your promised reward. I only need some time to arrange it." Belloc bit his lip, trying to see all the moving pieces again, trying to work out the final scenes of his play. "The queen must receive you first and then grant you your return to your family, all without James taking offense, as he expects you to be his physician in London someday. Be patient while this is arranged, please. We are trying to amuse many audiences here, each with their own taste in drama. I have to think a bit, but I will deliver to you what I promised. I promise it again, my friend."

Still the Turk was bent over the fire, showing only his shaking back. "Matt? Do you understand?"

Belloc took his crying agent's shoulders and turned him away from the fire, to face him. He put his hand around the back of Thatcher's neck and gently touched his lips to the crown of the Turk's head. "You have done something rare, Mr. Mahmoud Ezzedine. You have given my country a gift beyond measure. You have saved souls and bodies both. You are a hero."

Geoffrey held the old man up as he was choked and thrashed and racked by inexplicable sobs.

MAHMOUD EZZEDINE
and GOD

. . . .

Upon Thursday it was treason to cry "God save King James, King of England!" and upon Friday high treason not to cry so.

—THOMAS DEKKER, playwright

Nah, we'll no need the papists noo. . . . And as for the chess, I think it overfond, because it is overwise and philosophic a folly.

—JAMES I OF ENGLAND, formerly James VI of Scotland

1.

Elizabeth, in and out of sleep, received Cecil nearly alone in her chair, a few women in the shadows to catch her if she slipped. "My elf, do you credit these reports from your intelligencers? Let us see the dispatches themselves. Do they 'bear the glow and charm of truth'? That was a phrase of your dear father's."

Robert Cecil, Her Majesty's principal secretary, marveled that even now, old as she was, she was straining to charm him, as if she were still the woman his father had served, young and—by old men's reminiscences and lying portraits—not without beauty. A different court then. Cecil recalled some of it, his shy and anxious boyhood impressions of this woman, this seat, this room. It seemed much greater then, when he had stood in the back, already laughed at for his body. The room had also smelled different then, somehow. Cecil's father had been responsible for tracking the queen's menses, but now her head trembled simply from the effort to hold it still. The sheets of skin beneath her chin swayed like wind-pregnant sails in battle decades ago, when she had commanded fleets. "Robert, do you think Jane ever let Essex swive her?"

"Majesty." Cecil answered the first question to avoid the second, even though that might have been the queen's intention all along. "The news of the Spanish manipulations come from more than one source, and in this regard they would seem trustworthy, but in no case have I been able to interrogate the pretending witnesses my-self."

She looked at Cecil from beneath her sparse lashes, smiled with closed lips to hide her black teeth: "Read it to me, the most sugges-tive. I like to hear it from the spy's ink directly. I like to imagine their voices. Your father used to read them to me." She looked at her hands with something like wistfulness for the past, her old sec-retary, old secrets, secret emotions.

Cecil bowed to her lie and her theatrical gesture, false to her fin-gertips. His father never read any such thing to her. Walsingham and his father warned him never to titillate the queen with direct dispatches from spies. She had not the presence of mind, as a woman of so many passions (and now so many addling decades), to sweep away the many layers of uncertainty caking these words like succes-sive seasons of new soil. (Walsingham to young Cecil, a lesson taught to Walsingham by Cecil's own father: "Assume the spy is lying. Even if honest, the spy is reporting what he wishes were true, wishes it so fervently that he believes it to be so. Even if his vision is clear and true, the spy misunderstood what he saw. Even if accurate in his perspective, the spy is only accurately reporting someone else's lies to him. Even if reporting the truth, his words are badly chosen and imply some other facts when we decipher his letter. Even if accurately viewed and accurately transmitted in language, the spy has only seen one small corner of a vast tapestry, far too little to understand it. Even if the spy has seen it all and portrayed it all in truth, he is too late; events have changed, and his report is no longer of the slightest relevance. Finally, and least likely: The spy has presented to his master in London a perfectly complete, honest, perceptive, accurate, timely, and relevant picture of affairs. But his report is contradicted by three other false reports that arrived the same week, prepared by better writers.")

"Tell me, Robert: Do you miss your Lizzie?"

"But of course, Majesty. She was a good wife. And loving to you in her service."

"Yes. True. But I think it better for you, as it is for me, to be alone. We can only truly love England, you and I. My little pygmy."

When the secretary had been dismissed by the melancholy queen, his aide, Nicholas Faunt, was waiting for him in his office. "Belloc's returned. With *Clarity*." He handed Cecil a letter: "And this came from Nicolson today as well, by another route."

Cecil wouldn't let Faunt bring Belloc in until he had read Nicolson's letter and, more important, until he had propped himself in his chair elevated on the platform behind his writing table. Belloc was placed across from him again, on the low folding stool with its sling of leather. Pointless: There was no forcing a perspective that could make things otherwise. Cecil's back ached; the weight of his body hung unevenly from his spine. He bent. "Geoffrey, welcome home. Success, I read on your eager face."

Faunt closed the door quietly, backing away, eyes rising at the last second as the door shut, and Belloc was left alone with the queen's principal secretary. He took a breath and began: "Success, yes. Complete Clarity, and the result could not be happier."

Geoff, beginning that very night, did as Cecil requested and set about to calm his anonymous and violent friends with secret news and certain *Clarity*, courtesy of his successful plat. Cecil told Belloc in passing, as if he'd nearly forgotten to mention it: "Oh, yes, Geoff, you'd be doing everyone a service, her most of all, if you made it quietly clear for those who need to see clearly." That would be Geoff's pleasure, really, to put everyone's mind at ease, to serve up shares of his own newly acquired calm. With Robert Beale's death, Geoff became the only one who knew the names of all Beale's fellow doubters, some of whom sat on the council and therefore needed to know the new Clarity most urgently, before they caused any further difficulty for plans in motion. Others were the whispering courtiers and loitering lords who listened, rapt, in private dinners in the houses where Beale had been prized, where conversation ran frank and fearless. Geoff would let them all know that he was satisfied entirely and at last: The man up north was unquestionable—

unquestionably the heir, unquestionably right for the job, solid as steel. Word would float, drift. And finally the future would congeal in everyone's conception before it occurred; the future would come to pass more easily, more calmly, for having been understood and imagined first. The highest task of intelligence: to imagine a future and then smooth its approach.

Old Robert Beale's trusted spy Belloc—over wine, by fires, at games tables—had to accustom himself to spilling secrets, but after a few efforts he found the pleasure in it, spreading the truth to save spilled blood. "How the devil are you so sure of him, Geoff?" asked a man here and there, and of course Belloc wouldn't reveal the source of his certainty, but merely hearing Robert Beale's chosen man—who hated Catholics like cats hate mice, who had been gobbling them up since before most of these men were born—say that he was certain of James's Protestant bona fides was more than enough, as Robert Cecil had hoped it would be. It was like the voice of God saying the past was the past, and all was settled now, and men could look to the future and think of nothing but their wealth and their own position in the coming changes. There would be no more grumbles from those quarters of London, no murmurs that James was not the one, and most crucially no more talk of backing any other hopeful. That question was now closed, as it ought to be. Cecil could breathe, a little.

"Your man did extraordinary service," said Cecil to Belloc. "But it was you who drew the plot. Your talents, Geoffrey. We must think where to turn you next." Geoff's pleasure was legible as print. There were men like this, Cecil recognized, who spent so much time dissembling and conspiring that when they finally felt they were home, their faces relaxed into complete candor.

"I told the doctor we would find a way to send him back to Constantinople, with honor. I have written to our man Lello in Turkey."

"He wants to go back to the Turks? So he never did really convert? Hmm. But, yes, we can do that. A letter from Her Majesty to the sultan, to accompany him home. I'll see to it."

Up north, the Spanish ambassador and the papal legate wrote their own coded dispatches from Edinburgh: "God allowed me to bear witness to certain events," each man wrote to his master, unaware that his language was almost identical to his Catholic fellow's. "Any man would have thought he was doomed. The king was doomed. He prayed for absolution with his wife's priest. He took last rites." Both wrote in Latin, but with different ciphers. "His queen, Anna, has had her effect, as we have long hoped for him. His devotion to the Mother Church is complete at last. The heretics who murdered his blessed mother have only made his true faith all the stronger. He toys with them until he will reign over them. The heretics will find him their king before they realize what he truly is."

One hundred thirty miles southwest, Dr. Thatcher heard the story of his own adventures from Baron Moresby, who somehow had the news, too, but in his version, Thatcher was nowhere to be seen: "There was a miracle in Edinburgh, I have been told. Did you know of it, or was it after you had left? God's anointed, James, was taken with plague. But God spared the king's life, when any man would have succumbed. The prayers of the faithful were heard, and James is living proof of it." Moresby's family chapel was lit with candles and the reflected gleam of silver censers and the crucifix. The family priest that night dressed in all the splendor the old gowns could muster and spoke his Latin just a little more loudly than the accustomed murmur of more discreet days. Soon enough, James would restore God and sense to England.

"The work you did, Geoffrey," marveled Cecil. "Just wondrous. We can breathe again. But now we must shepherd your perfect intelligence carefully. It is not enough that we may rest easy. Now it is our sacred task to see to James's safety, that he has no trouble arriving here, when the day comes. Clarity is our friend here, in this office and in court and in his mind up north. But for the rest of the world, too much *clarity* may hurt us and him. Provoke our enemies. As he travels south someday, one might almost wish we could conjure a little *fog* to travel with him. Until he is safely arrived here.

Our enemy now is too much *clarity*. Will you have some wine? Our best hope for him to cover those miles when the day comes (God save the queen) is for *everyone* to applaud him and let him continue on in peace, in hopes that their secret desires come to pass. So we must encourage *everyone's* secret hopes. Something for everyone. *Maximum Fog* to shroud our friend."

2

BELLOC STOOD AMONG the groundlings, enchanted by the play-ers, by the sky.

It was not surprising that the master of revels had licensed this play. After all, it was set in unthreatening ancient Illyria. Consider-ing the demands on Ben Taylor—a play to learn in a morning, a different play to perform in the afternoon, and an evening to spend hip-deep in drink and boys—it was something of a miracle that he had written this one at all, even if it had been several months since he and Geoff had drunk by the river and vomited up its plot:

The Duke of Illyria lies in his garden, reclining on a chair of leopard skin. A goblet of gold falls from his fingers. He dozes, dreams of the doge's daughter, whom he would steal away from Venice by cover of night. He awakes with a start. There before him stands the Moor, who tells the startled duke:

> *I have within thy wine imbued such venom*
> *That yet no hour awaits thee on this earth*
> *But will be racked by grasps and tremors cold*
> *That from your pagan guts might spew such bloody tides*
> *And fiery bile as serpents would in screeching drown.*

But the Moor holds just out of the coughing duke's reach a vial, a clear and perfect antidote to the venom. If the Illyrian duke would

but answer truthfully a single question, he will have the cooling po-
tion to quaff, and in no time at all the venom that does even now
begin to squeeze his innards— The duke clutches his belly, falls
back, would rise but cannot. . . .

History is written by the *future,* and therefore distorted at its
start. There's no other way to write it, of course, but it always glows
with the unnatural clarity of having eliminated all the possibilities
that didn't happen. The present doesn't feel like a link in a chain
leading to the eventual coherent historical event, and unlived futures infinitely outnumber the one statistically improbable reality
that occurred.

James VI of Scotland became James I of England at the death of
Queen Elizabeth in 1603. He traveled south from Edinburgh to
London over land, gathering up the allegiance of the English nobility (Protestants and crypto-Catholics alike), along a route carefully
planned in conjunction with his early, unwavering, and well-
rewarded ally, Robert Cecil, the old queen's last principal secretary,
the new king's first principal secretary; her Mr. Cecil, his Earl of
Salisbury; her "pygmy," his "little beagle." Cecil had done his duty
to his queen as he saw fit, one by one eliminating all challengers to
James as her heir, secretly corresponding with James to reassure him
of his future, never discussing that future with Elizabeth while simultaneously convincing every powerful constituency—domestic
and foreign—that James would be exactly the king they wanted,
whatever that happened to be: Protestant, Catholic, tolerant, intol-
erant? Yes.

Cecil wagered early and secretly; it would have been excessively
prudent not to wager at all. And then he protected his dangerous
investment; it would have been excessively reckless not to.

To the end, both Elizabeth and the pope felt James was a co-
religionist and trusted ally. His procession rolled south, and all the
Catholic princes watching from the Continent resisted their urge to
interfere and place one of their own in London by force, trusting in
James's secret Catholic sense. Increasingly triumphant with each
mile, James faced each county, each lord, each town, and he won

them, *still* not honest to somebody, but he won their oaths, their men, their armor, their horse. By the time he reached London for his coronation, he could have pulled off a mask to reveal he was the pope and it would have been too late.

And the result was, upon uniting Scotland and England . . . James continued his lifelong Protestant religion. He was a Protestant, despite his Catholic wife; his winking secret negotiations with Catholic enemy countries; his tolerance of Catholic noblemen in his court and his bed; his Catholic father murdered by his Catholic mother, who was then executed in turn for her Catholic intrigue and treason against her own cousin-queen, Elizabeth; despite his Catholic birth and Catholic baptism, and the pope, and Spain, and France, and all the Catholic Englishmen who hoped he might restore the Old Religion or at least tolerate its open practice. It was never a ruse, or, if James did waver, he never wavered far enough or long enough, if he even knew he had wavered. He was, to his end, a Protestant. He even survived an extravagant assassination plot by a Catholic underground (a literal underground, maybe even the origin of the term, literal plotters under the literal floorboards).

BELLOC STAYED AFTER the play, climbed up behind the curtains to congratulate Ben Taylor for the writing and for his performance as the doomed Moor. "You'll drink with us tonight," Ben told him, wiping the burnt cork from his face. "I'll pay. I owe you a night of it, I think. You did help with this one."

The gift from King James to Queen Elizabeth, the gift of health or at least of deathly calm, began his own trek from Cumberland to London. After some days in Moresby Hall, where he stayed on to do what service he could to improve the baron's fading health and to correct his replacement physician in some matters of herbal medicine, Matthew Thatcher finally set off south to fetch the letter that would carry him to Constantinople.

There might await him in Constantinople honor for his loyalty to the new sultan's father, safety in his return. Perhaps Cafer bin

Ibrahim was long dead or had no influence in the new sultan's arrangements. But even if not, so be it. It was time to ask this much: that he might see them, his son and wife. If another had taken her as his own, if she had given herself by necessity to bin Ibrahim or someone else, if men had spoken ill of him to his son, if as soon as he saw them he was arrested and tried for crimes he never committed and even if the new sultan saw fit to slit his flesh into ten thousand strips or burn his eyeballs or smash his toes or un-nail his fingers then nail his hands, then that was as it would be, and Ezzedine would not deny that it was even as it should be. But he would have come back to them and kept all of his promises, to each and every person or god he had ever sworn anything.

It was Tuesday, so Geoffrey Belloc, heading home from the theater in the gathering dusk, came upon a spital sermon. A boy carried the collection box through the crowd, and Geoff added a few pennies to the fund to pay ransoms for English sailors held by Ottomans or Moors or Ishmaelites. He walked on, hoped his generosity might be noticed by God and bring him reward in some later day or only speed his man Thatcher safely home to his wife and boy in Turkey. He turned in to Silver Street before he realized with a wince that giving charity in hopes of reward could, perhaps, be viewed as more than a little bit Catholic.

Ben Taylor's play ends with the Duke of Illyria's revenge. Though in a bowdlerized version a century later, morality had shifted, and audiences preferred a different sort of ending, and another playwright pleased them with the duke's death and the Moor's righteous survival. Villainy and heroism had changed costumes in the passing years.

The poisoner—who never knew the courage with which the forewarned King of Scots had willingly licked the poison from his fingers so that all would be clear to those who required Clarity, who sacrificed himself as God's only Son had done, to pay in advance for the sins of those still to be born—left Moresby Hall to meet his confederates and receive his thirty pieces of silver. And if matters of state required the administration of justice to be secret, still justice would be administered. So Matthew Thatcher was met in an inn on his route, not far from the town of Lincoln, by men he knew well enough to welcome into his company. They had come from Edinburgh, too. It was a pleasant coincidence to find familiar faces here. In this tavern.

Matthew Thatcher died in the back room of a Lincoln tavern, a dagger driven through his eye and into his brain, at a divinely appointed monarch's vengeful whim, of course. It was a death disguised as several different sorts of murder to please a few distinct but vitally important possible audiences, the doctor's very death casting yet more protective *Fog* around James's intentions and his crucial travels south. The death of Mahmoud Ezzedine (for he may well have been the man of that name at his last breath) was painted carefully, for every Englishman's future; many of their very lives and deaths depended upon how various parties viewed and understood his end.

Or.

Or. A golden word: "Or." Opportunities, rebirths, other roads. Or Matthew Thatcher takes some slightly wiser step. He doesn't stop in Lincoln but carries on all the way to London without meeting those men he recalled vaguely from Edinburgh Castle, doesn't stop until he meets Mr. Leveret precisely where they had arranged.

Or, if he *does* stop in Lincoln, and the smiling men *do* ask him to drink with them, he declines, feigns exhaustion, retreats to his rooms, then sneaks away on horseback before the dawn and, for once in his life, tries to gallop. And he escapes. Escapes his murderers. Escapes England. Escapes Christendom.

Matthew Thatcher carries little onto the boat at Southampton. His leather bag. The letters to his son he'd never sent, which grew over years into a journal of hope and despair, of scientific drawings and anthropological studies of the Britons and their beliefs. He carries his license from the Privy Council, the loving letter to the sultan from the Queen of England, the money Geoff had given him with a final embrace of thanks. Matthew Thatcher has possessed other things in his years of embassy and exile. Some he has forgotten to bring, some he has forgotten existed, some he recalls but cannot say where he last saw them.

The agent of certainty, the front-most spy in a plat for intelligence out of Scotland called *Clarity,* the key with which Geoff Belloc opened James Stuart's innermost heart, begins his journey back to Constantinople. There is a boat that carries Matthew Thatcher from Southampton to Calais and horses that walk him from Calais to Marseille and another boat at Marseille that carries him onto the translucent blue Mediterranean, during which voyage he feels himself slowly becoming again Mahmoud Ezzedine, who once before rode these waves and who, like this older man, upon a boat the far side of Italy, bows to his Eastern God five times a day.

Or.

Or he is stopped before he boards the ship, by men he does not recognize from Edinburgh, who say they need just a word with him in private before he leaves. He complies, assumes they come from Mr. Leveret. And Matthew Thatcher never steps aboard the boat.

3

PROJECTED ONTO SOMETHING like a screen, or on a stage (but something inconceivably different from a stage), or as written text upon a sort of unimaginable page, all these possibilities play and mutate and then play again, over and over, in an infinity of perfect and total knowledge.

Mahmoud Ezzedine is granted by his Creator, over an infinity of time and contemplation, total perspective to understand his life's every moment and impulse, every choice and breath from every angle. On a scroll, or a reel, on a loom or a beam of projected light, on a feather or in golden writing on the walls of his heart, Mahmoud Ezzedine sees all that he ever did, the good and the bad and the unconsidered, in such fine detail and comprehension and empathy that any effort to winnow virtue from sin, consequence from intention, can only result in two equal and perfect infinities.

In paradise (nearly exactly as Cafer bin Ibrahim had correctly conceived it), Mahmoud Ezzedine also lives all the infinite lives he did *not* live, the lives where he never left Constantinople for England, where he let James of Scotland die, where he returned with the rest of the embassy and fought in his trial against the accusations of a jealous Cafer bin Ibrahim, where he never left Beirut as a child, where he grew old alone. All of these visions and every other possibility are granted to Mahmoud Ezzedine by his loving God.

ACKNOWLEDGMENTS

The author gratefully acknowledges the invaluable assistance of:
André Bernard, Lee Boudreaux, Julia Bucknall, BMC, Tony
Denninger, Benjamin Dreyer, Edward Hirsch and the Solomon
Guggenheim Foundation, Jennifer Hershey, Peter Magyar, Yuli
Masinovsky, Professor Nabil Matar, Mike Mattison, Eric Oleson,
FMP, ASP, DSP, MMP, FHP, OMP, Mihai Radulescu, Marly Ru-
soff, Professor James Shapiro, Dani Vetere, and Daniel Zelman.

ABOUT THE AUTHOR

ARTHUR PHILLIPS is the internationally bestselling author of *The Tragedy of Arthur; The Song Is You*, which was a *New York Times* Notable Book and named one of the best novels of the year by *The Washington Post; Angelica; The Egyptologist;* and *Prague*, which was also a *New York Times* Notable Book and the winner of the *Los Angeles Times* Art Seidenbaum Award for First Fiction. He lives in New York.

arthurphillips.info
Twitter: @arthurphillips

ABOUT THE TYPE

This book was set in Bembo, a typeface based on an old-style Roman face that was used for Cardinal Pietro Bembo's tract *De Aetna* in 1495. Bembo was cut by Francesco Griffo (1450–1518) in the early sixteenth century for Italian Renaissance printer and publisher Aldus Manutius (1449–1515). The Lanston Monotype Company of Philadelphia brought the well-proportioned letterforms of Bembo to the United States in the 1930s.